JOURNEY to HELL

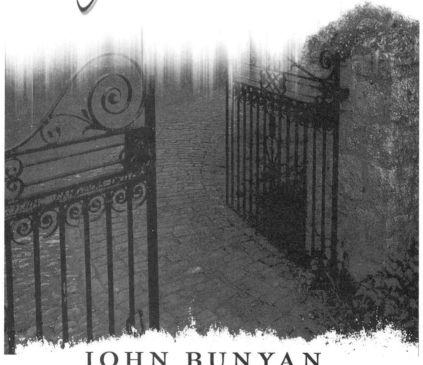

JOHN BUNYAN

WHITAKER HOUSE

Publisher's note:
This new edition from Whitaker House has been updated for the
modern reader. Words, expressions, and sentence structure have been
revised for clarity and readability.

Whitaker House wishes to thank Judith Bronte for the valuable
resources available on the Acacia John Bunyan Online Library.

Scripture quotations are taken from the King James Version (KJV)
of the Holy Bible.

JOURNEY TO HELL
(Originally titled *The Life and Death of Mr. Badman*)
trade paperback KJV edition

ISBN: 978-1-60374-044-9
Printed in the United States of America
© 1999 by Whitaker House

1030 Hunt Valley Circle
New Kensington, PA 15068
www.whitakerhouse.com

**The Library of Congress has cataloged a previous edition
of this book as follows:**

Bunyan, John, 1628-1688.
[Life and death of Mr. Badman]
Journey to hell / by John Bunyan; now in modern English.
p.   cm.
Formerly titled: The life and death of Mr. Badman.
ISBN 0-88368-583-3 (trade paper)
I. Title.
PR3329.L1 1999
828'.407–dc21
99-43318

---

2 3 4 5 6 7 8 9 10 11 **ய** 15 14 13 12 11 10 09 08

Contents

Sayings of John Bunyan

"Hell would be a kind of paradise if it were no worse than the worst of this world."

"A man would be counted a fool to slight a judge before whom he is to have a trial of his whole estate. The trial we have before God is of another kind of importance. It concerns our eternal happiness or misery, and yet we dare to affront Him?"

"I have often thought that the best of Christians are found in the worst of times. And I have thought again that one reason why we are no better is because God purges us no more. Noah and Lot–who was as holy as they in the time of their afflictions? And yet who so idle as they in the time of their prosperity?"

"In times of affliction, we commonly meet with the sweetest experiences of the love of God."

"Prayer will make a man cease from sin, or sin will entice a man to cease from prayer."

"Forsake not the public worship of God, lest God forsake you, not only in public, but in private."

The Life of John Bunyan

John Bunyan, a name familiar to every ear, was born in 1628 in the little village of Elstow, England, within a mile of Bedford. To use his own words, he was born "of a low inconsiderable generation," for his father followed the universally despised calling of a tinker (a mender of pots and pans). This occupation seems to have been held in low repute in those days, probably because of the wandering and unprincipled habits of most of the tinker fraternity. But Bunyan's father had a settled place of residence in Elstow and a good reputation among his neighbors.

In addition, he saw to it that John attended school at a time when it was much less common for parents in a humble position to avail themselves of the blessings of education for their children than, happily, it is now. John learned to read and write although he later said that he "did soon lose that little [that he had] learned."

It is clear, however, from his writings, that his memory must have been tenacious to an extraordinary degree and that the other powers of his mind were healthy and vigorous. It is likely that his assessment of what he remembered from school only reflects Bunyan's judgment that as a consequence of his youthful behavior, he lost all relish for learning. He felt that he had added nothing to his meager stock of knowledge until many precious years had been dissipated by him in evil and unprofitable courses. The reader will find a vivid and faithful narrative of his boyhood activities and the extreme distress he felt as a consequence of them in his spiritual autobiography entitled *Grace Abounding to the Chief of Sinners.*

God's Grace in Action

During his early life, he made some remarkable escapes from imminent danger. Twice he narrowly escaped drowning. When he served in the Parliamentary army, a soldier asked to take Bunyan's post, and that man was "shot into the head with a musket bullet, and died." Afterward, Bunyan looked back with a deep feeling of gratitude to a preserving and forbearing God who had not cut him off in his sins but had mingled mercy with judgment. Among those mercies, not the least of which was his being led while yet a very young man "to light upon a wife" who had been religiously educated. Her example and conversation persuaded Bunyan to go fairly regularly to church and to prefer his own fireside and her company to the alehouse and his drinking companions.

The young couple "came together as poor as poor might be, not having so much household stuff as a dish or spoon betwixt [them] both." His wife did have two books that she brought to their marriage: *The Plain Man's Pathway to Heaven* and *The Practice of Piety*. These books had a significant influence on Bunyan's spiritual development.

Bunyan was young, healthy, and had a trade by which he could always earn a decent livelihood. His wife was frugal, industrious, and good-tempered. What more was needed to light up their cottage with peace and contentment except the presence of true religion in both?

To true piety, however, John was yet a stranger. He had acquired a certain taste for churchgoing and a great respect, as he describes it, for "the high place, priest, clerk, vestment, service, and what else, belonging to the church." His strong and active imagination would often be powerfully excited by circumstances that would have made little impression on the average person's mind. But he was still an utter stranger to real religion.

His devotions were as formal as could well be imagined, and they often failed to keep his conscience quiet even though he felt a certain kind of pleasure in returning to them. His religious notions were exceedingly confused and contradictory. They seemed to have been accompanied by a strong leaning toward mysticism as well as bold speculation.

Sometimes he thought that words were spoken to him from heaven. At other times, he thought that new and mysterious objects were presented to his very senses. He would commit himself to prayer and Bible reading with something of a childlike willingness to be taught. Then, he would abandon his study of the Word to lose himself amid speculations utterly too high for him on the subject of the divine laws.

Times of Despair

Sometimes a gleam of light and hope shot across the darkness of his troubled soul, and he thought he could perceive what it was reasonable and expedient for him to do in order to be at peace with himself and his God. At other seasons, the darkness of despair's deepest midnight seemed to settle down on his soul, and in this fearful mood, he would argue thus insanely: "My state is miserable, miserable if I leave my sins, miserable if I follow them. I can but be damned; and if I must be so, I had as good be damned for many sins as for few." Thus, he said of himself on one occasion,

> I stood in the midst of my play, before all that were present, but yet I told them nothing; but having made this conclusion, I returned desperately to my sport again. And I well remember that presently this kind of despair did so possess my soul that I was persuaded I could never attain to other comfort than what I should get in sin, for heaven was gone already, so that on that I must not think. Wherefore I found within me great desire to take my fill of sin, still studying what sin was yet to be committed that I might taste the sweetness of it lest I should die before I had my desires.

A Changed Man

From this wretched course, he was rescued in an unusual manner. A woman, herself of very bad character, happened one day to scold him for swearing. She told him that he was "the ungodliest fellow that ever she heard in all her life" and fit to corrupt all the youth in the town. The criticism struck him so forcibly that from that hour, he began to discontinue the sin of swearing. He also pledged himself anew to the reading of his Bible. His conduct was so changed that his neighbors began to look on him as quite a reformed character.

Formerly, he had taken great delight in ringing the church bells. With his conscience growing very tender, he began to feel that "such practice was but vain." He abandoned that amusement and also quit dancing, considering it an ensnaring and frivolous recreation. A spirit of legality took possession of him; he began to think that "no man in England could please God better" than he. He did not know the necessity of a deeper, more powerful change of heart and nature than anything he had yet experienced; however, he felt certain misgivings and unrest as to his true condition in the sight of God. Happening to overhear some pious women talking about regeneration, he became at last convinced that his views of religion were very defective—that he "lacked the true tokens of a true godly man."

The women to whom Bunyan was indebted for his new light were members of a small Baptist congregation in Bedford of which John Gifford was pastor. Of this good man, Mr. Ivimey, in his *History of the English Baptists*, said,

> His labors were apparently confined to a narrow circle, but their effects have been very widely extended and will not pass away when time will be no more. We allude to his having baptized and introduced to the church the wicked tinker at Elstow. He was doubtless the honored evangelist who pointed Bunyan to the Wicketgate by instructing him in the knowledge of the Gospel, by turning him from darkness to light, and from the power of Satan unto God. Little did he think such a chosen vessel was sent to his house when he opened his door to admit the poor, the depraved, and the despairing Bunyan.

It is affirming too much to represent Mr. Gifford as having been the means of Bunyan's conversion; but that his conversation and preaching were greatly blessed to the once "wicked tinker of Elstow," we have the best authority for believing.

Bunyan endured great inward agitation of soul not only because of his own consciousness of sin but also because of the destructive talk of some antinomians (who taught that Christ's forgiveness eliminated the need for laws) into whose company he had fallen. But Bunyan had already studied the Scriptures with great diligence and fervent prayer, and by the blessing of God's Spirit, he gained a resting place for his troubled spirit in the scriptural assurance that "none ever trusted God and was confounded." (See Isaiah 45:17 and Psalm 25:20.)

Appointed to Preach

In 1655, Bunyan, then twenty-seven years of age, was admitted as a member of Mr. Gifford's church. Soon after, the church was deprived of its pastor by death, and the young brother so recently added to their fellowship was, after some trial of his qualifications, called on to undertake the office of occasional preacher or exhorter among them. About this appointment, Bunyan wrote,

> Some of the most able among the saints with us, I say the most able for judgment and holiness of life as they conceived, did perceive that God had counted me worthy to understand something of His will in His holy and blessed Word and had given me utterance in some measure to express what I saw to others for edification. Therefore they desired me, and that with much earnestness, that I would be willing at some times to take in hand in one of the meetings to speak a word of exhortation unto them; the which, though at the first it did much dash and abash my spirit, yet being still by them desired and entreated, I consented to their request.

When Bunyan first began to preach, people came from all over the countryside to hear him. Such was the visible success of his ministry that before long, "after some solemn prayer and fasting," he was specially set apart by the church for the regular exercise of an itinerant ministry in Bedford and the neighborhood.

In the beginning of his ministry, he dealt chiefly on the terrors of the law. About this aspect of his preaching, he wrote,

> This part of my work, I fulfilled with great sense; for I preached what I felt, what I smartingly did feel, even that under which my poor soul did groan and tremble to astonishment. I went myself in chains to preach to them in chains and carried that fire in my own conscience that I persuaded them to be aware of.

As his own spiritual horizon cleared up, his preaching took a better tone. He now labored, "still preaching what he saw and felt," to preach Christ, "the sinner's friend, while sin's eternal foe," and to persuade his hearers to lean entirely on the work and offices of Christ. He made it a leading object in his sermons "to remove those false supports and props on which the world does lean, and by them fall and perish."

A Dedicated Writer

He now had a sphere of constant activity and abundant usefulness opened to him. With his characteristic energy, he sought to fill it not only by preaching the Word but also by publishing short religious treatises. His first publication was entitled *Some Gospel Truths Opened according to the Scriptures*. To this treatise, John Burton, Mr. Gifford's successor in the regular ministry of the church at Bedford, prefixed a commendatory letter. Burton wrote,

> Having had experience with many other saints of this man's soundness in the faith, of his godly conversation, and his ability to preach the Gospel, not by human art but by the Spirit of Christ, and that with much success in the conversion of sinners, I say, having had experience of this and judging this book may be profitable to many others as well as to myself, I thought it my duty on this account to bear witness with my brother to the plain and simple and yet glorious truths of our Lord Jesus Christ.

The particular occasion of this treatise seems to have been the opposition that Bunyan experienced to his preaching from some

Quakers who told him that he "used conjuration and witchcraft" and that he "preached up an Idol, because he had said that the Son of Mary was in heaven with the same body that was crucified on the cross." Against such accusations and in defense of his views of Scripture concerning the death, resurrection, ascension, and mediation of Christ, Bunyan argued with great force as well as plainness of reasoning and with much less sharpness and lack of polish than might have been anticipated from the temper and education of the man and the character of the times in which he wrote.

His language is idiomatic but pure to an extraordinary degree for the first effort in composition by an uneducated man. A reply to Bunyan's pamphlet was published by one Edward Burroughs with the title *The True Faith of the Gospel of Peace Contended For in the Spirit of Meekness.* It was a railing and declamatory production, but Bunyan replied to it, and Burroughs rejoined, after which the controversy ended.

Sentenced to Prison

In 1657, Bunyan was indicted for preaching at Eaton. Nothing came of it, although Dr. Robert Southey, a biographer of Bunyan, labored to prove the existence of an extremely persecuting spirit at that time in the British Commonwealth. A few months after the Restoration, however, a warrant was issued against Bunyan, and he was arrested at Samsell in Bedfordshire and carried before Justice Wingate. When Bunyan refused to abstain from preaching, he was committed to the Bedford jail. At the quarter sessions, his indictment stated:

> John Bunyan of the town of Bedford, laborer, had devilishly and perniciously abstained from coming to church to hear divine service and was a common upholder of several unlawful meetings and conventicles [secret religious meetings not sanctioned by law] to the great disturbance and distraction of the good subjects of this kingdom, contrary to the laws of our sovereign lord the king.

On this ridiculous charge, he was returned to prison for three months and informed that if at the end of that period he did not submit to go to church and quit preaching, he would be banished from the realm.

A Faithful Wife

At this period, Bunyan was the father of four young children by his first wife. Mary, his oldest child, had been born blind. A year following his first wife's death, he had married a second wife. The birth of their child was approaching. News of Bunyan's imprisonment and the prospect of his impending banishment so affected her that she prematurely delivered a dead child. Yet in the middle of this complicated suffering, this noble-minded woman struggled hard to obtain her husband's deliverance. With simplicity of heart, she traveled to London to petition the House of Lords for her husband's liberation but was directed to apply to the judges at the judicial inquest. She then returned home, and with modesty and "a trembling heart," she put forth her request to the judges in the presence of many magistrates and gentry of the county. Sir Matthew Hale was one of them, but he shook his head and professed his inability to do anything for her husband.

"Will your husband leave off preaching?" asked Judge Twisden. "If he will do so, then send for him."

"My lord," replied the courageous woman, "he dares not leave preaching as long as he can speak."

Sir Matthew listened sadly to her, but Twisden brutally taunted her and said poverty was her cloak.

"Yes," observed she, "and because he is a tinker and a poor man, therefore he is despised and cannot have justice." Elizabeth Bunyan concluded her own account of this interview in these words:

> Though I was somewhat timorous at my first entrance into the chamber, yet before I went out, I could not but break forth into tears—not so much because they were so hard-hearted against me and my husband, but to think what a sad account such poor creatures will have to give at the coming of the Lord.

The Life of John Bunyan

A Productive Confinement

Bunyan remained in prison twelve years, but occasionally during that period, through the connivance of the jailer, he was allowed to steal out under cover of night. On one occasion, he was even able to pay a visit to the Christians in London. It was during this long imprisonment, while wasting the flower of his age in confinement and with no books except the Bible and *Foxe's Book of Martyrs*, that he penned his immortal work, *The Pilgrim's Progress*, besides many other treatises that have afforded much instruction and comfort to the people of God.

Freed from Prison

During the last year of his imprisonment (1671), he was chosen pastor of the Baptist church in Bedford. He appears to have been allowed to attend the church meetings for the last four years of his imprisonment. Doubtless, his word was considered a sufficient pledge that he would return every evening to prison. At last, his release was ordered. It is said that Barlow, Bishop of Lincoln, intervened on Bunyan's behalf. Soon after his release, a new chapel was built at Bedford, where he preached to large audiences during the remainder of his life.

Once every year, he visited London, where he preached with great acceptance, generally at the meetinghouse in Southwark. Also, he used to itinerate extensively in the surrounding counties. It is said that Dr. Owen was always among his metropolitan hearers. On being asked by Charles II how a learned man such as he could sit and listen to an illiterate tinker, that great scholar and divine replied, "May it please Your Majesty, could I possess that tinker's abilities for preaching, I would most gladly relinquish all my learning."

The writer of the first biographical sketch of Bunyan described his character and personal appearance in this way:

> He appeared in countenance to be of a stern and rough temper; but in his conversation, mild and affable, not given to talkativeness or much discourse in company unless

some urgent occasion required it; observing never to boast of himself or his parts, but rather seem low in his own eyes and submit himself to the judgment of others; abhorring lying and swearing; being just in all that lay in his power to his word; not seeming to revenge injuries; loving to reconcile differences and make friendships with all. He had a sharp quick eye, accompanied with an excellent discerning of persons, being of good judgment and quick wit. As for his person, he was tall of stature; strong-boned though not stout; somewhat of a ruddy face with sparkling eyes; wearing his hair on his upper lip after the old British fashion; his hair reddish, but in his later days, time had sprinkled it with gray; his nose well set, but not declining or bending; and his mouth moderate large; his forehead something high; and his habit always plain and modest.

His Work Lives On

Little is recorded of the remainder of Bunyan's life. It is not known whether he was again made a sufferer for conscience' sake when the spirit of persecution revived and waxed hot against the people of the Lord in the latter part of Charles's reign. He died in London on the twelfth day of August 1688 of a fever that he had caught by exposure to rain. He was buried in a churchyard in Bunhill Fields, in London. His widow survived him four years. The names of a few of his descendants appear in the books of the Baptist church at Bedford, but his last known descendant, Hannah Bunyan, a great-granddaughter, died in 1770 at the age of seventy-six.

In 1692, the year of Elizabeth Bunyan's death, her husband's collected works were published in two folio volumes by Ebenezer Chandler, his successor in the ministry at Bedford, and John Wilson, a fellow minister. These volumes contain about sixty pieces of various degrees of merit. All are richly impregnated with the unction of deep and fervent piety.

(Adapted from the introductory notes of the Reverend Thomas Scott in *Bunyan's Whole Allegorical Works*, Glasgow: Fullarton, 1840.)

The Author to the Reader

Dear Reader,

As I was considering what I had written in *The Pilgrim's Progress* about the journey of one traveling from this world to glory, and how that book has been helpful to many, it came to me to write about the life and death of the ungodly, and of their travels from this world to hell. As you will see, I have done that in this book entitled *Journey to Hell,* a title very appropriate for such a subject. I have written this allegory as a dialogue to make it easier for me to tell the story and hopefully for you to enjoy it. Although I have created the conversation between the two characters, I have tried to stay true to reality. As a matter of fact, what these fictitious characters relate has been acted on the stage of this world many times—even before my own eyes.

Here then, courteous reader, I present you with the life and death of Mr. Badman. I follow him in his life from his childhood to his death so that you may, as in a mirror, observe with your own eyes the steps that lead to hell and also discern, while you are reading about Mr. Badman's death, whether you yourself are walking on the same path.

Let me implore you to refrain from ridicule and mockery because Mr. Badman is dead; instead, gravely ask yourself if you are one of his lineage, for Mr. Badman has left many of his relatives behind. In fact, the world is overrun with his family. True, some of his relatives, as he, are gone to their eternal home, but thousands and thousands are left behind, including brothers, sisters, cousins, nephews, and innumerable friends and associates. I may say, and yet speak nothing but the truth in so saying, that there is scarcely a fellowship, community, family, or household where he has not left behind either a brother, nephew, or friend.

The target, therefore, that I shoot at is wide. It will be as impossible for this book to go into several families and not to arrest some as for government officials to rush into a houseful of traitors and find none but honest men there. I cannot but think that this shot will hit many, since our fields are so full of this game. How many it will kill to Mr. Badman's course and make alive to the Pilgrim's progress, I cannot determine. This secret is with the Lord our God alone, and only He knows to whom He will bless it to so good and so favorable an end. However, I have put fire to the pan, and I do not doubt but that the report will quickly be heard.

I told you before that Mr. Badman had left many of his friends and relatives behind. If I survive them, as that remains to be seen, I may also write of their lives; however, whether my life is long or short, this is my prayer at present: May God stir up witnesses against them who will either convert or destroy them, for wherever they live and wallow in their wickedness, they are a pest and a plague to that country.

England shakes and totters already because of the burden that Mr. Badman and his friends have wickedly laid upon it. Yes, our earth reels and staggers to and fro like a drunkard (see Psalm 107:27) because of the heaviness of its transgressions.

Courteous reader, I advise you now, even as we stand at the door and threshold of this house, that Mr. Badman lies dead within. Be pleased, therefore, if your leisure will permit, to enter and see the state in which he is laid, between his deathbed and the grave. He is not buried as yet, nor does he stink, as he surely will before he lies down in oblivion. As others have had their funerals commemorated according to their greatness and grandeur in the world, so likewise will Mr. Badman have his funeral according to his earthly deeds. Even he deserves not to go down to his grave in silence (Psalm 31:17).

The Author to the Reader

Four conventions are common at great men's funerals; I hope to allude to these customs without offense in the funeral of Mr. Badman.

First, the dead are sometimes presented to their friends in their completely adorned images, as lively as they can be by cunning men's hands. This act is done so that the remembrance of them may be renewed to their survivors—the remembrance of them and their deeds. I have endeavored to include a physical description in my memoir of Mr. Badman; therefore, I have described his features and actions from his childhood to his gray hairs. Here, therefore, you have him lively depicted in stages—from infancy, to the flower of youth, to his senior years, together with those actions of his life that he most customarily did in and under his present circumstances of time, place, strength, and opportunity.

Second, it is also customary at great men's funerals to display their badges and shields of honor, which they have received from their ancestors or have been thought worthy of for the deeds and exploits they have done in their lives. Mr. Badman has his collection, but they vary from those received by men of worth; his coat of arms heralds lack of merit in his actions. His honors all have decayed, and he has become *"an abominable branch"* (Isaiah 14:19) on his family tree. His deserts are the deserts of sin; therefore, his coat of arms is only that he died without honor, *"and at his end he [became] a fool"* (Jeremiah 17:11). *"Thou shalt not be joined with them* [the honored dead] *in burial....The seed of evildoers shall never be renowned"* (Isaiah 14:20). Consequently, Mr. Badman's funeral pomp will merely be the badges of a dishonorable and wicked life since *"his bones are full of the sin of his youth, which will lie down with him in the dust"* (Job 20:11).

Nor is it fitting that any should be his attendants, now at his death, except for those who conspired against their own souls in their lifetimes—persons whose transgressions have made them infamous to all who have known or will know what they have done. I have pointed out to the reader here in this little discourse those who were his associates in his life and attendants at his death. I have given a hint of some of the high villainy committed by them, as well as those judgments that have overtaken and fallen upon them from the just and revenging hand of God. All these things are either fully known by me as an eyewitness, or I have received the information from trustworthy sources whose accounts I am bound to believe.

Third, the funerals of persons of quality have been solemnized with suitable sermons at the times and places of their burials, but I have not come to that part as yet, having gone no further than to Mr. Badman's death. Since he must be buried, after he has stunk out his time before his onlookers, I do not doubt that some like those who we read are appointed to be at the burial of Gog will do this work in my place. (See Ezekiel 39.) They will leave neither skin nor bones above ground, but will *"set up a sign by it, til the buriers have buried it in the valley of Hamongog"* (Ezekiel 39:15).

Fourth, we usually hear mourning and crying at funerals, but once again Mr. Badman's funeral is different from others. His friends cannot lament his departure, for they do not have a sense of his damnable state. Instead, they ring him and sing him to hell in the sleep of death, in which he goes there. Good men count him no loss to the world. His workplace is better off without him. His loss is only his own. It is too late for him to recover that damage by a sea of bloody tears, even if he could shed them. Who then will lament for him, saying, "Oh, my brother"? He was but a stinking weed in his life and no better at all in his death. Those like him may well be thrown over the wall without sorrow (see 2 Samuel 20:21-22; 2 Kings 9:30-33), once God, in His wrath, has plucked them up by the roots (Jude 12).

Reader, if you are of the race, lineage, stock, or brotherhood of Mr. Badman, I tell you, before you read this book, you will neither tolerate the author nor what he has written about Mr. Badman. For he who condemns the wicked who die also passes the sentence upon the wicked who live; therefore, I expect neither credit nor approval from you for this narration of your kinsman's life. For your old love for your friend, his ways, and his actions will stir up in you enmity in your hearts against me. I imagine that you will tear up, burn, or throw away the book in contempt. You may even wish that for writing so notorious a truth, some harm may come my way. I expect that you may heap disdain, scorn, and contempt on me; that you will malign and slander me, saying I am a defamer of honest men's lives and deaths. For Mr. Badman, when he was alive, could not stand to be called a villain, although his actions told everyone that indeed he was one. How then should his friends who survive him, and who follow in his very steps, approve of the sentence that by this book is pronounced against him? Will they not rail at me for condemning him and imitate Korah, Dathan, and Abiram's friends who falsely accused Moses of wrongdoing? (See Numbers 16:1-33.)

I know it is dangerous to *"put* [your] *hand on the cockatrice's* [viper's] *den"* (Isaiah 11:8) and hazardous to hunt for wild boar. Likewise, the man who writes about Mr. Badman's life needs to be protected with a coat of armor and with the shaft of a spear so that Mr. Badman's surviving friends will be less able to harm the writer; but I have ventured to tell his story and to play, at this time, at the hole of these asps. If they bite, they bite; if they sting, they sting. Christ sends His lambs *"in the midst of wolves"* (Matthew 10:16), not to do like them, but to suffer by them for bearing plain testimony against their bad deeds. But does one not need to walk with a guard and to have a sentinel stand at one's door for protection? Verily, the flesh would be glad for such help, just as Paul was when the Jews conspired to kill him and the commander circumvented their plot. (See Acts 23.) But I am stripped naked of support, yet I am commanded to be faithful in my service for Christ. Well then, I have spoken what I have spoken, and now *"come on me what will!"* (Job 13:13). True, the Scripture says, *"He that reproveth a scorner getteth to himself shame: and he that rebuketh a wicked man getteth himself a blot. Reprove not a scorner, lest he hate thee"* (Proverbs 9:7-8). But what then? *"Open rebuke is better than secret love"* (Proverbs 27:5), and he who receives it will find it so afterward.

So then, whether Mr. Badman's friends will rage or laugh at what I have written, I know that the victory is mine. My endeavor is to stop a hellish course of life and to *"save a soul from death"* (James 5:20). And if for doing so I meet with malice from them, from whom reasonably I should receive thanks, I must remember the man in the dream who cut his way through his armed enemies and thus entered the beautiful palace (a reference to *The Pilgrim's Progress*); I must, I say, remember him and do the same myself.

Yet four things I will offer for consideration by Mr. Badman's friends before I turn my back on them.

Suppose that there actually is a hell—not that I question its existence any more than I wonder if there is a sun to shine, but I say it for the sake of argument with Mr. Badman's friends. I say, suppose there is a hell, such as the Scripture speaks of, one at the remotest distance from God and life eternal, one where the worm of a guilty conscience never dies and where the fire of the wrath of God is never quenched (Isaiah 66:24). Suppose, I say, that there is such a hell, prepared by God—as there is indeed—for the body and soul of the ungodly to be tormented in after this life. Suppose hell is real, and then tell me if it is prepared for you, if you are a wicked man. Let your conscience speak. Is it prepared for you? And do you think if you were there now that you could wrestle with the judgment of God? Why then do the fallen angels tremble there? (See Isaiah 24:21-22.) Your hands cannot be strong, nor can your heart endure in that day when God will deal with you (Ezekiel 22:14).

Suppose that a sinner who is now a soul in hell was permitted to come to earth to live again, and that he had a grant that, upon amending his way of life, the next time he died, he could exchange his place for heaven and glory. What do you say, O wicked man? Do you think anyone would follow the same course of life as before and risk being damned again for sins he had already been involved in before? Would he choose again to lead that cursed life that would once again rekindle the flames of hell for him and that would bind him up under the heavy wrath of God? He would not; he would not! The Scripture insinuates it (see Luke 16:19-31); reason itself would abhor and tremble at such a thought.

Suppose again that you who live and revel in your sin have as yet known nothing but the pleasures of sin. Imagine that an angel conveyed you to a place where you could easily view the joys of heaven and the torments of hell. Suppose that from this position you might have such a view that would fully convince you that both heaven and hell are realities as the Word declares them to be. Do you think you would, when brought to your home again, choose your former life, namely, to return to your folly again? No! If belief of what you saw remained with you, you would eat fire and brimstone first.

I will make one more suggestion. Suppose that there was a law and an official capable of imposing the punishment that for every known wickedness you committed, a certain portion of your flesh would be plucked from your bones with burning pincers. Would you continue in your bold way of lying, swearing, drinking, and whoring, as you delight to do now? Surely, you would not. The fear of the punishment would make you refrain, would make you tremble, even when your lusts were powerful. You would be sure to think about the punishment you would endure as soon as the pleasure was over.

But oh, the folly, the madness, the desperate insanity that is in the hearts of Mr. Badman's friends. In spite of the threats of a holy and sin-revenging God, and of the outcries and warnings of all good men, in spite of the groans and torments of those who are now in hell for their sins (see Luke 16:24), they continue on a sinful course of life, even though every sin is also a step of descent down to that infernal cave. How true is that saying of Solomon, *"The heart of the sons of men is full of evil;, and madness is in their heart while they live, and after that they go to the dead"* (Ecclesiastes 9:3). *"To the dead"*—that is, to the dead in hell, to the damned dead, the place to which those who have died as bad men are gone, and where those who now live as bad men are likely to go, when a little more sin, like stolen waters, has been imbibed by their sinful souls. (See Proverbs 9:16-18.)

I have written this book because wickedness, like a flood, is likely to drown our world. It already appears to be above the tops of the mountains. It has almost swallowed up everything; our youth, middle age, old age, and all are almost carried away by this flood. O debauchery, debauchery, what have you done? You have corrupted our young men and have made our old men beasts; you have deflowered our virgins and have made matrons madams of prostitution. You have made our earth *"reel to and fro like a drunkard, and...* [totter] *like a cottage; and the transgression thereof shall be heavy upon it; and it shall fall, and not rise again"* (Isaiah 24:20).

Oh, that I could mourn for our country, and for the sins that are committed here, even while I see that, without repentance, the men of God's wrath are about to deal with us, each one of them *"with a deadly weapon in his hand"* (Ezekiel 9:1). By God's assistance, I have written to warn people against sin, and I will pray that this flood of evil may lessen. If I could just see the tops of the mountains above it, I would think that the waters were abating.

It is the duty of those who can to cry out against this deadly plague, to lift their voices like a trumpet against it, so that people may be awakened and flee from it, as from that which is the greatest of evils. Sin pulled angels out of heaven, pulls men down to hell, and overthrows kingdoms. Who sees a house on fire and will not sound the alarm for those who live inside? Who sees the land invaded and will not signal a warning? Who sees the devil prowling like a roaring lion, continually devouring souls (1 Peter 5:8), and will not make an outcry? But above all, when we see sin, sinful sin, swallowing up a nation, sinking it, and bringing its inhabitants to temporal, spiritual, and eternal ruin, will we not cry out? Will we not say, *"'They are drunken, but not with wine; they stagger, but not with strong drink'* (Isaiah 29:9); they are intoxicated with the deadly poison of sin, which will, if its malignity is not by wholesome means subdued, bring soul and body, estate, country, and all to ruin and destruction"?

In and by this outcry, I will deliver myself from the ruins of those who perish, for a man can do no more in this matter—I mean a man in my capacity—than to detect and condemn the wickedness, warn the evildoer of the judgment, and flee from it himself. But oh, that I might not only deliver myself! Oh, that many would hear and turn from sin! Then they would be protected from the death and judgment that attend it.

The Author to the Reader

I have concealed most of the names of the persons whose sins or punishments I talk about in this book. The reasons I have handled the matter in this method are best known to me. In part, though, I have not revealed the names of many people because not all of their sins or their judgments are public; the sins of some were committed in private, and the judgments executed for them were kept confidential. Even though I could have learned some of their names, I would not have revealed them for this reason: I would not provoke those of their relatives who survive them. Nor would I lay them under disgrace and contempt, which would, as I think, unavoidably have happened to them had I revealed their names.

As for those whose names I mention, their crimes, or judgments, were made public as almost anything of that nature that happens to mortal men. Such, therefore, have published their own shame by their sins, and God has declared His anger by taking open vengeance. As Job said, God *"striketh them as wicked men in the open sight of others"* (Job 34:26). Therefore, I cannot imagine that my warning the world of their sins should turn to their detriment since their sins and judgments were so conspicuous. For the publishing of these things are, so far as my telling of them is concerned, intended for remembrances, so that they may recall the truth themselves, repent, and turn to God—lest the judgments for their sins should prove hereditary. For the God of heaven has threatened to visit *"the iniquity of the fathers upon the children unto the third and fourth generation of them who hate [Him]"* (Exodus 20:5).

Nebuchadnezzar's punishment for his pride was made public—because of his sin, he lost his kingly dignity and was driven from among men to eat grass like an ox and to keep company with the beasts (Daniel 4:30-33). Daniel did not hesitate to tell Belshazzar, Nebuchadnezzar's son, to his face about his sins and the sins of his father (Daniel 5:18-30) and to publish the account so that it might be read and remembered by generations to come. The same may be said of Judas (Acts 1:18-19), Ananias (Acts 5:1-5), and others who for their sins and punishments were known to all who lived in Jerusalem. It is a sign of desperate impenitence and hardness of heart that the offspring or relatives of those who have fallen into open, fearful, and immense sin will overlook, forget, pass by, or take no notice of such high costs imposed by God against them and their households. Thus Daniel increased Belshazzar's crime because Belshazzar hardened his heart in pride, though he knew that for that very sin and transgression his father had been brought down from his height and made to be a companion to asses. *"But thou his son, O Belshazzar, hast not humbled thine heart, though thou knewest all this"* (Daniel 5:22). This reproof hit home, but it was most fitting for Belshazzar's continued, open practice of sin.

Let those, then, who are the offspring or relatives of such, who by their own sins and the dreadful judgments of God have become a sign (Numbers 16:38-40) and have been swept like dung from the face of the earth, beware, lest when judgment knocks at their doors for their sins, as it did before at the doors of their progenitors, it falls with as heavy a stroke on them as on those who went before them— lest they, in that day, instead of finding mercy, find for their daring and offensive sins, *"judgment without mercy"* (James 2:13).

To conclude, let those who would not die Mr. Badman's death take heed of Mr. Badman's ways; for his ways led to his end. Wickedness will not deliver those who are given over to it even though they would cloak themselves with a profession of religion. If it was a transgression of old for a man to wear a woman's apparel, surely it is a transgression now for a sinner to wear a Christian profession for his coat. Wolves in sheep's clothing (Matthew 7:15) swarm in this day, wolves both as to doctrine and as to practice. Some men put on the cloak of Christianity in order to gain entrance into a profession. Then they try to build an estate even if in their dishonesty they ruin their neighbors. Let such take heed, for those who do such things will receive great damnation.

Christian, make your reputation shine with conduct that conforms with the Gospel (Philippians 1:27); otherwise, you will damage religion, bring scandal to your brothers, and become a *"stumbling-block"* (Romans 14:13). If you cause others to sin, *"it were better for* [you] *that a millstone were hanged about* [your] *neck, and that* [you]

The Author to the Reader

were drowned in the depth of the sea" (Matthew 18:6). Christian, a godly reputation is, in these days, a rare thing; seek it, put it on, and keep it *"without spot"* (1 Timothy 6:14). It will make you white and clean, and you will be an uncommon Christian indeed.

The prophecy of the end times, as I understand from 2 Timothy 3, is that even professing men will become vile, *"having a form of godliness, but denying the power thereof"* (verse 5). I urge you to *"continue thou in the things which thou hast learned"* (verse 14), not from depraved men, nor from licentious times, but from the Word and doctrine of God, that is, according to godliness. Then you will walk with Christ in purity. God Almighty gave His people grace, not to hate or malign sinners, nor to choose any of their ways, but to keep them pure from *"the blood of all men"* (Acts 20:26). God's people are to speak and act according to His name and His rules, which they profess to know and love for Jesus Christ's sake.

—John Bunyan

Chapter One

The Consequences of a Bad Man's Death

Mr. Wiseman. Good morning, my good neighbor, Mr. Attentive. Why are you out walking so early this morning? You look as if you are concerned about something. Have you lost any of your cattle, or is something else the matter?

Mr. Attentive. Sir, good morning to you. I have not as yet lost anything, but you are right. I am troubled in my heart, but it is because of the evil of the times. Sir, you, as all our neighbors know, are a very observant man. Please, therefore, tell me what you think of these times.

Wiseman. Why, I think, primarily, that they are bad times, and bad they will be, until men are better; for bad men make bad times. If people, therefore, would change, so would the times. It is foolish to look for good days as long as sin is so rampant and those who promote its growth so many. I pray for God to bring sin down, and for those who encourage it to repent. Then, my good neighbor, you will be concerned, but not as you are now. You are distressed now because times are so bad, but then you will be glad because times will be so good; now you are concerned and it causes you to be perplexed, but then your interest in the times will cause you to lift up your voice with shouting. I daresay, if you could see such days, they would make you exclaim with joy!

Attentive. Yes, so they would. I have prayed for and longed for such times, but I fear things will turn worse before they become better.

Wiseman. Make no conclusions, friend, for He who has the hearts of men in His hand can change them from worse to better; likewise, bad times into good. I pray that God will give long life to those who are good, especially to those who are capable of serving Him in the world. The grace and beauty of this world, next to God and His wonders, are those who glitter and shine in godliness.

Now as Mr. Wiseman said this, he gave a great sigh.

Attentive. Amen, amen. But why, good sir, do you sigh so deeply? Is it for the same reason that causes my apprehension?

Wiseman. I am as troubled as you are over the wickedness of the times, but that was not the reason for the sigh that you noticed. I sighed at the remembrance of the death of that man for whom the bell tolled in our town yesterday.

Attentive. I hope that your neighbor Mr. Goodman is not dead. I heard that he had been sick.

Wiseman. No, no, I am not referring to Mr. Goodman. Had it been he, I would have been concerned, but not as distressed as I am now. If he had died, I would only have mourned because the world would have lost a light. But the man whom I am concerned for now was one who was never good; therefore, he is one who is not only dead, but also damned. His natural death brought him into eternal death. (See 1 Corinthians 6:9.) He went from life to death, and then from death to death.

As Mr. Wiseman spoke these words, tears welled up in his eyes.

Attentive. Indeed, to go from a deathbed to hell is a fearful thing to think about. But, good neighbor Wiseman, please tell me who this man was and why you judge him to be so miserable in his death.

Wiseman. Well, if you can stay, I will tell you who he was and why I conclude that his end was wretched.

Attentive. My schedule will allow me to stay, and I am willing to hear you out. I pray to God that what you say will take hold of my heart so that I may be bettered by it.

So they agreed to sit down under a tree. Then Mr. Wiseman proceeded.

Wiseman. The man whom I mean is Mr. Badman. He has lived in our town a long time, and now, as I said, he is dead. But the reason for my concern over his death is not because he was related to me, or because any good conditions died with him, for he was far from them. But I greatly fear, as I hinted before, that he died two deaths at once.

Attentive. I see what you mean by two deaths at once. To speak honestly, it is a fearful thing to have grounds to think of any person going to hell. To die in such a state is more dreadful and appalling than anyone can imagine. Indeed, if a man had no soul, if his state was not truly immortal, the matter would not be so devastating. But since man has been made by his Maker to be a sensible being forever, for him to fall into the hands of revenging justice, punishing him in the dismal dungeon of hell to the utmost extremity that his sin deserves, will always be an unutterably sad and lamentable end.

Wiseman. Any man, I think, who is capable of perceiving the worth of one soul, must, when he hears of the death of an unconverted man, be stricken with sorrow and grief. As you have already well stated, man's state is such that he is a sensible being forever. For it is sense that makes punishment heavy. But yet sense is not all that the damned have; they have reason, too. So then, as sense receives punishment with sorrow, because it feels and bleeds under the pain, so by reason, and the exercise thereof, in the midst of torment, all present affliction is increased. That happens in three ways.

First, reason will consider thus with itself: For what am I being tormented? It will easily discover that it is for nothing but that base and filthy thing: sin. Now vexation will be mixed with punishment, greatly heightening the affliction.

Next, reason will consider the following question: How long

must this be my state? Then it will soon return this answer: This must be my state forever and ever. This realization will greatly increase the torment.

Finally, reason will consider this last thought: What more have I lost than present ease and quiet by the sins that I have committed? This answer will quickly come: I have lost communion with God, Christ, saints, and angels, and a share in heaven and eternal life. This awful thought must increase the misery of poor damned souls. And this is the case of Mr. Badman.

Attentive. I feel my heart shake at the thoughts of coming into such a state. Hell—what person who is yet alive knows what the torments of hell are? The word "hell" produces a very dreadful sound.

Wiseman. Yes, it does, in the ears of him who has a tender conscience. But if, as you say so truthfully, the very name of hell is dreadful, what is the place itself like, and what are the punishments that are inflicted there, without the least intermission, upon the souls of damned men, forever and ever?

Attentive. Before we go on with that subject, since I have the time to talk, please tell me what it is that makes you think that Mr. Badman has gone to hell.

Wiseman. I will tell you. But first, do you know which of the Badmans I mean?

Attentive. Why, was there more than one of them?

Wiseman. Oh yes, a great many, both brothers and sisters, and yet all of them were the children of a godly parent, which makes the truth even more pitiful.

Attentive. Which of them therefore was it who died?

Wiseman. The eldest, old in years, and old in sin; but the sinner who dies a hundred years old will be accursed.

Attentive. But what makes you think he has gone to hell?

Wiseman. His wicked life and fearful death, especially since the manner of his death so corresponded to his life.

Attentive. Please let me know the manner of his death, if you know the details accurately.

Wiseman. I was there when he died. While I live, I hope I never see another man die in the way he did.

Attentive. Please tell me about it.

Wiseman. You say you have time and can stay; therefore, if it is agreeable with you, we will examine his life and then proceed to his death, because hearing about his death may affect you more once you have heard about his life.

Attentive. Did you know him well during his life?

Wiseman. I knew him when he was a child. When he was a boy, I was a man, so I had the opportunity to observe him for his whole life.

Attentive. Then please let me hear an account of his life, but be as brief as you can, for I am interested in hearing about the manner of his death.

Chapter Two

A Bad Boy

Wiseman. I will endeavor to answer your questions about his life and death. But first, I will tell you that even as a child, he was very bad. His beginning was ominous and foretold that no good end was likely to follow. Several sins that he was prone toward when but a young boy showed him to be notoriously infected with original corruption. I daresay he learned none of them from his father or mother, nor was he allowed to play with other children who were morally corrupt and thus learn to sin from their examples; on the contrary, if at any time he mingled among others, he would be the inventor of bad words and the leader in bad actions. From the time he was a child, he was the ringleader and master sinner.

Attentive. He had a bad beginning indeed and demonstrated that he was, as you say, polluted, very much polluted with original corruption. To speak my mind freely, I confess that it is my opinion that children come into the world defiled with sin, and that often the sins of their youth, especially while they are very young, are by virtue of indwelling sin, rather than by examples that are set before them by others. Not that they do not learn to sin by example, too; however, example is not the root, but rather the temptation to wickedness. The root is sin within, for as the Scripture says,

> *For from within, out of the heart of men, proceed evil thoughts, adulteries, fornications, murders, thefts, covetousness, wickedness, deceit, lasciviousness, an evil eye, blasphemy, pride, foolishness. All these evil things come from within, and defile a man.* (Mark 7:21-23)

Wiseman. I am glad to hear that you are of this opinion, and I will also confirm what you have said by a few truths from the Word of God: Man in his birth is compared to an ass, an unclean beast (Job 11:12), and to a wretched infant polluted in its own blood (Ezekiel 16:4-6). Besides, all the firstborn of old who were offered to the Lord were to be redeemed at the age of one month, and that was before they were sinners by imitation (Exodus 13:13, 15; 34:20; Numbers 18:15-16). The Scripture also affirms that *"as by one man sin entered into the world, and death by sin"* (Romans 5:12), and it conveys this reason for judgment: *"death passed upon all men, for that all have sinned"* (verse 12).

The objection that Christ by His death has taken away original sin is without foundation. First, it has no grounds because it is not in the Scriptures. Second, it makes children incapable of salvation by Christ, for none but those who in their own persons are sinners are to receive salvation by Him. Many other things might be added, but among persons who agree as well as you and I do, these reasons may suffice at present. But when an antagonist comes to deal with us about this matter, then we have other strong arguments for him, if he is an opponent worthy of our taking notice.

Attentive. But, as you suggested before, Badman used to be the ringleader of sinners, or the master of evil among other children, yet these are general descriptions. Please tell me about the specific sins of his childhood.

Wiseman. I will. When he was only a child, he was so addicted to lying that his parents hardly knew when to believe he was telling the truth. He would boldly invent, speak, and stand behind the lies that he created. Looking at the shamelessness and boldness in his face as he told his lies, one might recognize the symptoms of a hard and desperate heart.

Attentive. This was an immoral beginning indeed, and shows that he had begun to harden himself in sin at an early age. For a lie cannot be knowingly told and maintained by one—and I perceive that this was his way of lying—unless he, as it were, forced his own heart to it. Yes, he must have made his heart hard and bold to do it. He must have arrived at an exceeding degree of wickedness to do so, since he did all this against the good training that he had received from his father and mother.

Wiseman. The lack of good education, as you have intimated, is many times the reason that children do so easily, and so soon, become bad—especially when there is not only a lack of moral instruction, but also bad examples to follow. Sadly, this is the case in many families; consequently, poor children are trained up in sin and nursed in it for the devil and hell.

But it was otherwise with Mr. Badman, for to my knowledge, his way of lying was a great grief to his parents, and they were disheartened by their son's early tendency toward sin. There was no lack of good counsel and correction from them in their efforts to make him better. I often heard him told repeatedly that *"all liars shall have their part in the lake which burneth with fire and brimstone"* (Revelation 21:8), and that no one who *"defileth, neither...worketh abomination or maketh a lie, but* [only] *they which are written in the Lamb's book of life"* (verse 27) will enter the heavenly Jerusalem. He was taught well that *"whosoever loveth and maketh a lie"* (Revelation 22:15) will never be a part of that great city. But all these lessons availed nothing with him.

When an opportunity or an occasion to lie came to him, he would invent, tell, and stand by his lie as steadfastly as if it had been the biggest of truths that he told. The hardening of his heart and face amazed those who stood by. He would boldly lie even when under *"the rod of correction"* (Proverbs 22:15), which is appointed by God for parents to use in order to keep their children from hell (Proverbs 23:13-14).

Attentive. Truly, it was, as I said, a bad beginning. He served the devil early; in fact, he became nurse to one of his brats, for a spirit of lying is the devil's brat. As the Scripture says, "[The devil] *is a liar, and the father of it"* (John 8:44).

Wiseman. Right, he is the Father of Lies indeed. A lie is sired by the devil as the father and is brought forth by the wicked heart as the mother. Another Scripture says, *"Why hath Satan filled thine heart to lie?"* (Acts 5:3). Yes, Peter called the heart that is big with a lie, a heart that has *"conceived"* (verse 4), that is, has conceived by the devil. Peter said to Ananias, *"Why hast thou conceived this thing in thine heart? Thou hast not lied unto men, but unto God"* (verse 4). True, his lie was a lie of the highest nature, but every lie has the same father, *"for* [the devil] *is a liar, and the father of it"* (John 8:44).

A lie then is the brat of hell, and it cannot be in the heart before the person has committed a kind of spiritual adultery with the devil. The soul, therefore, that tells a known lie, has collaborated and conceived it by lying with the devil, the only father of lies. For a lie has only one father and mother, the devil and the human heart. Do not be surprised, therefore, if the hearts that hatch and bring forth lies share the complexion of the devil. Yes, do not be astonished that God and Christ have so denounced liars in their Word and pronounced the same punishment on them as on murderers: *"Thou shalt destroy them that speak* [falsehood]*; the* LORD *will abhor the bloody and deceitful man"* (Psalm 5:6). A liar is wedded to the devil himself.

Attentive. It seems astonishing in my eyes that since a lie is the off-spring of the devil, and since a lie brings the soul to the very den of devils, namely, the dark dungeon of hell, that men should be so desperately wicked as to accustom themselves to so horrible a thing.

Wiseman. It seems also staggering to me, especially when I observe for how little a matter some men will study, contrive, and tell a lie. Some will lie over and over just for a penny's profit. They will lie and stand by their word, although they know that they lie. In fact, some men will not hesitate to tell lie after lie, even though they get nothing for doing it. They will tell lies in their ordinary conversations with their neighbors. Their news, their jokes, and their stories need to be adorned with lies or else they seem to sound displeasing to the ears and lack imagination to those to whom they are told. Alas! What will these liars do, when, for

A Bad Boy

their lies, they will be tumbled down into hell, to the devil who begot those lies in their hearts, and so be tormented by fire and brimstone (Psalm 11:6; Revelation 20:10) with him forever and ever because of their lies?

Attentive. Can you give an example of God's judgments upon liars, so that one may tell it to liars when one hears them lie? Perhaps, then, the liars will become afraid and ashamed to lie.

Wiseman. Examples! Why Ananias and his wife are examples enough to put a stop, one would think, to a spirit addicted to lying, for they both were stricken down dead for telling a lie, and that by God Himself in the middle of a group of people (Acts 5:1-10). But if God's threatening of liars with hellfire and with the loss of the kingdom of heaven will not prevail with them to stop lying and making up lies, it is doubtful that liars will stop lying because they are breaking any earthly laws. Now, as I said, lying was one of the first sins that Mr. Badman was addicted to, and he could make them and tell them boldly.

Attentive. I am sorry to hear this fact about him, and even more because I fear that this sin alone did not reign in him. Usually, one who is accustomed to lying is also accustomed to other evils besides. If this were not so with Mr. Badman, it would indeed be a surprise.

Wiseman. You speak the truth, for the liar is captive to more than the spirit of lying; consequently, Badman, since he was a liar from a child, was also a thief. What he could, as we say, handsomely lay his hands on, he considered to be his own; whether they were the possessions of his playmates or his neighbors, he would take them away. You must understand, he started with stealing small items. Since he was just a child, he attempted to steal no significant things at first. But as he grew in strength and cleverness, so he attempted to pilfer things of more value than at first. He took great pleasure in robbing gardens and orchards, and as he grew up, in stealing poultry from the neighborhood. Even what belonged to his father could not escape his fingers; all was fish that came to his net, so hardened, at last, was he in this evil.

Attentive. Your account of him makes me wonder more and more. What, he played the thief, too! And so soon! He had to have known, even though he was only a child, that what he took from others was not his own. Besides, if his father was a good man, as you say he was, he would have heard from him that to steal was to transgress the law of God (Exodus 20:15), and that in so doing, he was running the risk of eternal damnation.

Wiseman. His father did not miss the opportunity to reclaim him. He often earnestly entreated him, as I have been told, to obey the law God gave to Moses, *"Thou shalt not steal"* (Exodus 20:15). He also was taught: *"This is the curse that goeth forth over the face of the whole earth: for every one that stealeth shall be cut off"* (Zechariah 5:3). The light within his nature also, though he was little, must have shown him that what he took from others was not his own, and that he would not willingly have been treated in this way himself. But all was to no purpose. Let father and conscience say what they would to him, he would go on, he was resolved to go on, in his wickedness.

Attentive. But his father would, as you intimate, sometimes rebuke him for his wickedness. How would the boy react to correction?

Wiseman. How? Why, like a thief who is caught in the act. He would stand gloating inwardly, while outwardly, he would hang down his head in a sullen, pouting manner. As we used to say, one could read the picture of bad luck in his face, and when his father demanded an answer to such questions concerning his wickedness, the boy would grumble and mutter at him, and that would be all he would say.

Attentive. But you mentioned that he would also rob his father. I think that was an unnatural thing.

Wiseman. Natural or unnatural, both are the same thing to a thief. Besides, you must know that he had companions to whom he was, for the wickedness that he saw in them, more firmly related than he was to either his father or mother. He would not have cared if his father and mother had died for grief over him. Their deaths would have been, as he would have counted, great release and liberty for him. The truth is, they and their counsel were his bondage. And if I remember correctly, I have heard some say that when he was, at times, among his friends, he would greatly rejoice to think that his parents were old and could not live long. Then, he said, "I will be my own man, to do what I like, without their control."

Attentive. Then it seems that he considered robbing his parents to be no crime.

Wiseman. None at all; therefore, he fell directly under this sentence: "*Whoso robbeth his father or his mother, and saith, It is no transgression; the same is the companion of a destroyer*" (Proverbs 28:24). His lack of respect for them and for their advice was a sign that at that time he was of a very abominable spirit, and that some judgment waited to take hold of him in time to come. (See 1 Samuel 2:25.)

Attentive. But can you imagine his self-conceit, his vanity—I do not speak now of the suggestions of Satan, by which undoubtedly he was urged to do these things—that caused him to think that his stealing was no great matter?

Wiseman. It was because the things that he stole were small—robbing orchards and gardens, stealing chickens, and the like. These he counted tricks of youth, nor would he be dissuaded by anything people would say. They would tell him that he must not covet or desire (Exodus 20:17), yet to covet is less than to take, and that if he did steal anything, even the least thing that belonged to his neighbor, it would be a transgression of the law (verse 15). But coveting and stealing were one and the same to him. Through the wicked talk of his companions, and the delusion of his own corrupt heart, he would go on in his pilfering course. Where he felt secure, he would talk and laugh about what he had done.

Attentive. I heard once that a man who was on the ladder with the hangman's rope around his neck confessed that what had brought him to that end was his accustoming himself, when young, to stealing small things. To my best remembrance, he said that he began the trade of a thief by stealing shoelaces. He warned all the youth who were gathered together there to see him die to take heed of beginning with little sins because by tampering at first with little ones, the way is made for the commission of bigger ones.

Wiseman. Since you have told me a story, I will tell you one. Though I was not there when it happened, I fully believe the person who told the account to me. It is about a man called old Tod, who was hanged about twenty years ago or more, at Hertford, for being a thief. At a summer trial held at Hertford, while the judge was sitting upon the bench, old Tod came into court, clothed in a green suit. He had his leather belt in his hand, his shirt front was open, and he was all covered in sweat as if he had run for his life. Once he entered the room, he spoke aloud as follows:

> My lord, I am the worst rogue who breathes upon the face of the earth. I have been a thief since I was a child. When I was but a little one, I spent my time robbing orchards and doing other similarly wicked things. I have continued to be a thief ever since. My lord, there has not been a robbery committed for many years within miles of this place, but that I have either been at it or known about it.

The judge thought the fellow was mad, but after conferring with some of the justices, he agreed to indict him on several felonious actions to all of which he heartily confessed guilt. He was hanged on the same day.

Attentive. This is a remarkable story indeed, and you think it is a true one?

Wiseman. It is not only remarkable, but relevant to our discussion. This thief, like Mr. Badman, began his trade early. He also began with the same type of theft that Mr. Badman did as a child—robbing orchards and other such things—which brought him, as you may perceive, from sin to sin, until at last it led him to the public shame of sin, which is the gallows.

As for the truth of this story, the relater of it told me that he was in the court, standing within less than two yards of old Tod, when he heard him utter the words aloud.

A Bad Boy

Attentive. These two sins of lying and stealing were a bad sign of an evil end.

Wiseman. So they were, yet Mr. Badman came to his end unlike old Tod, though I fear his end was even worse than death on the gallows. His death was less discerned by spectators, but more about that by and by. You talk of these two sins of lying and stealing as if they were all that Mr. Badman was addicted to in his youth. Alas, he swarmed with sins, even as a beggar does with vermin, and that when he was but a boy.

Attentive. Why, what other sins was he addicted to while he was still a child?

Wiseman. You need not ask what other sins he was inclined toward, but rather to what sins he was not addicted to that suited his age. A man may safely say that nothing that was vile was out of place for him, if he was but capable of doing it. Indeed, there are some sins that children do not know how to tamper with, but I speak of sins that he was capable of committing. I will name two or three more.

First, he could not endure the Lord's Day because of the holiness associated with it. The beginning of that day was to him as if he were going to prison. Reading the Scriptures, hearing sermons, listening to godly conversations, and repeating prayers were things that he could not avoid. The only good thing for him was that he could escape the attentions of his mother and father by lurking among his companions until holy duties were over. Sometimes, in spite of his father's diligence, the boy would give his father the slip. When his father did keep him strictly to the observation of the day, Mr. Badman would plainly show by his posture that he was highly discontent. He would sleep during prayer, would talk foolishly with his brothers, and, as it were, think every godly opportunity seven times as long as it was, resenting it until it was over.

Attentive. His abhorrence of that day was not, I think, because of the day itself, but because God has put sanctity and holiness upon the Sabbath. Also, it is the day above all the days of the week that ought to be spent in holy devotion, in remembrance of our Lord's resurrection from the dead.

Wiseman. Yes, that was why he was such an enemy to it. Also, more restraint than was possible to place on him on all the other days was exercised over him on that day, which kept him from his wicked ways.

Attentive. By instituting a day for holy duties, does not God reveal how the hearts and inclinations of spiritually poor people react to holiness of heart and conduct in holy duties?

Wiseman. Undoubtedly so, and a man will show his heart and his life for what they are more by one Lord's Day than by all the other days of the week. On the Lord's Day there is a special restraint placed on men as to their thoughts and lives, more than on other days of the week. Also, men are commanded on that day to practice a stricter performance of holy duties, and restraint from worldly business, than on other days. Thus, if their hearts are not inclined naturally toward good, they will show it, and they will appear as what they are.

The Lord's Day is a kind of symbol of the heavenly Sabbath above, and it clearly reveals the heart's attitude toward eternal holiness. More is seen in one's observance of the Sabbath than one's performance of earthly activities. On other days, a man may begin and end his prayers within a quarter of an hour, but the Lord's Day is, as it were, a day that directs one to a perpetual practice of holiness. *"Remember the sabbath day, to keep it holy. Six days shalt thou labour and do all thy work: but the seventh day is the sabbath of the Lord thy God"* (Exodus 20:8-10). This commandment is not annulled by Christ, but changed, into the first of the week, not as it was given in particular to the Jews, but as it was sanctified by Him from the beginning of the world. (See Genesis 2:2-3; Exodus 31:13-17; Mark 2:27-28; 16:1-2; Acts 20:7; 1 Corinthians 16:1-2; Revelation 1:10.) Therefore, the way a man keeps the Sabbath is a greater proof of the frame and character of his heart, and does more to reveal to what he is inclined, than does his other performance of duties.

A Bad Boy

Thus, God puts a great difference between those who truly call this day holy, count it honorable, and walk in holiness, and those who do not. Sincere believers consider the day to be an opportunity to show how they delight to honor God in that they have not only an hour, but a whole day, to devote to Him (Isaiah 58:13-14). God puts a great difference between true worshippers and those who say, "When will the Sabbath be over so that we may engage in our worldly business?" (See Amos 8:5.) The first He calls blessed, but brands the others as unsanctified worldlings. Indeed, to delight ourselves in God's service on His holy days gives a better proof of a sanctified nature than to begrudge its coming and to be weary of the holy duties of such days, as Mr. Badman did.

Attentive. There may be something in what you say, for he who cannot stand to keep one day holy to God, has, to be sure, given a sufficient proof that he is an unsanctified man, and, as such, what should he do in heaven since that is the place where a perpetual Sabbath is to be kept to God? I say, it is to be kept forever and ever. (See Hebrews 4:1, 3-11.)

For all I know, one reason why one day in seven has been set apart by our Lord for holy observances may be to give people conviction that there is enmity in the hearts of sinners toward the God of heaven, for he who hates holiness, hates God Himself. They pretend to love God, and yet they do not love His holy day. They do not love to spend that day in one continuous act of holiness to the Lord. It would be better for them to say nothing than to call Him *"Lord, Lord,"* and not do the things that He commands (Matthew 7:21).

Mr. Badman was such a one. He could not stand this day, nor any of the duties of it. Indeed, when he could get with his friends and spend it in all manner of idleness and profanity, then he would be well pleased. But what were these actions other than a turning of the day into night? He refused to take the opportunity at God's command not to follow the earthly impulses to satisfy his lusts and delights of the flesh. I take the liberty to speak this

45

way about Mr. Badman based on what you have said to be true of him.

Wiseman. You do not need to apologize for your censuring of Mr. Badman, for all who knew him will confirm what you say to be true. He could not tolerate either the Lord's Day or anything else that had the stamp or image of God upon it. To sin and to do worthless acts were what he delighted in, from the time he was a little child.

Attentive. For his own sake, and also for the sake of his relatives, I am sorry to hear that. They must have been heartbroken over such actions as these. *"For because of these things cometh the wrath of God upon the children of disobedience"* (Ephesians 5:6). Undoubtedly, he must be in hell if he died without repentance. To bear a child for hell is a sad thing for parents to consider.

Wiseman. As I said, I will tell you about his dying presently, but now we are talking about his life, and the manner of his life in his childhood, even of the sins that attended him then. Indeed, I have mentioned some already, but there are more to follow that are not at all any less serious than what you have already heard.

Attentive. What were they?

Wiseman. Why, he was greatly given, even as a lad, to grievous swearing and cursing. He made no more of swearing and cursing than I do of counting my fingers. He would swear without provocation and considered it a distinction to swear and curse. It was as natural to him as to eat, drink, or sleep.

Attentive. Oh, what a young villain he was! Here is an example, as the apostle Paul said, of a yielding of one's *"members as instruments of unrighteousness unto sin"* (Romans 6:13). This is proceeding *"from evil to evil"* (Jeremiah 9:3). This argues that he was a foulmouthed young wretch indeed.

Wiseman. He was so, and yet, as I told you, he judged this kind of sinning to be a badge of honor. He considered himself a man's man when he had learned to swear and curse boldly.

Attentive. I am persuaded that many think as you have said, that to swear is a thing that bravely becomes them, and that it is the best way for a man, when he wants to put authority or terror into his words, to stuff them full of the sin of swearing.

Wiseman. I agree; otherwise, I think, men would not belch out their blasphemous oaths as they do. They take pride in it. They think that to swear is gentlemanly, and having once accustomed themselves to it, they seldom forsake the practice all the days of their lives.

Attentive. Well, now that we are considering it, please show me the difference between swearing and cursing. There is a difference, is there not?

Wiseman. Yes, there is a difference between swearing and cursing. Now, vain and sinful swearing, such as young Badman accustomed himself to, is a frivolous and wicked calling upon God to witness our vain and foolish attesting of things. These things fall into two categories: things that we swear are or will be done, and things that we swear are either true or false.

First, there are things that we swear are or will be done. We swear that we have done such a thing, or that such a thing is so or will be so. It does not matter what these men swear about; if it is done lightly, wickedly, and groundlessly, it is vain, because it is a sin against the third commandment, which says, *"Thou shalt not take the name of the LORD your God in vain; for the LORD will not hold him guiltless that taketh his name in vain"* (Exodus 20:7). For this is a profane use of that holy and sacred name, and so a sin for which, without sound repentance, there is not, nor can be rightly expected, forgiveness.

Attentive. Then it seems that a man can swear truthfully, but if he swears lightly and without justification, his oath is evil, and by it, he sins.

Wiseman. Yes, men may say, *"As the LORD liveth,"* (Jeremiah 5:2), and that statement is true, but in so saying, they *"swear falsely"* (verse 2) because they swear vainly, needlessly, and without reason. To swear out of necessity, which a man does when he

47

calls God as his witness, that is tolerated by the Word. But this was not the case with Mr. Badman's swearing, and therefore we are not concerned about that now.

Attentive. I see by the Scripture from the prophet Jeremiah that a man may sin in swearing to a truth (Jeremiah 5:2). Therefore, those who swear to confirm their jests and lies must be sinning most horribly, and they think they are doing it to beautify their foolish talking!

Wiseman. They sin high-handedly, for they presume to imagine that God is as wicked as they, namely, that He is an avower of lies. For, as I said before, to swear is to call God to witness, and to swear to a lie is to call God to witness that that lie is true. This action, therefore, is offensive, for it affronts the holiness and righteousness of God; therefore, His wrath must expel them (Zechariah 5:3).

This kind of swearing is equated with lying, killing, stealing, and committing adultery; therefore, it must not go unpunished (Jeremiah 7:9–15; Hosea 4:2–3). For if God *"will not hold him guiltless that taketh his name in vain"* (Exodus 20:7), which a man may do when he swears to a truth, how can it be imagined that God should hold those guiltless who, by swearing, appeal to Him for lies that are not true, or who swear out of their frantic and wildly foolish madness? It would distress and provoke any sober man to anger if one should swear to a notorious lie and then confirm that that honest man would corroborate it as the truth. Yet men deal with the holy God in this way. They tell their jokes, tales, and lies, and then they swear by God that their words are true. Now, this kind of swearing was as common with young Badman as it was for him to eat when he was hungry or go to bed when he was tired.

Attentive. I have often pondered what makes men take up the habit of swearing when those who are wise will not believe them any smarter for doing it.

Wiseman. It cannot be anything that is good, you may be sure, because the thing itself is abominable; therefore, it must be from the promptings of the spirit of the devil within them. Also, it flows sometimes from hellish rage, when the tongue "*setteth on fire the course of nature; and it is set on fire of hell*" (James 3:6). But commonly, swearing flows from that daring boldness that defies the law that forbids it. Swearers think, too, that by their belching of blasphemous oaths out of their black and polluted mouths, they show themselves to be more valiant men. They imagine, also, that by these outrageous kinds of villainies, they will conquer those with whom they associate and make them believe their lies are true. They also swear frequently to profit thereby, and when they meet with fools, they overcome them in this way. But if I might give advice in this matter, no buyer should lay out one cent to someone who is a common swearer, especially with such a master of oaths who endeavors to swear away his merchandise to another, and who would swear his peddler's money into his own pocket.

Attentive. All these causes of swearing, as far as I can see, grow from the same root as do the oaths themselves, even from a hardened and desperate heart. But please show me now how wicked cursing is to be distinguished from this kind of swearing.

Wiseman. Swearing, as I said, has immediately to do with the name of God, and it calls upon Him to witness to the truth of what is said, that is, if those who swear, swear by Him. Some, indeed, swear by idols, by saints, beasts, birds, and other creatures, but the usual way of profane ones is to swear by God, Christ, faith, and the like. By whatever they swear, cursing is distinguished from swearing thus.

To curse profanely is to sentence another or ourselves for evil or to evil or to wish that some evil might happen unjustly to the person or thing under the curse. It is to sentence for evil or to evil without a cause. Thus Shimei cursed David. He sentenced him unjustly, when he said to him,

> Come out, come out, thou bloody man, and thou man of Belial: the LORD hath returned upon thee all the blood of the house of Saul, in whose stead thou hast reigned; and

> the LORD *hath delivered the kingdom into the hand of*
> *Absalom thy son: and, behold, thou art taken in thy mis-*
> *chief, because thou art a bloody man.* (2 Samuel 16:7–8)

David called Shimei's words *"a grievous curse"* (1 Kings 2:8).
David said to Solomon his son, *"Thou hast with the Shimei the*
son of Gera, a Benjamite of Bahurim, which cursed me with a
grievous curse in the day when I went to Mahanaim" (verse 8).

But what was this curse? First, it was a wrong sentence passed on
David. Shimei called him *"a bloodthirsty man"* (2 Samuel 16:7)
when he was not. Second, Shimei sentenced him to the evil that
at that time was supposedly upon him for being *"a bloodthirsty*
man," that is, for being against the house of Saul, when that evil
had overtaken David for quite another thing. And we may thus
apply this point to the profane ones of our times, who in their
rage and envy have little else in their youths but an unjust sentence against their neighbor for evil. How common it is with
many, when they are a little offended with one, to cry, "Hang
him; damn him, rogue!" This is both a sentencing of him for evil
and to evil and is in itself a vicious curse.

The other kind of cursing is to wish that some evil might happen
to and overtake a person or thing. This kind of cursing Job considered to be a wicked sin. He said, *"Neither have I suffered my*
mouth to sin by wishing a curse to his soul" (Job 31:30). This,
then, is a wicked cursing, to wish that evil might either befall
another or ourselves. And this kind of cursing young Badman
accustomed himself to.

He would wish that evil might happen to others: he would wish
that they would break their necks, have their brains removed,
or be consumed by disease. These kinds of devilish curses have
become one of the common sins of our age. He would also as often
wish a curse on himself, saying, "I wish I would be hanged, or
burned, or that the devil might come for me," and the like. When
bold swearers in their hellish fury say, "God damn me," "God
kill me," or something similar, they curse rather than swear; yes,
they curse themselves with a wish that damnation might happen

to them. In a little while, they will get their wish and end up in hellfire, if they do not repent of their sins.

Attentive. But did this young Badman accustom himself to such filthy language?

Wiseman. I think I may say that nothing was more frequent in his mouth, and that he cursed with the least provocation. He was so versed in this kind of language that neither his father, nor mother, nor brother, nor sister, nor servant, no, not even the very cattle that his father owned, could escape these curses of his. I say that even the brute beasts, when he drove them or rode them, if they did not please his mood, would be sure to receive his curses. He would wish their necks and legs to be broken, their intestines to be torn out, or that the devil might carry them away. It is no surprise that he spoke in this way, for one who is so brazen to wish damnation or other bad curses on himself or his dearest relatives will not hesitate to wish evil on any beasts.

Attentive. Well, I can see that this Badman was a desperate villain. Kind sir, since you have gone this far, please show me where this evil of cursing comes from and also what dishonor it brings to God. I easily discern that it brings damnation to the soul.

Wiseman. This evil of cursing arises in general from the desperate wickedness of the heart, but particularly from envy, which is, as I understand, the leading sin to witchcraft. It also comes from pride, which was the sin of the fallen angels. Additionally, it arises from scorn and contempt of others (Ecclesiastes 7:21-22). But a man's curses of himself must come from desperate madness.

The dishonor that it brings to God is that it takes away His authority, in whose power resides the only right to bless and curse—not to curse wickedly, as Mr. Badman, but justly and righteously, giving by His curse the due reward of their deeds to those who are wicked.

Besides, these wicked men, in their evil cursing of their neighbors, curse God Himself in His handiwork (James 3:8-9). Man is made in God's image (Genesis 1:27), and to wickedly curse the image of God is to curse God Himself. Therefore, when men wickedly swear, they tear apart God's name and make Him, as much as in their lies, the avower and approver of all their wickedness. He who curses and condemns his neighbor in this way or who wishes his neighbor evil, curses, condemns, and wishes evil on the image of God; consequently, he judges and condemns God Himself. Suppose that a man would say with his mouth, "I wish that the king's picture was burned." Would not this man's words make him an enemy of the king? It is the same with those who, by cursing, wish evil on their neighbors or on themselves. They condemn the image, even the image of God Himself.

Attentive. But do you think that the men who do curse in this way realize that their words are so vile and abominable?

Wiseman. The question is not what men believe concerning their sins, but what God's Word says about sin. If God's Word says that swearing and cursing are sins, though men consider them virtues, their reward will be the just reward for sin, namely, the damnation of the soul. To curse another and to swear vainly and falsely are sins against the conscience. Whoever curses another knows when he does so that he would not want to be cursed himself. To swear also is a sin against the same law, for nature will tell me that I should not lie, much less swear to confirm it. Even the heathens have looked on swearing as a solemn ordinance of God, and therefore not to be lightly or vainly used by men, except to confirm a matter of truth. (See Genesis 31:43–55.)

Attentive. But I wonder, since cursing and swearing are such evils in the eyes of God, why He does not make examples to others of those who commit such wickedness.

Wiseman. So He has, a thousand times over, as may be easily gathered by any observant people in every age and country. I could present you with several myself, but waving the abundance that might be mentioned, I will present you with two. One was that dreadful judgment of God upon one N. P. at Wimbleton in Surrey. After a horrible fit of swearing and cursing at some people who did not please him, he suddenly fell sick, and in little time died raving, cursing, and swearing.

A Bad Boy

Then there is the shocking story of Dorothy Mately, an inhabitant of Ashover, in the county of Derby. She was known by the people of the town to be a great swearer, curser, liar, and thief—just like Mr. Badman. The work that she usually did was to wash the rubbish that came out of the lead mines in order to retrieve fragments of lead ore. Her usual way of asserting things was with the following kinds of curses: "May I sink into the earth if what I say is not so," or "May God open the earth and swallow me up if I am not telling the truth."

On March 23, 1660, Dorothy was washing ore on the top of a steep hill, about a quarter of a mile from Ashover. She was accused by a lad of taking two single coins out of his pocket, for he had laid his pants aside and was working in his undergarments. She violently denied it and wished that the ground would swallow her up if she had stolen his money. She had said the same wicked words on several other occasions that day.

Now one George Hodgkinson, of Ashover, a man of good reputation, accidentally came by where Dorothy was working. He stood still awhile to talk with her, and as she was washing the ore, a little child also stood there by the side of her tub. Another distance from her, a woman called to the child to come away. Then George took the little girl by the hand to lead her away to the one who had called her. They had not gone more than ten yards from Dorothy before they heard her crying out for help. Looking back, George saw the woman, her tub, and her sieve twirling around, sinking into the ground. He called to her, "Pray for God to pardon your sin, for you are never likely to be seen alive again."

So she and her tub twirled around and around, until they sunk about three yards into the earth and stayed there for a while. Then she called for help again. Now the man, though greatly amazed that she was still alive, began to think how to help her, but immediately a great stone appeared in the earth, fell on her head, and broke her skull. Then the earth fell in upon her and covered her. She was afterward dug up and found about four yards deep in the ground. The boy's two single coins were discovered in her pocket, but her tub and sieve were never located.

Attentive. That story brings to mind another sad story that I will tell you. Not far from where I once lived, there was an obscure tavern, and the man who operated it had a son whose name was Edward. Edward, or Ned, as he was called, was foolish both in his words and behavior. Certain jovial companions would come once or twice a week to the tavern. The boy's father would entertain them by calling for Ned to amuse them with his foolish words and gestures. So when these raucous men came to this man's house, the father would call for Ned. Ned would come forth, and the villain was devilishly addicted to cursing, yes, to cursing his father and mother, and anyone else who crossed him. Even though he was dim-witted, he saw that his practice was pleasing, and he would do it with all the more audacity.

Well, when these brave fellows came at various times to this tippling-house, as they called it, to get drunk and make merry, then Ned had to be called out. Because his father was closest to him and best knew how to provoke him, he would usually ask him certain questions or command him to do some work, which would be sure to provoke him indeed. Then Ned, after his foolish manner, would curse his father most bitterly, at which the old man would laugh, and so would the rest of the guests. They would continue to ask that Ned might be provoked to curse so that they might be provoked to laughter. This was the manner the old man used to entertain his guests.

The curses Ned used to curse his father, and at which the old man would laugh, were these, and others like them: "The devil take you," or "The devil fetch you." He would also wish plagues and destruction on his father. Well, it came to pass, through the righteous judgment of God, that Ned's wishes and curses were in a little time fulfilled toward his father. Not many months passed before the devil did indeed take and possess him. In a few days, he carried him out of this world by death. I say Satan took him and possessed him. I mean, it was judged so by those who knew

A Bad Boy

him and had contact with him in his final, lamentable condition. Ned's father felt the devil like a live thing go up and down inside of his body. He often had tormenting seizures, and during them, it seemed as if the devil would settle like a hard lump in the soft place of his chest. I saw it happen. The pain would tear at him and make him roar, until he finally died.

I told you before that I was an eyewitness of what I have just told you, and so I was. I have heard Ned in his roguery cursing his father, and his father laughing at it most heartily, provoking Ned to curse so that his mirth might be increased. I saw his father, also, when he was possessed. I saw him during one of his fits, and saw his flesh as it appeared to be gathered up into a heap by the devil, about the size of half an egg, to the unutterable torture and affliction of the old man.

There was also one man, who was more than an ordinary doctor, who was sent for to cast out the devil, and I was there when he attempted to do it. This is what took place. They carried the possessed man outside and laid him on his belly upon a form, with his head hanging over the form's end. Then they bound him to it. When that was done, they set a pan of coals under his mouth and put something in the pan that caused a great amount of smoke. By this means, they said they could exorcise the devil. They kept the man in that position until he was almost smothered in the smoke, but no devil came out of him. The doctor was somewhat embarrassed, the man was greatly afflicted, and I went away confused and fearful. In a little time, what possessed the man carried him out of the world, according to the cursed wishes of his son. And this was the end of the hellish mirth.

Wiseman. These are all sad judgments.

Attentive. These are dreadful judgments indeed.

Wiseman. Yes, and they remind me of the judgment found in Psalm 109. Although these verses applied mainly to Judas, they make me think of Mr. Badman:

> As he loved cursing, so let it come unto him; as he delighted not in blessing, so let it be far from him. As he clothed

*himself with cursing like as with his garment, so let it come
into his bowels like water, and like oil into his bones.*

(Psalm 109:17–18)

Attentive. It is a fearful thing for youth to be trained up in the way of cursing and swearing.

Wiseman. Trained up in them! I cannot say that Mr. Badman was, for his father often in my presence bewailed the disobedience of his children, and of this naughty boy in particular. I believe that the thoughts of the wickedness of his children made him go to bed many nights with a heavy heart and rise in the morning with an equal heaviness. But neither fatherly sorrow nor wholesome counsel would make this graceless son mend his ways.

There are some indeed who do train their children to swear, curse, lie, and steal; great is the misery of such poor children whose hard fortune it is to be ushered into the world by and under the tutelage of such ungodly parents. It would have been better for such parents had they not borne them, and better for such children had they not been born. I think that for a father or a mother to train up a child in the very way that leads to hell and damnation is so horrible! But Mr. Badman was not brought up in this way by his parents.

Attentive. But I think that since this young Badman would not be ruled at home, his father should have tried to send him abroad. He should have arranged for an apprenticeship for him with someone with whom he was acquainted, who he knew would be able to command the boy and keep him hard at work at some employment. That way, at least he would have prevented him from having the time to do those evil deeds that could not be done without the time in which to do them.

Chapter Three

Badman's Apprenticeship to a Pious Master

Wiseman. His father did arrange for one of his friends to take the boy as an apprentice. He requested that the man treat the boy with love and take care to keep him from immoral ways. The man's business was run honestly, and he had many employees. Young Badman had no unoccupied periods or idle hours given to him during which he would have opportunities to get into trouble. This arrangement did not make any difference to him, though, because as he had begun to be vile in his father's house, he continued in that way when he was in the house of his employer.

Attentive. I have known some children who, though they have been very bad at home, have changed when they have been apprenticed abroad, especially when they have been placed into a family where the father has made it a principle to maintain the worship and service of God in his household. Perhaps this was not the case in Mr. Badman's master's house.

Wiseman. Indeed, some children greatly reform when put under other men's roofs, but, as I said, this naughty boy did not, nor did his badness continue because he lacked an employer who both could not or did not correct it. For his master was a very good and devout person. He led his family in the worship of God and also walked humbly before God (Micah 6:8). He was a very meek and merciful man, one who never prodded young Badman in business, nor kept him working unreasonable hours.

Attentive. This case is rare. Personally, I have seen few who can parallel in these things with Mr. Badman's master.

Wiseman. Nor I; indeed, Mr. Badman had a good supervisor. For the most part, employers nowadays pay attention to nothing but their worldly concerns, and if apprentices carry out their work responsibilities, souls and religion may go where they will. Yes, I greatly fear that there have been many promising lads placed by their parents with such masters, who have quite undone them as to their spiritual values and eternal destinations.

Attentive. More is the pity. But since you have touched upon this subject, show me how an employer may be the ruin of his poor apprentice.

Wiseman. I cannot tell you about all the ways, but I will mention some of them. Suppose, then, that a friendly lad becomes an apprentice with one who is reputed to be a godly man; that boy may yet be ruined in many ways if his master is not circumspect before his apprentice in all things both in respect to God and man.

If he is not moderate in the use of his apprentice, if he drives him beyond his strength, if he makes him work unreasonable hours, if he will not allow him a convenient time to read the Word and to pray—these are all ways to destroy him, especially in those years of tender beginnings of good thoughts about spiritual things.

If he permits his house to be scattered with profane and wicked books that stir up lust and wantonness; that teach idle, lewd, and lascivious talk; that have a tendency to provoke to profane humor and joking; or that tend to corrupt and pervert the doctrine of faith and holiness; all these things will eat like a canker, and will quickly spoil, in youth, those good beginnings that may be sprouting within.

If there is a mixture of good and bad workers in the same place, that is another way to undo such tender lads, for those who are bad and sordid will exercise harmful influences. They have the opportunity to practice their deceit before others and to promote the use of their profane and wicked words, which will easily stick in the minds of youth and corrupt them.

Badman's Apprenticeship to a Pious Master

If the master has one way of speaking and acting outside of his home and another manner inside his home—that is, if his religion hangs in his house as his coat does and he seldom wears it except when he is away—young men will notice and stumble at this example. We say, "Hedges have eyes," and "Little pitchers have ears"; indeed, children make a greater inspection into the lives of fathers, teachers, and others than often those people are aware of. Therefore, employers should be careful lest they may destroy the good beginnings in their employees.

If the master is unconscionable in his dealings and trades with lying words, or if bad merchandise is avouched to be good, or if he seeks after unreasonable gain, his employees see it, and it is enough to undo them. Eli's sons *"were sons of Belial"* (1 Samuel 2:12) before the congregation; their actions made men despise the sacrifices of the Lord (verses 12-17).

These things may serve as a warning to masters to take heed that they do not take in apprentices and then lead to the destruction of their souls. But young Badman had none of these hindrances. His father took care and provided well for him. He had a good master; he did not lack for good books, good instruction, good sermons, good examples, or good companions, but all these things would not do.

Attentive. It is a wonder that in such a family, amid so many spiritual helps, nothing could take hold of his heart! Not good books, good instruction, good sermons, good examples, or good companions—nothing did him any good!

Wiseman. He did not pay attention to any of these things; no, they were all detestable to him. Good books could lay in his master's house until they rotted, and he would not take any time to read them; on the other hand, he would acquire all the bad and abominable books that he could, such as beastly romances and books full of debauchery that immediately tended to set all fleshly lusts on fire. True, he did not dare to let his master know that he had them. He would never let them be seen, but would keep them in hidden places and read them in secret.

He appreciated good instruction as much as he liked good books! His preference was to hear as little beneficial teaching as possible and to forget what he heard as soon as it was spoken. Yes, I have heard some who knew him then say that one could obviously discern by the look on his face and by his gestures that good counsel caused him to be ill at ease, even tormented. He never considered himself at liberty except when far removed from wholesome words. He would hate those who rebuked him and count them his deadly enemies. (See Proverbs 9:8; 15:12.)

The good examples, which were frequently set for him by his master, both in religious and civil matters, these young Badman would laugh at, and he would also make derogatory proverbs of them when he was in a place where he felt safe to do so.

His master would make him go with him to hear sermons and to where he thought the best preachers were, but this ungodly young man was, I think, a master of all evil. He used various wicked ways to hinder himself from hearing the sermons, even when the preacher thundered loudly. First, when he came into the meetinghouse, he would sit down in some corner and then fall fast asleep. Another of his devious tricks was to fix his adulterous eyes on some beautiful object that was in the place. Then, during all of the sermon, he would be feeding his fleshly lusts. Finally, if he could sit near to someone who he had observed would match his humor, he would be whispering, giggling, and playing with him until the sermon was finished.

Attentive. Why, he grew to a monstrous height of wickedness!

Wiseman. He did, and what aggravated everything was that he was accomplished in these evil practices as soon as he came to his master—he was as ready to do all these things before he came to him as if he had served an apprenticeship to learn them.

Attentive. As you tell about his sins, one must be added to them: rebellion. It was as if he had said, "I will not hear; I will not pay attention to good; I will not change; I will not repent; I will not be converted."

Wiseman. What you say is true. I do not know to whom more aptly to compare him than to that man who, when I myself rebuked him for his wickedness, in a great huff replied, "What would the devil do for company if it was not for such as I?"

Attentive. Did you really hear someone say that?

Wiseman. Yes, I did, and this young Badman was as like him as an egg is like an egg. Alas, the Scripture mentions many who by their actions speak the same. *"They say unto God, depart from us; for we desire not the knowledge of thy ways'"* (Job 21:14). Another passage states:

> *They refused to harken, and pulled away* [shrugged] *the shoulder, and stopped their ears that they should not hear. Yea, they made their hearts as an adamant stone, lest they should hear the law, and the words which the LORD of hosts hath sent in his spirit by the former prophets: therefore came a great wrath from the LORD of hosts.*
>
> (Zechariah 7:11–12)

What are all these but men like Badman, and like the young man I just mentioned? That young man was my companion when I was consoling myself in my sins. I mention him to my shame, but he has a great many friends just like him.

Attentive. Young Badman was like him indeed. Both of them walked as if their wickedness was their guiding light. I do not think your former companion would have replied to you as he did if he had not been desperate. On what occasion did you give him such a rebuke?

Wiseman. It was a while after God had parted him and me by calling me by His grace, still leaving him in his sins. As far as I know, he died as he lived, even as Mr. Badman did, but we will leave him and return again to our conversation.

Attentive. Poor obstinate sinners! Do they think that God cannot be fair with them?

Wiseman. I do not know what they think, but I know that God has said, *"'As he cried* [out], *and they would not hear; so they cried* [out], *and I would not hear,' saith the LORD of hosts"* (Zechariah

7:13). Doubtless, there is a time coming when Mr. Badman will cry for God's help.

Attentive. But I wonder that he should have been so expert in wickedness so soon! Alas, he was but a youth. I suppose he was not yet twenty.

Wiseman. No, nor eighteen either; but, as with Ishmael, and as with the children who mocked the prophet, the seeds of sin sprouted early in him. (See Genesis 21:9; 2 Kings 2:23-24.)

Attentive. Well, he was as wicked a young man as one would commonly hear about.

Wiseman. You will say so when you know the whole story.

Attentive. If there is more, please let me hear it.

Wiseman. Why then, I will tell you. He had not been with his master much more than a year and a half before he became acquainted with three young villains, who will here be nameless. They taught him to add to his sin much of the same kind as he already was doing, and he aptly received their instructions. One of them was chiefly given to immorality, another to drunkenness, and the third to stealing from his master.

Attentive. Alas, poor wretch! He was bad enough before, but these, I suppose, made him much worse.

Wiseman. That they made him worse you may be sure of, for they taught him to be a rogue, a chief one in all their ways.

Attentive. It was an ill fortune that he ever became acquainted with them.

Wiseman. You must say it in this way instead: it was through the judgment and anger of God that he became acquainted with them. He had a good master, and before that, a good father. From these two men, he had wise counsel given to him for months and years together, but his heart was set upon evil. He loved wickedness more than goodness, even when his iniquity came to be hateful; therefore, it was from the anger of God that he became acquainted with these companions of his.

Paul said, *"They did not like to retain God in their knowledge"* (Romans 1:28). And what follows? *"God gave them over to a reprobate mind, to do those things which are not convenient"* (verse 28). And again, *"As for such as turn aside unto their crooked ways, the LORD shall lead them forth with the workers of iniquity"* (Psalm 125:5). This, therefore, was God's hand upon him, that he might be destroyed and be damned, *"because* [he] *received not the love of the truth, that* [he] *might be saved"* (2 Thessalonians 2:10). God chose his delusions and deluders for him (Proverbs 12:20), even the company of base and foolish men, that he might be destroyed.

Attentive. I cannot but think indeed that it is a great judgment of God for a man to be given up to the company of vile men, for what are they but the devil's decoys, even those by whom he draws the simple into his net? A man who consorts with prostitutes, drunkards, and thieves entangles himself in the devil's bait, by which he catches them.

Wiseman. You speak the truth, but this young Badman was not simple, if by simple you mean one who is uninstructed, for he often had good counsel given to him. However, if by simple you mean one who is a fool as to the true knowledge of and faith in Christ, then he was a simple one indeed. He chose death rather than life (Deuteronomy 30:19; Romans 6:23), and to live in continual opposition to God rather than to be reconciled to Him. According to Solomon, *"Fools hate knowledge"* (Proverbs 1:22) and do *"not choose the fear of the Lord"* (verse 29). And what judgment more dreadful can a fool be given up to than to be delivered into the hands of men who have skill to do nothing but to ripen sin and hasten its finishing to damnation? Therefore, men should be afraid of offending God because He can in this manner punish them for their sins.

Once I knew a man who was awakened to his sinful condition. Yes, I knew two who were so convicted, but in time they began to draw back and to turn again to their lusts; therefore, God gave them up to the company of three or four men, who in less than three years' time, led them thoroughly to the gallows, where they were hanged like dogs because they refused to live like honest men.

Attentive. But such men do not believe that they are being given up by God in judgment and anger. They consider it to be their liberty, and they count it their happiness. They are glad that their cords are loosed and that their reins are free. They are glad that they may sin without control and that they may choose such company as can make them more expert in evil ways.

Wiseman. Their judgment is, therefore, so much the greater, because blindness of mind and hardness of heart are added to their wicked ways. They are walking on the way of death, but they cannot see where they are going. They must go as *"an ox goeth to the slaughter, or as a fool to the correction of the stocks, till a dart strike through his liver; as a bird hasteth to the snare, and knoweth not that it is for* [would cost] *his life"* (Proverbs 7:22-23). This, I say, makes their judgment double.

They are given up by God for a while to sport themselves with what will assuredly make them *"mourn at the last, when* [their] *flesh and* [their bodies] *are consumed"* (Proverbs 5:11). These are they whom Peter spoke about, who *"shall utterly perish in their own corruption"* (2 Peter 2:12). They *"count it pleasure to riot in the day time. Spots they are and blemishes, sporting themselves with their own deceivings while they feast with you"* (verse 13).

Attentive. Well, but I ask now about these three villains who were young Badman's companions. Tell me more particularly how he was swayed by them.

Wiseman. How was he influenced by them? Why, he did as they did. I intimated as much before, when I said they made him a rogue, a chief one in their ways. First, he became a frequenter of taverns and would stay there until he was as drunk as a beast. And if he could not get out by day, he would be sure to get out at night. Yes, he became so common a drunkard at last that everyone knew he was one.

Attentive. How like a swine, for drunkenness is so beastly a sin. It is a sin so much against nature that I wonder how anyone who has the appearance of a man can give up himself to so beastly, yes, worse than beastly, a thing.

Wiseman. It is a contemptible vanity indeed. I will tell you another story. There was a gentleman who had a drunkard as his groom. When he came home one night very much intoxicated with beer, his master saw it. "Well," said his master to himself, "I will leave you alone tonight, but tomorrow morning I will convince you that you are worse than a beast."

When morning came, he asked his groom to go and water his horse. He watered the horse, but when he returned to his master, he was commanded to water the horse again. The fellow rode the horse into the water a second time, but his master's horse would not drink anymore, so the fellow came up and told his master. Then, his master said,

> You drunken sot, you are far worse than my horse. He will drink to satisfy his thirst, but you drink to the abuse of nature; he will drink to refresh himself, but you to hurt and damage yourself; he will drink so that he may be more serviceable to his master, but you drink until you are incapable of serving either God or man. You beast, how much worse are you than the horse on which you ride!

Attentive. Truly, I think that his master treated him well, for in doing as he did, he showed him plainly that he was less able to govern himself than the horse was able to control his nature; consequently, the beast lived more according to the law of his nature by far than did his groom. But, please, go on with what you have to say.

Wiseman. Why, I say, there are four things, which, if they were well considered, would make drunkenness to be abhorred in the thoughts of the children of men. First, it greatly tends to impoverish and beggar a man. As Solomon said, *"The drunkard and the glutton shall come to poverty"* (Proverbs 23:21). Many who have come into the world with plenty have gone out of it in rags because of drunkenness. Many who have been born to good estates have become beggars because of this beastly sin of their parents.

Second, this sin of drunkenness results in many great and incurable diseases, by which men do, in little time, come to their end, and no one can help them. Because they are excessively wicked, they die before their time (Ecclesiastes 7:17).

Third, drunkenness is a sin that is often accompanied by an abundance of other evils. As Solomon said,

> *Who hath woe? who hath sorrow? who hath contentions? who hath babbling? who hath wounds without cause? who hath redness of eyes? They that tarry long at the wine; they that go to seek mixed wine.* (Proverbs 23:29-30)

Fourth, by drunkenness, men often shorten their days. They go out of the tavern drunk and break their necks before they get home. Not a few instances might be given of this, but this point is so clear that no more needs to be said.

Attentive. But what is worse than all is that drunkenness prepares men for everlasting hellfire (1 Corinthians 6:10).

Wiseman. Yes, and it so stupefies and muddles the soul that a man who is far gone in drunkenness is hardly ever recovered to God. Tell me, when did you ever see an old drunkard converted? No, one like that will sleep until he dies, though he sleeps on the top of a mast (Proverbs 23:34-35). Even when his dangers are great, and death and damnation are near, he will not be awakened out of his sleep. If a man has any concern for his credit, health, life, or salvation, he will not be a drunkard. But the truth is, where this sin gets the upper hand, men are, as I said before, so intoxicated and bewitched with the seeming pleasures and sweetness thereof, that they have neither heart nor mind to think of what is better in itself or what would, if embraced, do them good.

Attentive. You said that drunkenness leads to poverty, yet some make themselves rich by drunken bargains.

Wiseman. I said so, because the Word says so. As to some men's profiting from drunken deals, that is indeed rare and ignoble, and the end of such transactions will be contemptible. The Word of God is against such ways, and the curse of God will be the end of such doings. An ill-gotten inheritance may sometimes be acquired, but the end thereof will not be blessed (Proverbs 1:19). Listen to what the prophet said, *"Woe to him that coveteth an evil covetousness to his house, that he may set his nest on high"* (Habakkuk 2:9). Whether he makes drunkenness or something else the agent and decoy to get it, he brings shame to his own house, spoils his family, and damns his own soul. What he accumulates by working iniquity, he acquires by the devices of hell; therefore, he who gains by an evil course gains nothing for himself or his family. But this was one of the sins that Mr. Badman was addicted to after he became acquainted with these three fellows, nor could all that his master do break him of this beastly sin.

Attentive. But where, since he was but an apprentice, could he get money to indulge in this practice? Drunkenness is a very costly sin.

Wiseman. His master paid for it all. As I told you before, Badman learned from these three villains to be a beastly drunkard. He also learned from them how to steal from his master. Sometimes he would sell off his master's goods, but keep the money, that is, when he could. Other times, he would trick his master by stealing from his cash box. When he could do neither of these things, he would remove some of his master's possessions, those that he thought would be missed the least, and send or carry them to houses where he knew they would be credited to his drinking tab. Then, at appointed times, he would meet and make merry with these fellows.

Attentive. This was as bad, no, I think, even worse than his former sins, for by taking from his master, he not only brought himself under the wrath of God, but also endangered the monetary security of his master and his family.

Wiseman. Sins do not travel alone, but follow one another as do the links of a chain. He who would be a drunkard must have money, either his own or some other man's—either his father's, mother's, master's, or a stranger's whose he can steal in some way.

Attentive. I fear that many an honest man is undone by this kind of servant.

Wiseman. I am of the same mind as you, but this should make a merchant more wary as to the kind of servants he keeps, and what kind of apprentices he takes. It should also teach him to look carefully to the management of his shop, and to take strict account of all things that are bought and sold by his servants. The master's neglect herein may embolden his servant to be bad, and may also bring him in short time to rags and a morsel of bread.

Attentive. I am afraid that there is much of this kind of pilfering among servants in these days of ours.

Wiseman. Now, while it is on my mind, I will tell you a story. When I was visiting in prison, a woman who was in a great deal of trouble came to me. So I asked her, since she was a stranger to me, what she had to say. She said she was afraid she would be damned. I asked her the reason for her fears. She told me that she had, some time ago, lived with a shopkeeper at Wellingborough and had robbed his cash box in the shop several times. She asked me what she should do.

I told her that she should go to her master and make things right. She said she was afraid, and I asked her why. She said that she feared that he would have her hung. I told her that I would intercede for her life and would make use of other friends to do the same, but she told me that she dared not try it. Then I volunteered to go to her master, and while she remained out of sight, to make amends for her. I asked her her master's name, but all that she said in answer to this was, "Please leave the matter alone until I come to you again." Away she went, without telling me either her master's name or her own. This happened about ten or twelve years ago, and I have never seen her again. I tell you this story for this reason—to confirm your fears that too many of this kind of servant exist, and that sometimes, God causes them, like old Tod, of whom mention was made before, through the terrors that He lays upon them, to confess and turn themselves in. I could tell you of another who came to me with a similar story concerning herself and the robbing of her mistress, but at this time, let this one suffice.

Attentive. But what was that other villain addicted to, I mean young Badman's third companion?

Wiseman. Immorality. I told you before, but it seems that you have forgotten.

Attentive. Now I remember. Immorality is another kind of filthy sin.

Wiseman. It is, and yet it is one of the most prominent sins of our day.

Attentive. So they say, and amazingly, it is prevalent among those who one would think had more sense, even among some important leaders.

Wiseman. More is the pity, for usually examples that are set by those in leadership spread sooner and more universally than do the sins of other men; yes, and when such men who are in important positions transgress boldly and audaciously, sin walks with a brazen face through the land. As Jeremiah said of the disobedient prophets, it can be said of these, *"From the prophets of Jerusalem is profaneness gone forth into all the land"* (Jeremiah 23:15).

Attentive. But please, let us return to Mr. Badman and his companions. You say one of them was very vile in the commission of impure actions.

Wiseman. Yes, not that he was not also a drunkard and a thief, but he was the foremost villain in this sin of uncleanness. This roguery was his masterpiece, for he was a ringleader to all of them in the beastly sin of meeting with prostitutes. He was also best acquainted with the houses where prostitutes worked, and so he could readily lead the rest of his gang to them. Because the Jezebels knew this young villain, they would quickly reveal themselves in all their whorish pranks to those whom he brought with him.

Attentive. That is a deadly thing to young men, when such beastly queens will, with words and poses that are openly tempting, expose themselves to them; it is hard for a man to escape their snare.

Wiseman. That is true; therefore, the wise man's counsel is the best: *"Remove thy way far from her, and come not nigh the door of her house"* (Proverbs 5:8). For they are, as you say, very tempting, as is seen in the Proverbs. The wise man said,

> For at the window of my house I looked through my casement, and beheld among the simple ones, I discerned among the youths, a young man void of understanding, passing through the street near her corner; and he went the way to her house in the twilight, in the evening, in the black and dark night: and, behold, there met him a woman with the attire of a harlot, and subtle of heart. (She is loud and stubborn; her feet abide not in her house: Now is she without, now in the streets, and lieth in wait at every corner.) So she caught him, and kissed him, and with an impudent face said unto him, I have peace offerings with me; this day have I payed my vows. Therefore came I forth to meet thee, diligently to seek thy face, and I have found thee. I have decked my bed with coverings of tapestry, with carved works, with fine linen of Egypt. I have perfumed my bed with myrrh, aloes, and cinnamon. Come, let us take our fill of love until the morning: let us solace ourselves with loves.   (Proverbs 7:6–18)

There was a bold beast! Indeed, the very eyes, hands, words, and ways of such are all snares and bands to youthful, lustful fellows. And with these was young Badman greatly snared.

Attentive. This sin of immorality is mightily cried out against, both by Moses, the prophets, Christ, and His apostles; yet, as we see, for all that, men run headlong to it!

Wiseman. You have said the truth, and I will add that God, to hold men back from so filthy a sin, has set such a stamp of His indignation on it, and commanded such evil effects to follow it, that, were not they that use it bereft of all fear of God and love of their own health, they could not but stop and be afraid to commit it. In addition to the eternal damnation that attends this behavior in the next world, for these have no *"inheritance in the kingdom of Christ and of God"* (Ephesians 5:5), the evil effects in this world are dreadful as well.

Attentive. Please describe some of the consequences of this sin to me so that, as the occasion presents itself, I may explain them to others for their good.

Wiseman. So I will. First, it brings a man to poverty. *"For by means of a whorish woman a man is brought to a piece of bread"* (Proverbs 6:26). The reason is that a prostitute will not yield without being paid, and men, when the devil and lust is in them, and God and fear of Him is far away from them, will not refuse to give their seal, their cords, and their staff to pledge (Genesis 38:18), rather than miss the fulfillment of their lusts so that they may accomplish their desire.

Second, by this sin men diminish their strength and bring upon themselves a multitude of diseases. King Lemuel's mother warned her son of this. She said, *"What, my son? and what, the son of my womb? and what, the son of my vows? Give not thy strength unto women, nor thy ways to that which destroyeth kings"* (Proverbs 31:2-3). This sin is destructive to the body.

Give me permission to tell you another story. I have heard of a great man who was a very unclean person, and he had lived so long in that sin that he had almost lost his sight. So his physicians were sent for, to whom he told his disease, but they told him that they could do him no good unless he would leave these women alone. "No, then," he said, "farewell, sweet sight." Observe that this sin is destructive to the body, and also that some men are so addicted to it that they will have it even though it destroys their bodies.

Attentive. Paul said that he who sins this sin, sins against his own body. He wrote, *"Flee sexual immorality. Every sin that a man does is outside the body, but he who commits sexual immorality sins against his own body"* (1 Corinthians 6:18). But what of that? He who commits this sin risks destroying his body and runs the hazard of eternal damnation of his soul. If Badman did not fear the damnation of his soul, do you think that the consideration of impairing his body would have deterred him from this evil practice?

Wiseman. You speak the truth. But I think that if men would consider the bad results that come from the commission of this sin, it would at least cause them to stop making a career out of it.

Attentive. What other evil consequences follow this sin?

Wiseman. Outward shame and disgrace. First, the foul disease called syphilis often follows this terrible sin. This disease is so disgusting and offensive, so infectious to the whole body, and so frequently transmitted by the sin of prostitution that, to their shame, many unclean women have more or less a touch of it.

Attentive. That is a foul disease indeed! I knew a man once who rotted away from it, and another whose nose was eaten off, and his mouth almost closed up because of it.

Wiseman. Where this disease is found, its cause is generally known to be immorality. This disease declares to all who see a man suffering from it that he is an odious, beastly, unclean person. Job spoke of the punishment for this sin as a *"destruction to the wicked, and a strange punishment to the workers of iniquity"* (Job 31:1-3).

Attentive. Do you think that the disaster that Job spoke of refers to this foul disease?

Wiseman. I do think so, and for this reason. We see that this disease is inherent to this most beastly sin, nor is there any disease as related to any other sin as this disease is to this sin. That Job referred to this sin of immorality, you will easily perceive when you read these verses:

> I have made a covenant with my eyes; why then should I think upon a maid? For what portion of God is there from

above? and what inheritance of the Almighty from on high? (Job 31:1-2)

Job then answered his own question: *"Is not destruction to the wicked, and a strange punishment to the workers of iniquity?"* (verse 3). This *"strange punishment"* is venereal disease. Also, I think that this foul disease is what Solomon intended when he said, speaking of the unclean and beastly creature who commits adultery, *"A wound and dishonour shall he get; and his reproach shall not be wiped away"* (Proverbs 6:33). Job called it *"strange punishment"*; Solomon called it *"a wound and dishonour"*; and they both saw it as a judgment on this sin.

Attentive. What other things follow the commission of this beastly sin?

Wiseman. Why, often it is attended with murder, with the murder of the baby conceived on the defiled bed. How common it is for the bastard-begetter and the bastard-bearer to consent together to murder their children will be better known on the day of judgment, yet something of it is known now.

I will tell you another story. An old man, one of my acquaintances, a man of good reputation in our country, had a mother who was a midwife. She was mostly employed in assisting prominent persons. One day, a brave young gentleman on horseback rode to this woman's house to take her to help a young lady. She prepared herself to go with him, whereupon he lifted her up behind him on the horse, and away they rode into the night. Now they had not ridden far before the gentleman got off his horse, and, lifting the old midwife off the horse, he turned her around several times and then set her back up on the horse again. Then he got back up, and away they went until they came to a stately house, into which he led her. He took her into a room where a young lady was in labor. He then told the midwife to do her job, and she demanded help. He drew out his sword and told her that if she did not hurry up and do her job alone, she would find nothing but death.

To make a long story short, this old midwife helped the young woman to deliver a fine, sweet baby. Now this room was heated by a very great fire. The gentleman picked up the baby, went and took coals from the supply, cast the child into the fire, covered the baby with the coals, and that was the end of that.

When the midwife had finished her work, he paid her well for her efforts, but locked her in a dark room all day. When night came, he placed her on the horse behind him again, and carried her away until she had arrived almost at home. Then he turned her around and around as he did before to disorient her. He brought her to her house, set her down, bid her farewell, and away he went. She could never tell who he was or where he had taken her. The midwife's son, who was a minister, told me this story and attested to its truthfulness.

Attentive. Murder often follows as the fruit of immorality. But sometimes God brings even these adulterers and adulteresses to shameful ends. I heard of one case in or near to Colchester of a pharmacist and his mistress, who had three or four illegitimate children between them and had murdered them all. At last, they were hung for their crimes. The truth came out this way: the harlot was so afflicted in her conscience about it that she could not be quiet until she had told the whole truth. Thus many times God makes the actors of wickedness their own accusers and brings them to just punishment for their own sins by their own tongues.

Wiseman. I was once in the presence of a married woman who lay sick of the illness from which she died. Being smitten in her conscience for the sin of infidelity, which she had often committed with other men, I heard her, as she lay upon her bed, cry out, "I am a whore, and all my children are bastards. I must go to hell for my sin, and look, there stands the devil at the foot of my bed to receive my soul when I die."

Attentive. These are sad stories. Tell no more of them now, but if you please, show me some other evil consequences of this beastly sin.

Wiseman. This sin is such a snare to the soul, that unless a miracle of grace intercedes, the person unavoidably perishes in the enchanting and bewitching pleasures of it. This truth is manifest by these and similar texts:

> For by means of a whorish woman a man is brought to a piece of bread; and the adulteress will hunt for the precious life. (Proverbs 6:26)

> But whoso committeth adultery with a woman lacketh understanding; he shall give all the substance of his house. (Proverbs 6:32)

> For a whore is a deep ditch; and a strange woman is a narrow pit. (Proverbs 23:27)

> Her house inclineth unto death, and her paths unto the dead. None that go unto her return again, neither take they hold of the paths of life. (Proverbs 2:18-19)

> She hath cast down many wounded; yea, many strong men have been slain by her. Her house is the way to hell, going down to the chambers of death. (Proverbs 7:26-27)

Attentive. These are dreadful sayings and show the terrible state of those who are guilty of this sin.

Wiseman. Truly, they do. But what makes the whole situation more shocking is that men are given up to this sin because they are abhorred by God, and because abhorred, they will fall into the commission of it and will live there. "*The mouth* [that is, the flattering lips] *of strange women is a deep pit: he that is abhorred of the LORD shall fall therein*" (Proverbs 22:14). Therefore, it is said again of such that they do not have "*any inheritance in the kingdom of Christ and of God*" (Ephesians 5:5).

Attentive. When we take all these facts together, it is a horrible thing to live and die in this transgression.

Wiseman. True, but suppose that instead of all these awful judgments, this sin had attached to it all the joys of this life, and no bitterness, shame, or disgrace was mixed with it. Even still, one hour in hell would spoil it all. Hell, hellfire, damnation in hell, is such an inconceivable punishment that, were it but thoroughly believed, it would nip this sin, along with others, in the bud. But here is the evil result: those who give themselves to these things harden themselves in unbelief and atheism about the punishments that God has threatened to inflict upon the committers of such sins. At last, they arrive at almost an absolute and firm belief that there is no judgment to come hereafter; otherwise, they would not, they could not, attempt to commit this sin by saying such abominable things as some do.

I heard of one who would say to his young lady when he tempted her to commit this sin, "If you will risk your body, I will risk my soul." I myself heard another say, when he was tempting a young woman to commit an immoral act with him—it was in the days when Oliver Cromwell was Lord Protector—that if she did become pregnant, he would tell her how she could escape punishment, which was then severe. He told her to say when she came before the judge that she was with child by the Holy Spirit. I heard him say this, and it greatly troubled me. I had a mind to have accused him for it before some judge, but he was an important man, and I was poor and young, so I let it alone, but it upset me very much.

Attentive. That is the most horrible thing that I have ever heard in my life! How different these men were from the spirit and grace that Joseph demonstrated (Genesis 39:6-10).

Wiseman. How true. When Joseph's master's wife tempted him, yes, tempted him daily, even touching him and saying, *"Lie with me"* (Genesis 39:12), he refused. He refused to sleep with her or to be with her. Mr. Badman would have taken the opportunity.

Here is something more to be said about Joseph. Here was a young woman, an important woman, the wife of the captain of the guard. I guarantee that she was beautiful. Here is a woman who had whorish affections for Joseph even though he had never flirted with her. Without his encouragement, she invited him to come and lie with her. Joseph was a young man, full of strength, and therefore more in danger to be enticed. This temptation from her continued for days, yet Joseph refused. He said no heartily, violently, and constantly to her daily temptation, her daily solicitation, and her daily provocation.

One day, when she asked him to lie with her, he had the perfect opportunity because there were no other men in the house at this time (Genesis 39:11). But when she grabbed him by the coat, saying, *"Lie with me"* (verse 12), he left his garment in her hand and got out. Although contempt, treachery, slander, accusation, imprisonment, and danger of death followed—for a whore does not care what trouble she causes when she cannot have her way—yet Joseph would not defile himself, sin against God, and hazard his own eternal salvation (verse 9).

Attentive. Blessed Joseph! I wish there were more men like him!

Wiseman. Mr. Badman has more men like him than Joseph; otherwise, there would not be as many harlots as there are. Though I do not doubt that some women are bad enough on their own, yet I truly believe that many of them are first led astray by the flatteries of men like Badman. Unfortunately, many women plunge into this sin at first by the promise of marriage. They are flattered by promises and even forced into consenting to these villainies. Once they have fallen, their hearts grow hard until, at last, they give themselves up, even as wicked men do, to engage greedily in this kind of wickedness. But Joseph, as you see, was of another mind, for the fear of God was in him.

Before I leave this point, I will tell you two noteworthy stories. I hope Mr. Badman's companions will hear them. They are found in Clarke's *Looking Glass for Sinners*. Mr. Cleaver, said Clarke, reports of one whom he knew who had committed an immoral act. Then the horror of his actions troubled his conscience to the point that he hanged himself. He left this note, which said,

> Indeed, I acknowledge it to be utterly unlawful for a man
> to kill himself, but I am bound to act the magistrate's part,
> because the punishment of this sin is death.

On the same page, Clarke mentioned two more who, as they were committing adultery, were immediately struck dead during the very act with fire from heaven. Their bodies were found, half burned, emitting a most loathsome odor.

Attentive. These are memorable stories indeed.

Wiseman. So they are, and they are as true as they are remarkable.

Attentive. If young Badman's master knew him to be such a wretch, I wonder how he could allow him into his house.

Wiseman. They got along as well as fire and water do. Young Badman's ways were odious to his master, and his master's ways were unbearable to young Badman. Thus, in these two were fulfilled that saying of the Holy Spirit: *"An unjust man is an abomination to the just: and he that is upright in the way is abomination to the wicked"* (Proverbs 29:27). Mr. Badman could not tolerate the good man's ways, and the good man could not accept the bad ways of his wicked apprentice. Yet his master would have kept him and also taught him his trade if he could have.

Attentive. If he could have? Why could he not?

Wiseman. Alas, Badman ran away from him once, then twice, and he would not be disciplined at all. So the next time he ran away, his master let him go. He gave him no reason to run away, except that he tried to hold him to the good and honest rules of life. If the decision had been yours to make, I think you would have let him go, too. For what could a man do who had concern for his own peace, his children's welfare, and the preservation of the rest of his servants from evil, but let him go? Had he stayed, a reform school would have been the best place for him, but his master was unwilling to send him there because of the love and respect that he felt for Badman's father. I think a reform school would have been the most appropriate place for him, but his master let him go.

Attentive. He ran away, you say, but where did he go?

Chapter Four

Badman's New Master

Wiseman. Badman ran away to one who was a master in Badman's chosen occupation, and also to one who was as evil as he. Thus he joined forces with the wicked (Proverbs 11:21), and there he served out the remaining time of his apprenticeship.

Attentive. Then, did he have his heart's desire since he was living with one who was like himself?

Wiseman. Yes, he did, but God gave it to him in His anger.

Attentive. What do you mean?

Wiseman. I mean what I said before, that for a wicked man, by the providence of God, to be turned out of a good man's house to live in a wicked man's house is a sign of the anger of God. For God, by this and similar judgments, says, in effect, to such a person,

> You wicked one, you do not love Me, My ways, or My people. You cast My law and good counsel behind your back. Come, I will dispose of you in My wrath. You will be turned over to the ungodly, you will be schooled by the devil, and I will leave you to sink and swim in sin, until I visit you with death and judgment.

This was, therefore, another judgment that came upon young Badman.

Attentive. You have said the truth, for by such a judgment as this, God takes evildoers out of the hand of the just and binds them in the hand of the wicked, and where they will be carried then, one can only imagine.

Wiseman. For several reasons, this is one of the saddest expressions of God's anger that happens to this kind of person. First, by this judgment, one is removed from the means that ordinarily are useful to the good of the soul. For a family where godliness is professed and practiced is God's ordinance; it is the place that He has appointed to teach young ones the way and fear of God. (See Genesis 18:19.) Now, to be taken from such a family and moved into a bad, wicked one, as Mr. Badman was, must be a sign of the judgment and the anger of God. In ungodly families, men learn to forget God, to hate goodness, and to estrange themselves from the ways of those who are good.

Second, in bad families there are continually fresh examples of evil, and also incitements and new encouragement to practice it. Moreover, in such places, evil is commended, praised, and well-thought-of. Those who do it are applauded; and this, to be sure, is an overwhelming judgment.

Next, such places are the haunts and walks of the infernal spirits, who are continually poisoning the thinking and minds of one or more in such families, so that they may be able to poison others. Therefore, observe this: usually, in wicked families, one or two members are more prone to wickedness than the others who live there. Such are Satan's channels, for by them he conveys the spawn of hell, through their being crafty in wickedness, into the ears and souls of their companions. When they have conceived wickedness, they labor in it, as a woman does with child, until they have brought it forth. *"Behold, he travaileth with inquity, and hath conceived mischief, and brought forth falsehood"* (Psalm 7:14). Some men, as is suggested here in this verse, have a kind of mystical but hellish copulation with the devil, who is the father, and their soul is the mother of sin and wickedness; they, as soon as they have conceived by him, bring forth sin, and by it, their own damnation (James 1:15).

Attentive. How much then does it concern those parents who love their children to see that they are apprenticed to good families, so that they may early learn to shun evil and to follow what is good!

Wiseman. It concerns them indeed. It also concerns those who take children into their families. They must be careful of the kind of children they accept. For a man may soon, by a bad boy, be damaged both in his name, estate, and family. He may also be hindered in his peace and pursuit after God and godliness by the offensive behavior of a wicked and filthy apprentice.

Attentive. True, for *"one sinner destroyeth much good"* (Ecclesiastes 9:18), and *"a poor man is better than a liar"* (Proverbs 19:22). But many times a man cannot help taking a bad apprentice, for at the beginning, he promises to be very fair. Then, in a little time, he proves to be a rogue, like young Badman.

Wiseman. That is true also, but when a man has done the best he can to prevent a problem, he may confidently expect the blessings of God to follow. Moreover, he will given all the more peace if things go contrary to his desires.

Attentive. Did Mr. Badman and his new master get along well since they were birds of a feather? I mean, since they were so well-suited for wickedness?

Wiseman. This second master was bad enough, but he would often disagree with young Badman, his servant. He would scold, and sometimes beat him, too, for his disobedience.

Attentive. What! He would act that way when he was so bad himself! This is like the proverb, "The devil corrects vice."

Wiseman. I assure you, it is as I say. For you must know that Badman's ways did not always suit his master's gains. Could he have done as the slave girl that we read of in Acts 16:16, in other words, filled his master's purse through his badness, he would certainly have been his master's favorite. But it was not so with young Badman; therefore, though his master and he got along well enough for the most part, yet in certain points, they differed.

Young Badman neglected his master's business, went to houses of prostitution, deceived his master, and attempted to seduce his master's daughters. No wonder they disagreed in these points. Not so much that his master had an antipathy against the actions themselves, for he had done the same kinds of things when he was an apprentice. He was more irate because his servant, through his sins, robbed him of his commodities, and so caused damage to him.

If young Badman's wickedness had worked exclusively to his master's advantage, he could have sworn, lied, deceived, cheated, and defrauded customers for his master—and indeed sometimes he did so. Had that been all that he had done, he would never have heard a cross word from his master, but this was not always Mr. Badman's way.

Attentive. That was well said, and the distinction was made clear between the wickedness of the master and wickedness of the servant.

Wiseman. How sad it is when men who are wicked themselves greatly hate it in others, not simply because it is evil, but because it opposes their interest. Do you think that the masters of the *"damsel possessed with a spirit of divination"* (Acts 16:16) would have been troubled at the loss of her, if they had not lost, along with her, their profit? No, I'll warrant you, she could have gone to the devil for them; but *"when her masters saw that the hope of their gains was gone"* (verse 19), then they persecuted Paul and Silas for freeing her of her evil spirit. (See Acts 16:16-24.) But Mr. Badman's master sometimes lost money because of Badman's sins, and then the two would be at odds.

Attentive. Poor Badman! Then it seems he could not always please others who were as bad as he.

Wiseman. No, he could not, because of the reason I have told you.

Attentive. But do not bad masters condemn themselves in condemning the badness of their servants?

Wiseman. Yes, in that they condemn in others what they permit themselves to do (Romans 2:1-3). The time will come when that very sentence that has gone out of their own mouths against the sins of others—while they themselves take pleasure in the same actions—will return with violence upon their own heads

(Matthew 7:1-5). The Lord pronounced judgment against Baasha because of all his evils in general, but for this reason in particular: because he was *"like the house of Jeroboam; and because he killed them"* (1 Kings 16:7). This is the same case as Mr. Badman's master's; he was like Badman, and yet he beat him. He was like his servant, and yet he railed at him for being bad.

Attentive. But why did young Badman not run away from this master, as he ran away from the other?

Wiseman. If I am not mistaken, the reason was that there was godliness in the house of his first master, and young Badman could not endure that. He had better food, lodging, work, free time, and more overall from his first master's allotment than he ever had by his second, but he was never satisfied because of the godliness that was fostered there. He could not tolerate the praying, the reading of Scriptures, and the listening to and discussing of sermons. He could not bear to be told about his transgressions in a sober and godly manner.

Attentive. There is a great deal in the manner of reproof; wicked men both can and cannot accept having their transgressions spoken about.

Wiseman. There is much difference indeed. Mr. Badman's last master would tell him of his sins in Mr. Badman's own dialect; he would swear, curse, and damn when he told him of his sins, and this manner of speech Badman could bear better than to be told of his sins in a godly way. Besides, that last master would, when his passions and rage were over, laugh and joke about the sins of his servant Badman, and that would please young Badman well. Nothing offended Badman but beatings, and he received only a few of those at this point because he was pretty well grown up. For the most part, when his master raged and swore, Badman would return oath for oath, and curse for curse, at least secretly, letting him go on as long as he would.

Attentive. This was a hellish way to live.

Wiseman. It was terrible indeed. One might say that with this master, young Badman perfected himself more and more in wickedness, as well as in his trade. By the time his apprenticeship was completed, what with his own inclination to sin, his acquaintance with his three companions, and the wickedness he saw in his last master, Badman became an inveterate sinner. Before he finished his time of service, I believe he was responsible for fathering an illegitimate child.

Attentive. Well, it seems he lived to finish his time, but what happened to him then?

Wiseman. Why, he went home to his father, who was a loving and tenderhearted man, and he welcomed him home.

Attentive. And how did he conduct himself there?

Wiseman. Why, the reason he went home was to get money to set himself up in business. He stayed only a little while at home, and during that time, he restrained himself as well as he could. He did not reveal his depraved character for fear that his father would be offended and refuse to give, or for a while refrain from giving, him money. Yet even then he would have his times, and companions, and gratify his lusts with them. He would cover his cavorting by saying that he was just renewing old acquaintances. Using civility as an excuse, he would oblige them with a bottle or two of wine or a dozen or two drinks.

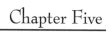

Chapter Five

The Tricks of a Wicked Businessman

Attentive. And did his father give him money to set up his business?

Wiseman. Yes, more than several thousand dollars.

Attentive. I think that the old man was out of his mind. Had I been his father, I would have held him at arm's length until I had had far better proof of his good behavior. I perceive that his father knew what a disobedient boy he had been, both by what he used to do at home and because he left a good master for a bad. He should not, therefore, have given him money so soon.

What if he had had to pinch his pennies a little, and had worked as a journeyman for a time so that he might have learned the value of money by earning it himself? Then, in all probability, he would have known better how to spend it. By that time, perhaps, he would have matured and deliberated over how he should live in the world. Yes, and who knows but that he might have come to himself, as the Prodigal did (Luke 15:11-19), and have asked God and his father for forgiveness for the crimes that he had committed against them.

Wiseman. If his father could have dealt with him in this way and made it beneficial so that the son would have reached the ends that you have described, then I would think the same way as you do. But unfortunately, you talk as if you never knew or at the present have forgotten what the tenderness and compassion of a father are like. Why, did you treat your own son like this?

It is evident that we are better at giving good counsel to others than at taking good counsel ourselves. But, my honest neighbor, suppose that Mr. Badman's father had done as you say and by so doing had driven his son to evil choices. How would he have helped either himself or his son in so doing?

Attentive. That is true, but it does not necessarily follow that if the father had done as I said, the son would have reacted as you said. But if he had done as you supposed, how would things be worse than they already were?

Wiseman. He turned out bad enough, that is true. But suppose his father had given him no money, and suppose that young Badman had thrown a fit, and in anger had gone over the sea where his father neither saw nor heard of him again. Or suppose that in a spirit of resentment, he had robbed travelers of their money, and thus had brought himself to the gallows, and his father and family to great contempt. If he had not been caught stealing, then he still would have added this crime to his other evils acts. What comfort could his father have had if any of these things had happened? Besides, when his father had done for him what he could, with desire to make him an honest man, he would then, whether his son had proved honest or not, have laid down his head with far more peace than if he had taken your advice.

Attentive. I think I should not have been so brash as to have offered counsel in this case. But since you have given me such a clear account of his evildoing, I cannot help but be angry with him.

Wiseman. In an angry mood, we may soon wear ourselves out, but this poor wretch has gone to his eternal punishment. But, as I said, when a good father has done what he can for a bad child, even if that child never proves to be better, the father can lie down with far more peace than if, through severity, he had driven him to trouble.

I remember that I once heard of a good woman, who had, as did Badman's father, a wicked and ungodly son. She prayed for him, counseled him, and showed a mother's heart for him for several years, but still he remained bad. At last, after she had been praying for his conversion, as she was accustomed to doing, she went to him and began to admonish him. She said,

> Son, you have been and are a wicked child. You have cost me many prayers and tears, yet you remain wicked. I have done my duty well. I have done what I can to save you. Now, I am satisfied that if I see you damned on the day of judgment, instead of being grieved for you, I will rejoice to hear the sentence of your damnation on that day.

Hearing those words and knowing the love and pain in her heart, her son became converted.

I tell you that if parents act lovingly toward their children, mixing mercy with loving rebuke, and their loving rebuke with fatherly and motherly compassion, they are more likely to save their children than by being churlish and severe toward them. But if their children are not saved, if their mercy does them no good, yet it will greatly comfort them at the day of death to recall that they have done in love as much as they could to save and deliver their children from hell.

Attentive. Well, I yield to your opinion. But please, let us return again to Mr. Badman. You said that his father gave him a portion of his inheritance so that he might establish his business.

Wiseman. Yes, his father did give him a part of the family fortune, and he did set up his business, and almost as soon closed it down. He was not open for business long because of his mismanagement of money—both at home and with his extravagant spending abroad. He became so far in debt, and had so little in his shop to sell, that he was hard put to keep himself out of prison. But when his creditors heard that he was about to marry well and to get a rich wife, they said among themselves, "We will not be hasty with him; if he marries a rich wife, he will pay us all."

Attentive. But how could he so quickly run out of money? For I perceive it was in a small amount of time by what you have said.

Wiseman. It was a short period indeed. I think it was not more than two and a half years, but the reason is apparent: he was a wild young man, and now that his bridle was loose, and he was wholly controlled by his lusts and vices, he gave himself up to the ways of his heart and to the sight of his eyes, forgetting that for all these things God would bring him to judgment (Ecclesiastes 11:9). And he who does this, you may be sure, will not be able to stand on his feet for long.

Besides, he now had additional companions, companions who were most like himself in manners. They did not care who sank as long as they themselves could swim. These friends often visited him, and even hung around his shop when he was absent. They would frequently egg him on to the tavern, but make him pay everyone's tab. They would also borrow money from him, but never bother to repay them, except by spending more time with him, which he liked very well. Consequently, his poverty came *"as one that travelleth* [prowls]*, and* [his] *want as an armed man"* (Proverbs 6:11). But all the while, they observed his disposition and saw that he loved to be flattered, praised, and commended for his wit, manhood, and personality. All this was like stroking his ego. Thus they associated with him and wheedled their way into his life. Like parasites, they bled him dry, taking what his father had given him. They brought him down quickly, almost to where he was living among beggars.

Attentive. Then were the sayings of Solomon, the wise man, fulfilled: *"He that keepeth company with harlots spendeth his substance"* (Proverbs 29:3), and *"A companion of fools shall be destroyed"* (Proverbs 13:20).

Wiseman. Yes, and this verse, too: *"A companion of riotous men shameth his father"* (Proverbs 28:7). For he, poor man, had both grief and shame in seeing how his son, now at his own hand, behaved himself in the enjoyment of those good things, in and under the lawful use of which he might have lived to God's glory, his own comfort, and credit among his neighbors. *"But he that followeth after vain persons shall have poverty enough"* (Proverbs 28:19). The way that he took led him directly into this condition; for who can expect other things of one who follows such a course? Besides, when he was in his shop, he could not stand to work; he was naturally given to idleness. He loved to live high, but his hands refused to labor. What other end can such a one come to except what the wise man said? *"The drunkard and the glutton shall come to poverty: and drowsiness shall clothe a man with rags"* (Proverbs 23:21).

Attentive. But now, I think, when he was brought so low, he should have considered the hand of God that was gone out against him, struck his breast in sorrow, and returned to the ways of God.

Wiseman. Consideration, good consideration, was far from him. He was as obstinate and proud now as ever in all his life. He was as active in his pursuit of sin as when he was in full bloom; only now he moved like a broken-down horse. The devil had almost knocked him off his feet.

Attentive. Well, what did he do when almost everything he owned was gone?

Wiseman. Two things now occupied his time. First, he spent his time swearing, cracking jokes, and lying. He convinced others that he had succeeded rather than failed in business, and he had at his beck and call some of his companions who would swear to his lies as fast as he could tell them.

Attentive. This was double wickedness. He sinned in saying it and sinned in swearing to it.

Wiseman. That is true, but what evil will he not do who is bereft of God, as I believe Mr. Badman was?

Chapter Six

Badman Deceives a Good Woman

Attentive. What was the other thing he was engaged in doing?

Wiseman. Why, what I hinted before. He was looking for a rich wife, which brings me to more of his inventive, imaginative, contrived, and abominable roguery, such that will reveal him to have been a most desperate sinner.

This was the thing: it was not so much a wife he wanted, but rather money. As for women, he could summon prostitutes with a whistle. But, as I said, he wanted money, and the only way he could get it was to marry a wife. Nor could he so easily find a wife either, except by becoming an artist of disguises; but camouflaging himself did not work among people who could conceal themselves as well as he.

But a young lady lived not far from him, who was both godly and had a good dowry. Figuring out how to get her would require deception and ingenuity. He began by calling together a council of some of his most trusty and cunning companions, and he revealed his plan—namely, that he had a desire to marry. He also told them to whom, but he asked them how he could accomplish his end since she was religious, and he was not. Then one of them replied,

> Since she is religious, you must pretend to be so, too, and continue to do so for some time before you approach her. Pay attention to where she goes each day to hear sermons, and you go there also. But you must be sure to behave

yourself and act soberly. Pretend that you like hearing the Word of God wonderfully well. Stand where she will be able to see you, and when you come home, be sure that you walk down the street very sedately. Try to stay within sight of her. After doing these things for a while, then go to her, and first talk of how sorry you are for your sins. Show great love for her religion, speaking well of her preachers and of her godly friends, bewailing your hard luck that it was not your lot to be acquainted with her and her fellow believers sooner. This is the way to get her.

Also you must write down sermons, talk about Scriptures, and solemnly affirm that you came courting her only because she is godly. Tell her that you would count it your greatest happiness if you might be wed to her. As for her money, ignore it; that is the best way to acquire it the soonest, for she will be suspicious at first that you desire her only for her money. You know what she has, but do not say a word about it. Do this, and see if you do not quickly ensnare the lass.

Thus was the trap laid for this poor, honest girl, and she was quickly caught in his pit.

Attentive. Did he take this advice?

Wiseman. Did he? Yes, and after a while, he went boldly to her wearing a mask of religion, as if he had been, for his honesty and godliness, one of the most sincere and upright men in England. Paying careful attention to detail, he followed the advice of his counselors and quickly obtained her hand in marriage. For he was naturally attractive; he was tall and handsome, and wore plain, but very good, clothes. It was even easier for him to don his religion because he had seen true Christianity practiced in the house of his father and his first master; thus, he could more readily pretend to be a devout believer himself.

So he chose the day and went to her, which he could easily do since she did not have a living father or mother to oppose his advances. When he arrived, he politely informed her of his esteem and told her why he had come. Then he apprised her of the great deal of love he felt for her and said that of all the women in the world, he had chosen her. If she agreed, he wanted to make her his beloved wife. The reasons, as he told her, that he had settled upon her were her religious and personal qualities; therefore, he entreated her to take his offer into her tender and loving consideration.

As for his worldly affairs, he said,

> I have a very good trade and can maintain myself and my family well, while my wife sits still on her seat. I have accumulated much already, and money comes in every day, but that is not the thing at which I aim. I am seeking an honest and godly wife.

Then he would present her with a good book or two, pretending how much benefit he had received by reading them himself. He would also often speak well of godly ministers, especially of those whom he perceived she enjoyed and loved the most. In addition, he would often tell her what a godly father he had, and what a new man he had become himself; thus did this treacherous wheeler-dealer conduct himself with this honest and good girl, to her great grief and sorrow, as later you will hear.

Attentive. But did the young lady have no friends to look after her?

Wiseman. Her father and mother were dead, and that he knew well enough, so she was the more easily overcome by his deceiving, lying tongue. But even if she had had an abundance of friends, she might still have been beguiled by him. It is too much the custom of young people now to think that they are wise enough to make their own choices and that they need not ask counsel of those who are older and wiser than they. This is a great fault in them, and many of them have paid dearly for it. Well, to be brief, in a little time, Mr. Badman obtained his desire, captured this honest girl and her money, married her, brought her home, gave a feast and entertained her royally, but her money paid for it all.

Attentive. This was an amazingly deceitful act. One will seldom hear of anything like it.

Wiseman. By doing these things, he showed how little he feared God, and what little regard he had for His judgments. By all this behavior and all these words, he demonstrated his premeditated evil. He knew that he had lied; he knew that he had disguised himself; and he knew that he had abused the name of God, religion, good men, and good books. He acted like a stalking-horse in order to better catch his game. In all his glorious pretense of religion, he was but a gloriously painted hypocrite, and hypocrisy is the highest sin that a poor carnal wretch can achieve. It is also a sin that most dares God, and that also brings great damnation. Now he was *"like unto white sepulchres, which indeed appear beautiful outward, but are within full of dead men's bones, and of all uncleanness"* (Matthew 23:27). Now he was *"as graves which appear not, and the men that walk over them are not aware of them"* (Luke 11:44). For this poor, honest, godly lady little imagined that her peace and comfort, her property and liberty, her very personhood were going to die when she married Mr. Badman. Yet it was so. She was happy for only a short time before she became dead and buried to what she had once enjoyed.

Attentive. Certainly some astonishing judgment of God must be in store for and overtake such wicked men as these.

Wiseman. You may be sure that they will receive full judgment for all these things when the day of judgment comes. But as for judgment upon them in this life, it does not always come, not upon those who are worthy of it. *"And now we call the proud happy; yea, they that work wickedness are set up; yea, they that tempt God are even delivered"* (Malachi 3:15). But their punishments are reserved until the day of wrath. Then, for their wickedness, God will repay them to their faces.

> *The wicked is reserved for the day of destruction; they shall be brought forth to the day of wrath. Who shall declare his way to his face? and who shall repay him what*

*he hath done? Yet shall he be brought to the grave, and
shall remain in the tomb.* (Job 21:30-32)

That is, ordinarily they escape God's hand in this life. Only a few examples are made so that others may be cautioned and take warning thereby. But on the day of judgment, they must be rebuked for their evil with the lashes of devouring fire.

Attentive. Can you give me any examples of God's wrath falling upon men who have acted in tragically wicked ways like Mr. Badman?

Wiseman. Yes, Hamor and Shechem, and all the men of their city, for attempting to make God and religion the stalking-horse to get Jacob's daughters as their wives. Together, they were slain with the edge of the sword. The judgment of God fell upon them, no doubt, for their disguising the truth in that matter. (See Genesis 34:1-29.) All manner of lying and pretense is dreadful, but to make God and religion a disguise, thereby hiding one's deceitful ways from others' eyes, is highly provoking to the Divine Majesty. I knew one man, who lived not too far from our town, who procured a wife in the same way that Mr. Badman got his, but he did not enjoy her for long. One night as he was riding home from his companions, with whom he had been in a neighboring town, his horse threw him to the ground, and he was found dead at daybreak. He was frightfully and lamentably mangled by his fall, and besmeared with his own blood.

Attentive. Interesting, but please return to Mr. Badman's tale. How did he treat his wife after he married her?

Wiseman. Let us take things as we go. Badman had not been married for long before his creditors came after him for their money. He deferred them for a little while, but at last things came to the point that he had to give them their money or else they would harm him. So he arranged a time for them to come for their money. Right before her eyes, he paid them with her money for those goods that he had profusely spent among his whores long before he was married. He used up all that his father had given him as well.

Attentive. This beginning was bad, but what will I say? It was like Mr. Badman himself. Poor woman! This was a bad beginning for her. I fear it filled her with trouble enough, as I think such a beginning would have done to one even stronger than she.

Wiseman. Trouble, yes, you may be sure of it, but then it was too late to change her mind. She should have thought more about her decision when being cautious would have done her good. Her misery may be advantageous to others who will learn to take heed thereby, but for herself, she had to suffer the consequences— even such a life into which her husband would lead her, and that was bad enough.

Attentive. This beginning was bad, yet I fear it was but the beginning of her troubles.

Wiseman. You may be sure that it was but the beginning of sorrow, for other evils followed. For instance, it was only a short time after he was married that Badman hung his religion on the bushes. In other words, he treated his faith like some men deal with their old clothes: they cast them off or give them to others to wear. For his part, he would be religious no longer.

Therefore, he removed his mask and began to show himself for what he was: a base, wicked, debauched fellow. The poor woman then saw that she had been betrayed indeed. Also, his old companions began to flock about him, and to frequent his house and shop as they had before. And who joined them but Mr. Badman?

Now those good people who used to accompany his wife began to be amazed and discouraged. He would frown and scowl at them as if he hated the sight of them, so that, before long, he drove all good company away from her, and made her sit in solitude. He also began to go out at night to visit the prostitutes to whom he had gone before and with whom he would stay sometimes until midnight or even until near daybreak. Then he would come home as drunk as a swine. This was the path Mr. Badman followed.

Chapter Seven

Badman's Disguise
Is Removed

Wiseman. Now when he came home drunk, if his wife just spoke a word to him about where he had been and why he had so abused himself, though her words were always spoken in nothing but meekness and love, then she was "a whore, a wench, and a horse"! Sometimes he would also bring his ruffian friends home to his house, and woe to his wife after they left if she had not entertained them with an assortment of good foods and also served it diligently to them. Thus this good woman was made by Badman, her husband, to possess nothing but disappointment as to all that he had promised her or that she had hoped to have at his hands.

But what added a pressing weight to all her sorrow was that, as he had cast away all religion himself, so he attempted, if possible, to make her do the same. He would not permit her to go out to the preaching of the Word of Christ, nor to the rest of the meetings where she might have received nourishment for the salvation of her soul. He would ridicule her preachers and speak of them disparagingly, and would incite scandals about them, much to her great grief and sorrow.

At this point, she hardly dared to visit an honest neighbor's house or have a good book in her hand, especially when he had his companions in their house, or he had a little drink in his head. Also, when he perceived that she was dejected, he would speak tauntingly and mockingly to her in the presence of his friends, calling her his "religious wife," his "demure dame," and the like. He would make sport of her among his wanton friends outside of the house, too.

If she did ask him, as sometimes she would, to let her go out to hear a sermon, he would in a churlish manner reply, "Stay at home, keep the house, and look to your business here. We cannot make a living by hearing sermons." If she still urged him to let her go, then he would say to her, "Go, if you dare." He would also accuse her of giving what he had to her ministers, when, vile wretch, he had knowingly spent it on his vain companions. This was the life that Mr. Badman's good wife lived within a few months after he had married her.

Attentive. This was a disappointment indeed.

Wiseman. As great a disappointment as ever I think a poor woman has had. One would think that the knave might have given in to her a little since her ways were nothing but honest, and since she had brought him such a pleasing lump sum of money—for she had brought thousands of dollars into his house. I say, one would think he would have let her have her own way once in a while, since she desired it only in the service and worship of God. But could she persuade him to grant her that? No, not a bit, even if it would have saved her life.

True, sometimes she would steal out when he was away from home, on a journey, or among his drunken companions, but with all secrecy imaginable. One advantage the poor woman had was that her neighbors, though many of them were carnal, would not betray her, or tell of her going out to hear the Word preached, if they saw her going. Instead, they would endeavor to hide it from Mr. Badman himself.

Attentive. His treatment of her was enough to break her heart.

Wiseman. It was enough to do it indeed. In fact, it did eventually kill her in time, and, all of the time, it was killing her. Often, when she sat by herself, she would mournfully bewail her condition, saying,

"Woe is me, that I dwell in Meshech, that I dwell in the tents of Kedar! My soul hath long dwelt with him that hateth peace" (Psalm 120:5-6). I am a woman grieved in spirit. My husband has bought me and sold me for his lusts. It was not me, but my money, that he wanted. Oh, that he had had money of his own, so that I could have kept my freedom!

This she said, not in contempt of his person, but of his conditions, and because she saw that, by his hypocritical tongue, he not only had brought her almost to beggary, but had also robbed her of the Word of God.

Attentive. It is a deadly thing, I see, to be *"unequally yoked together with unbelievers"* (2 Corinthians 6:14). If this woman had had a good husband, how happily might they have lived together! Such a husband would have prayed for her, taught her, and also encouraged her in the faith and ways of God. But now, poor creature, instead of this, there was nothing but the contrary.

Wiseman. It is a deadly thing indeed, and therefore, by the Word, God's people are forbidden to be joined in marriage with unbelievers. The Bible says,

For what fellowship hath righteousness with unrighteousness? and what communion hath light with darkness? and what concord hath Christ with Belial? or what part hath he that believeth with an infidel? And what agreement hath the temple of God with idols? (2 Corinthians 6:14-16)

There can be no agreement where such matches are made. Even God Himself has declared the contrary from the beginning of the world. In speaking of the enmity between Christ and the devil, He said, *"I will put enmity between* [the serpent] *and the woman, and between thy seed and her seed"* (Genesis 3:15). In another place, He said, *"They shall not cleave one to another, even as iron is not mixed with clay"* (Daniel 2:43). I say they cannot agree, and they cannot be one; therefore, believers should be aware from the start, and not lightly receive such into their affections. God has often made such matches bitter, especially to His own. Such matches, as God said of the punishment of those who do not keep His covenant, will *"consume the eyes, and cause sorrow of heart"* (Leviticus 26:16). Oh, the wailing and lamentation of those who have been thus yoked, especially if they deliberately joined in marriage against their inner light and good counsel.

Attentive. Alas, he deluded her with his tongue and feigned reformation!

Wiseman. Yes, but she should have shown more wariness in making her decision to marry him. What if she had sought advice from some of her best, most knowing, and godly friends? What if she had engaged a godly minister or two to have talked with Mr. Badman? Also, what if she had waited to see if he was the same person behind her back that he was to her face? And besides, I truly think—since *"in the multitude of counsellors there is safety"* (Proverbs 11:14)—that if she had informed the congregation about her decision and asked them to spend some time in prayer to God about it, she would have had more peace for the rest of her life. She should have sought the judgment of others as to his godliness rather than relied on her own opinion. She should have trusted the godly wisdom of judicious and unbiased men rather than to trust in her own poor, inexperienced judgment as she did. Love is blind and will see nothing wrong where others may see a hundred faults. Therefore, I say, she should not have trusted in her own judgment alone in the matter of his goodness.

As to his personality, she would be the best judge because she was the person to be pleased, but as to his godliness, there the Word was the best judge, and those who could best understand it, because God was the One to be pleased. I wish that all young ladies would be careful about being beguiled with flattering words, with counterfeit and lying conversations, and take the best way to preserve themselves from being bought and sold by wicked men as she was, lest they regret their actions along with her. In this case, their change of mind will do them no good, and their ill-advised decisions will lead them sorrowing to their graves.

Badman's Disguise Is Removed

Attentive. Although things are past with this poor woman and cannot be recalled, let others learn from her misfortune, lest they, too, fall into her distress.

Wiseman. Yes, let them take heed, lest they suffer for their poor judgment, as this poor woman has done. And oh, I think that those who are still single persons, and who are tempted to marry men like Mr. Badman, should inform and warn themselves before they entangle themselves by going to some who are already in the snare and by asking them how it is with them. They should ask how suitable or unsuitable their marriages are and seek their advice. Surely they would sound an alarm in their ears about the inequality, unsuitableness, disadvantages, anxieties, and sins that attend such marriages, which would make them beware as long as they live. But the bird in the air does not know the notes of the bird in the snare until she comes there herself. Besides, to make up such marriages, Satan, along with carnal reason, lust, and, at the least, carelessness, has the chief hand. Where these things hold sway, destructive plans will plunge forward; therefore, I fear that little notice will be taken by young girls of Mr. Badman's wife's affliction.

Attentive. But are there no dissuasive arguments to present to prevent their future misery?

Wiseman. Yes, the law of God forbids marriage with unbelievers both in the Old Testament and in the New. The Old Testament reads, "*Neither shalt thou make marriages with them; thy daughter thou shalt not give unto his son, nor his daughter shalt thou take unto thy son*" (Deuteronomy 7:3).

The New Testament states,

> Be ye not unequally yoked together with unbelievers: for what fellowship hath righteousness with unrighteousness? and what communion hath light with darkness? And what concord hath Christ with Belial? or what part hath he that believeth with an infidel? And what agreement hath the temple of God with idols? for ye are the temple of the living God; as God hath said, I will dwell in them, and

walk in them; and I will be their God, and they shall be my people. Wherefore come out from among them, and be ye separate, saith the Lord, and touch not the unclean thing; and I will receive you. (2 Corinthians 6:14-17)

The New Testament also explains that *"a wife is bound by law as long as her husband lives; but if her husband dies, she is at liberty to be married to whom she wishes, only in the Lord"* (1 Corinthians 7:39).

Here now are prohibitions plainly forbidding believers to marry unbelievers; therefore, they should not do it. These kinds of unwarrantable marriages are condemned even by irrational creatures, who will not couple except with their own sort. Will the sheep mate with a dog, the partridge with a crow, or the pheasant with an owl? No, they will strictly partner only with those of their own kind. Yes, it sets all the world to wondering when they see or hear anything contrary. Only man is the most likely creature to condone or allow these unlawful mixtures of men and women because only man is sinful. Therefore, he, above all, will take it upon himself by rebellious actions to contradict, or rather to oppose and violate, the law of his God and Creator. Sinful man will not regard the following question worthy of his consideration: What fellowship, what concord, what agreement, what communion can there be in such marriages?

Further, the dangers that those who rebel against God's laws commonly run into should be a dissuasive argument to others to stop them from doing the same. In addition to the miseries of Mr. Badman's wife, many who have had very hopeful beginnings for heaven have, by virtue of the discord that has attended these unlawful marriages, miserably and fearfully failed to achieve their purposes. Soon after such marriages begin, conviction, the first step toward heaven, ceases; prayer, the next step toward heaven, stops; hungering and thirsting after salvation, another step toward the kingdom of heaven, comes to an end. In a word, such marriages have alienated them from the Word, from their godly and faithful friends, and have brought them once again into carnal company, among carnal friends, and also into carnal delights, where, and with whom, they have both sinfully remained and miserably perished.

And this is one reason why God has forbidden these kinds of unequal marriages. *"For they,"* said He, meaning the ungodly, *"will turn away thy son from following me, that they may serve other gods: so will the anger of the LORD be kindled against you, and destroy thee suddenly"* (Deuteronomy 7:4). Now notice, there were some in Israel who, in spite of this prohibition, risked marrying heathens and unbelievers. But what happened?

> *And they served their idols: which were a snare unto them. Yea, they sacrificed their sons and their daughters unto devils, And shed innocent blood, even the blood of their sons and of their daughters, whom they sacrificed unto the idols of Canaan: and the land was polluted with blood. Thus were they defiled with their own works, and went a whoring with their own inventions. Therefore was the wrath of the LORD kindled against his people, insomuch that he abhorred his own inheritance.* (Psalm 106:36–40)

Attentive. But let us return to the story of Mr. Badman's life. Did he have any children by his wife?

Wiseman. Yes, seven.

Attentive. I imagine they were badly brought up.

Wiseman. One of them loved his mother dearly and always obeyed her teachings. She had the opportunity to instruct this child in the principles of Christian religion, and he became a very gracious child. But Mr. Badman could not tolerate him. Seldom would he speak a pleasant word to this child, but instead, he would scowl and frown at the child, speaking gruffly and rigidly to him. Even though the boy was the most frail of the seven, he often felt the weight of his father's hand. Three of his children followed his steps directly and began to be as vile as he was in his youth. The others became a kind of mix—not as bad as their father, nor as good as their mother. They had their mother's ideas and their father's actions, and they were much like those whom you read about in the book of Nehemiah: *"And their children spake half in the speech of Ashdod, and could not speak in the Jews' language, but according to the language of each people"* (Nehemiah 13:24).

Attentive. What you say in this matter is observable within many families. If I do not miss my mark, it often happens in this way where such unlawful marriages are contracted.

Wiseman. It sometimes does so, and the reason, with respect to their parents, is this: Where one of the parents is godly, and the other is ungodly and vile, though they can agree in having children, yet they contend for their children when they are born. The godly parent devotes himself to the child, and by prayers, counsel, and good examples, labors to make the child holy in body and soul, thus fit for the kingdom of heaven. But the ungodly parent desires that the child will be like himself—wicked, base, and sinful; so they both give instructions according to their purposes. Instructions, did I say? Yes, and examples, too.

Thus, the godly, like Hannah (1 Samuel 1:27-28), present their children to the Lord, but the ungodly offer their children to Molech (Jeremiah 32:35), to an idol, to sin, to the devil, and to hell. Thus one listens to the law of his mother and is preserved from destruction, but the other follows in the ways of his father. Thus did Mr. Badman and his wife divide their children between them, but as for the three who were, as it were, mongrels, caught between the beliefs of both parents, they were like those whom you read about in Kings: they feared the Lord, but served their own idols (2 Kings 17:32-33).

They had, as I said, their mother's beliefs, and I will add, profession, too, but their father's lusts, and something of his life. Now their father did not like them because they had their mother's way of speaking, and the mother did not like that they still had their father's heart and life; nor were they fit company for either good or bad. The good would not trust them because they were bad; the bad would not trust them because they were good. In other words, the good would not trust them because they were bad in their actions, and the bad would not trust them because they were good in their words. So they were forced, with Esau, to join in affinity with Ishmael (Genesis 28:9); that is, to look for people who were hypocrites like themselves, and with them they matched, lived, and died.

Attentive. Poor woman, she could not have been but bewildered.

Wiseman. Yes, and poor children, who were sent into the world as the offspring of these two and under the control of such a father as Mr. Badman.

Attentive. You speak the truth, for such children lie under almost all manner of disadvantages, but we must say nothing, because this also is the sovereign will of God.

Wiseman. We may not by any means oppose God, yet we may talk of the advantages and disadvantages that children have by having for their parents either godly or ungodly ones.

Attentive. Yes, we may speak so, and now, since we are discussing it, let us talk briefly about the advantage those children whose parents are godly have above others.

Wiseman. I will, only I must first set forth these few points: Children born of godly parents do not have the advantage of election for their fathers' sakes. They are born as others, the *"children of wrath"* (Ephesians 2:3), though they come from godly parents. Grace comes to them not as an inheritance because they have godly parents. These things established, I will now proceed.

The children of godly parents are the children of many prayers. They are prayed for before and prayed for after they are born, and the prayers of a godly father and godly mother accomplish much (James 5:16). They have the advantage of what restraint is possible, from what evils their parents see them inclined to, and that is a second mercy. They have the advantage of godly instruction, and of being told what are and what are not the right ways of the Lord. They also have those ways commended to them that are good, and spoken well of in their hearing. Such children are also, as much as is possible, kept away from evil company, from evil books, from being taught the ways of swearing and lying, from breaking the Sabbath, and from mocking good men and good things. All these things are a very great mercy. They also have the benefit of godly lives set before them doctrinally by their parents, and that doctrine is backed with godly and holy examples. And all these things are very great advantages.

The children of ungodly parents lack these benefits, so they are more in danger of *"being led away with the error of the wicked"* (2 Peter 3:17). For ungodly parents neither pray for their children, nor do or can they heartily instruct them. They do not after a godly manner restrain them from evil, nor do they keep them from evil company. They are not grieved at, nor yet do they forewarn their children to beware of, such evil actions that are an abomination to God and to all good men. They permit their children to break the Sabbath, to swear, to lie, and to be wicked and foolish. They do not commend a holy life to their children, or set a good example before their eyes. No, they do just the opposite. They alienate their children from the love of God and all good men as soon as they are born.

Attentive. These are the actions of terrible parents. Well, before we leave the topic of Mr. Badman's wife and children, I have a mind, if you please, to ask a few more questions that I am sure you can answer.

Wiseman. What are they?

Attentive. You said a while ago that Mr. Badman would not permit his wife to go out to hear godly ministers as she liked to do. You mentioned that he told her that if she did go, it would be better for her not to come back. Did her husband often mistreat her like this?

Wiseman. He did say such things, and he said them frequently. I got sidetracked telling you about other things.

Attentive. I understand. Please go on.

Wiseman. So I will. Once, on the Lord's Day, she was going to hear a sermon, and Mr. Badman was unwilling for her to go. It seems, though, that on this occasion, she had more courage than she usually did. Therefore, after she had used up many fair words and entreaties in an effort to persuade him to let her go, but all to no avail, at last she announced that she would go. She gave him this reason:

> I have a husband, but I also have a God. My God has commanded me to be subject to His authority and to continually worship Him, and that upon threat of damnation (Romans 13:1-2; Hebrews 10:23-30). I have a husband, but I also have a soul, and my soul ought to be of more value to me than all the world. This soul of mine I will look after, care for, and, if I can, provide a heaven for its eternal habitation. You are commanded to love me as you love your own body (Ephesians 5:28), and so am I to love you (verse 22). But I tell you the truth: I prefer my soul before all the world, and its salvation I will seek (Psalm 40:16).

At this, he pronounced a frightful curse on her and then fell into a fearful rage. Moreover, he swore that if she did go, he would make both her and all her "damnable brotherhood"—for so he liked to call them—regret that they had met together to worship.

Attentive. But what did he mean by that?

Wiseman. You may easily guess what he intended. He meant that he would turn informer, and so either make those whom she loved weary of meeting together to worship God or make them pay dearly for doing so. He knew that if he carried out these threats, it would break her heart.

Attentive. But do you think Mr. Badman would have been so morally reprehensible?

Wiseman. Truly, he had enough malice and enmity in his heart to do it, but he was a businessman. He knew that he must live among his neighbors, and so he had enough sense to restrain his anger and not carry out his threats. But, as I said, he had enough malice and envy in his heart to have made him do it, only he thought it might make things worse for his business. Yet he did do other terrible things. He would urge others to persecute and abuse her friends. He would be happy when he heard that any troubles happened to them. Also, he would laugh at her when he saw her concerned about her friends. And now I have told you how Mr. Badman tormented her for her faith.

Attentive. But was he not afraid of the judgments of God that occurred at that time?

Wiseman. He showed no regard for the judgment or mercy of God, for if he had, he would not have done as he did. But what judgments do you mean?

Attentive. Such judgments that, if Mr. Badman had paid serious attention to them, might have made him ashamed.

Wiseman. Why, have you heard of any such persons whom the judgments of God have overtaken?

Attentive. Yes, and I believe you have, too.

Wiseman. I have indeed heard about some, to my astonishment and wonder.

Attentive. If you please, tell me what you know; then, perhaps, I will have more to add.

Wiseman. In our town there was one W. S., a man who lived a very wicked life. At that time, it was sanctioned to be an informer. Well, he turned into one and was as diligent in his business as most of them could be. He would watch at night, climb trees, and roam the woods during the days in his efforts to seek out believers. Yes, he would curse them bitterly and swear most fearfully, saying what he would do to them when he found them.

After he had gone on like a madman in his course and had caused some trouble to the people, he was stricken by the hand of God in this manner. First, although his tongue was naturally under the control of his will, he was able to speak for weeks only in a flattering way—just like a man who was drunk. Then he started to drool, or slobber. Sometimes the slobber would hang from his mouth almost halfway to the ground. Then he had such weakness in the tendons of his neck that often he could not look up unless he clapped his hand hard upon his forehead and held up his head that way using the strength of his hand. After this point, his speech disappeared completely, and the only sounds he made sounded like a pig or a bear. Therefore, like one of them, he would grunt and squeal, according to his moods, whether he was offended or pleased or wanted something to be done.

He continued in this way for about a half a year or thereabouts. Other than his speech, he was well overall and could go about his business, except once when he fell from the bell as it hung in our steeple. It was a wonder that he was not killed. But after that accident, he also walked about, until God had made a sufficient example of him and his sin. Then he was stricken suddenly and died miserably. That brought an end to him and his doings.

I will tell you another illustration. About four miles from St. Neots in Cambridgeshire, there was a gentleman who had a manservant. This servant was an energetic man who wanted to be an informer. An informer he became, and he caused much distress for some people. He made such a thorough case against them that there was nothing further for the police to do but to bring charges against these people. The informer pressured the police to act quickly so that he might receive money or goods as his reward for providing the information.

Now, while he was in the middle of his work, he stood by the fireside one day. Meat was cooking on the spit, and he had a taste for some of it. As he prepared to take some of the cooked meat, a dog—some say his own dog—took dislike over something, and bit his master in the leg. Although much effort was made to cure the wound, it turned to gangrene. The bite resulted in his death, and it was a dreadful one. The person who told me this story said that the young man suffered in a terrible condition from the initial bite, until his flesh rotted off him, and he departed from this world.

There is no need for me to give any more specific examples when the judgment of God against informers was made clear, if not in all, yet in nearly every county in England where such poor creatures as these were. But I wish, if it had been the will of God, that neither I nor anybody else could relate more of these stories— even though they are true and are neither lies nor fiction.

Attentive. I have also heard both of these accounts myself, and I could tell even more that are just as remarkable if I had any inclination to tell them. Instead, let us leave those who are behind to others, or to the coming of Christ, who then will justify or condemn them, as the merit of their works will require. If they have repented and have found mercy, I will be glad to know about it, for I do not wish any curses on the soul of my enemy.

Wiseman. There can be no pleasure in telling such stories, though to hear them may do us some good. They may remind us that there is a *"God that judgeth in the earth"* (Psalm 58:11), who regards *"the prayer of the destitute"* (Psalm 102:17). These examples also carry along with them both caution and counsel to those who are the survivors. Let us tremble at the judgments of God, and be afraid of sinning against Him, and our fear will be our protection. *"It shall be well with them that fear God, which fear before Him"* (Ecclesiastes 8:12).

Attentive. Well, sir, as you have intimated, so I think we have spoken enough about this kind of men. If you please, let us return to Mr. Badman himself, if you have any more to say of him.

Wiseman. More! We have scarcely begun with anything that we have said. All the particulars are in themselves so full of badness that we have only looked at the surface of them, but we will proceed. You have heard of the sins of his youth, of his apprenticeship, how he deceived the wife whom he had married, and the kind of life he led with her. Now I will tell you some more of his malicious acts. He had the very knack for knavery. As I said before, if he had been bound to serve an apprenticeship to all these things, he could not have been more cunning, nor more artful at them.

Attentive. Just as none can teach goodness as God Himself can, so none can teach evildoing to a man as the devil can. I perceive that Mr. Badman went to the devil's school from his childhood to the end of his life. But, sir, please continue.

Wiseman. So I will. You may remember that I told you what a desperate condition he was in for money before he married, and how, when he got a rich wife, he paid his debts with her money. Having some money left, he set up shop again as briskly as ever. He operated a great trade, but ran up enormous debts. He was not indebted to one or two, but to many. Eventually, he came to owe some thousands of dollars, yet he continued in business a good while.

To pursue his ends better, he began to study how to please people and to fit into any group. If he listened carefully, he could act and speak as they did. And listen he would, when he thought that by doing so he might either make them customers of his merchandise or his creditors. If he dealt with honest men, as with some honest men he did, then he would act as they did. He would mimic their talk by seeming to be as sober as they. He would speak of justice and religion and against debauchery. Yes, he would appear to show a dislike of those who spoke or acted in an evil way or were anything but honest.

When he did happen upon those who were bad, then he would be as bad as they. He was just more secretive and cautious, except among those of whose trust he was sure. Then he would conduct his evil behavior openly, acting as they did, cursing, and damning others along with them. If they railed on good men, he would, too; if they railed on religion, so would he; if they talked vainly, so would he; if they favored drinking, swearing, whoring, or any other similar villainies, so did he. This was now the path on which he walked, and he could do it all as proficiently as any man alive. He thought of himself as a perfect man. Before, he had considered himself just a boy. What do you think of Mr. Badman now?

Attentive. Think! Why I think he was an atheist, for no one but an atheist could act as he. I judge that a man like Mr. Badman must be an obscene and stinking atheist. If one believes in the existence of God and the devil, heaven and hell, death and the judgment after, he cannot do as Mr. Badman did. If he could do these things without reluctance or being checked by his conscience, if he did not feel sorrow and remorse for such abominable sins as these, then I think he would have to have been an atheist.

Wiseman. Not only was he very far from reluctance and remorse of conscience for his deceptions, but he also counted them excellent achievements, the quintessence of his wit, his rare and singular virtues, such as few besides himself could be the masters of. Therefore, as for those who hesitated to do such things, who could not in good conscience act that way for fear of death and judgment, he would call them fools and simpletons. He would ridicule them for being afraid of goblins and would challenge them to act like men. He told them that they would have to work hard to attain his level of artistry.

He would often entertain himself with thoughts of what he could do in this matter, saying, "I can act both religious and irreligious; I can be anything or nothing; I can swear and denounce swearing; I can lie and censure lying; I can drink, keep company with prostitutes, be immoral, and defraud, and not be troubled by any of these actions. I enjoy myself and am the master of my own ways. They do not master me. I have attained this position through much study, great care, and considerable effort."

But he said these things only to himself or to his wife, whom he knew did not dare to divulge it, or among his close friends to whom he knew he could say anything.

Attentive. Did I call him an atheist before? I may now call him a devil, or a man possessed with one, if not with many. I think that this kind of evil exists in only a few men. True, it is said of King Ahaz that *"in the time of his distress did he trespass yet more against the LORD"* (2 Chronicles 28:22). It is also said that Ahab *"[sold] himself to work wickedness in the sight of the LORD"* (1 Kings 21:25), and that *"the men of Sodom were wicked and sinners before the LORD exceedingly"* (Genesis 13:13).

Badman's Disguise Is Removed

Wiseman. He was an atheist, no doubt—if there is such a thing as an atheist in the world. In spite of all his boasting about his perfection and his security in his wickedness, I believe that at times God sent down fire from heaven to sting his conscience. True, I believe he would quickly put it out and grow more wicked and desperate afterward, but the hardening of his heart also turned to his destruction, as later you will hear. (See Job 21:17.)

But I do not think as you do that there are few men like him in this world, unless you are referring to the degree of wickedness he had attained. For otherwise, no doubt, there is an abundance of men like him—men of the same mind, of the same principles, and of the same conscience, which allow them to practice their evil. Yes, I believe that there are many who are endeavoring to reach the same depth of wickedness, and all of them are like him as far as the law of God is concerned, nor will their lack of hellish wit excuse them on the day of judgment.

You know that in every science, some are more proficient than others. So it is in the art and practice of wickedness as well. Some are two-fold and some seven-fold the children of hell compared with others, yet all are the children of hell. (See Matthew 23:15.) Otherwise, they would all be teachers, leaving no students in the school of wickedness. There must be instructors, and there must be learners. Mr. Badman was a master in this art, and therefore it follows that he must have been a principal leader in the school of evil.

Attentive. You are right, for I perceive that some men, though they desire it, are not so accomplished in the practice of wickedness as others, but are, as I suppose they call them, fools and dunces to the rest. Their heads and capabilities will not serve them to act as wickedly. But Mr. Badman did not lack a wicked head to contrive, nor a wicked heart to do, his wickedness.

Wiseman. True, but yet I say such men will on the day of judgment be judged, not only for what they are, but also for what they wanted to be. For if *"the thought of foolishness is sin"* (Proverbs 24:9), undoubtedly, the desire of foolishness is more sin; and if

113

the desire is more, the endeavor after it must be even more. He then who is not a consummate atheist and sinner but desires to be one, if he endeavors to pursue this goal, will be judged and condemned to hell for it. For the law judges men according to what they want to be. The Scripture says, *"Whosoever looketh on a woman to lust after her hath committed adultery with her already in his heart"* (Matthew 5:28).

By the same rule, he who would steal does steal; he who would cheat does cheat; he who would swear does swear; and he who would commit adultery does commit adultery. For God judges a man according to the working of his mind, and says, *"As he thinketh in his heart, so is he"* (Proverbs 23:7). That is, so is he in his intentions, in his desires, and in his endeavors. God's law imputes blame for man's desires, intentions, and endeavors, even as it attributes responsibility for the act of wickedness itself (Matthew 5:19-48). A man, then, who desires to be as wicked as Mr. Badman, even though he never attains to that proficiency in wickedness, will be judged for being as bad a man as he desired to be, because it was in his heart to be so wicked.

Attentive. But this height of wickedness in Mr. Badman will not leave my mind. This hard, desperate, or, what should I call it, diabolical frame of heart was in him a foundation, a groundwork for all acts and deeds that were evil.

Wiseman. The heart, and the desperate wickedness of it (Jeremiah 17:9), is the foundation and groundwork of all evil. Atheism, professed and practical, both spring out of the heart, yes, and all manner of evil besides. For bad deeds do not make a bad man, but he is already a bad man who does bad deeds. A man must be wicked before he can do wickedness. *"Wickedness proceedeth from the wicked"* (1 Samuel 24:13). It is an evil tree that bears evil fruit (Matthew 7:16). Men do not *"gather grapes of thorns, or figs of thistles"* (verse 16). The heart, therefore, must be evil before the man can do evil, and good before the man does good (verses 16-18).

Attentive. Now I see the reason why Mr. Badman was so base as to

Badman's Disguise Is Removed

get his wife through trickery and to abuse her like a villain after he had married her: he was prepared to act wickedly because of his wicked heart.

Wiseman. You may be sure of it. As the Scriptures say,

> *That which cometh out of the man, that defileth the man. For from within, out of the heart of men, proceed evil thoughts, adulteries, fornications, murders, Thefts, covetousness, wickedness, deceit, lasciviousness, an evil eye, blasphemy, pride, foolishness: All these evil things come from within, and defile the man.* (Mark 7:20-23)

And a man, as his wicked mind inclines him, makes use of these evil actions to gratify his lust, to promote his designs, to revenge his malice, to make himself rich, or to wallow in the foolish pleasures and pastimes of this life. And all these Mr. Badman did, even to the utmost, if either opportunity, resources, or treachery would help him obtain his purpose.

Attentive. Resources! Why, he could not but have had enough funds to do almost whatever he desired because of having married a wife with so much money.

Wiseman. Wait a minute, please. Some of Mr. Badman's sins were costly, such as his drinking, whoring, and keeping other bad company, although he was a man who had many ways to get money, as well as many ways to spend it.

Attentive. Did he do well in business then, even though he was such a bad man? Was his occupation so prosperous as to always keep his wallet full, even though he was an extravagant spender?

Wiseman. No, it was not his business that did it, although his trade was good. He had other ways to get rich that brought in bushels of money at a time.

Attentive. He was not a robber, was he?

Wiseman. I will be sparing in my speech as to that question, although some have rumored that he would go away overnight now and then, but no one but himself knew why. Then he would

115

come home all dirty and weary the next morning. But that is not the point I am making.

Attentive. What did you want to tell me?

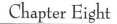

Chapter Eight

Badman Uses Bankruptcy to Gain Money

Wiseman. Badman was an artist when it came to declaring bankruptcy.

Attentive. What do you mean by Mr. Badman's bankruptcy? Do you mean that he was spiritually bankrupt?

Wiseman. No, my words are clear. If you prefer even plainer language, it is this: when Mr. Badman had squandered and whored away most of his wife's dowry, he began to feel that he could not maintain his indulgent way of life and keep up his business and reputation in the world—such as it was—unless he came up with a new plan. His wickedly ingenious solution was to go bankrupt.

Therefore, he proceeded to incur substantial debts to several men. All the while, he managed to look successful by selling many things for less than they cost him in order to establish credit by blinding his creditors' eyes to what was really going on. His creditors, seeing that he was doing a great business and thinking that in due time it would have to yield a significant profit, trusted him freely, and so did others, too, lending him enormous amounts of money to conduct his trade.

When Mr. Badman had feathered his nest with other men's goods and money, after a little time, he would declare bankruptcy. Before long, the word would spread that Mr. Badman had closed his shop, was gone, and was no longer in business. Now, by that time, news of his bankruptcy would reach the ears of his creditors. Through his skill as a finagler, he made sure of what he had and that his creditors could not touch a penny of it. When his money was hidden, he would send pathetic, sugary letters to his creditors, informing them of what had happened to him. He requested their leniency, for he assured them of his honesty and his intention to pay his debts as far as he was able.

He sent his letters through one of his accomplices, someone who could make both the best and worst of Mr. Badman's case; that is, the best for Mr. Badman and the worst for his creditors. When he came to them, he would bemoan their problem, while at the same time grieving for Mr. Badman's condition. He would tell them that unless things were drawn to a speedy conclusion, Mr. Badman would be unable to satisfy their claims. Presently, he both could and would resolve the issue satisfactorily to the utmost of his power, and to that end, he requested that they would meet with him.

Well, his creditors appointed a time to come over. Meanwhile, he authorized another person to negotiate with them. He would not show up himself, unless it was on a Sunday; otherwise, they might have been able to serve him with a writ, summoning him to court. So his delegated friend negotiated with them about their concern over Mr. Badman's debts.

First, he told them of the great care that Mr. Badman had taken to satisfy them and all men for whatever he owed, as far as was humanly possible, and for how little a time he expected to be in this impoverished condition. He pleaded with them to consider the greatness of Badman's expenses, the huge cost of taxes, the poor economic conditions of the times, and the severe losses that he had suffered from many of his customers. Some had died in his debt, others had run away, and he could never expect to collect a penny from many who were alive. Nevertheless, he would prove himself to be an honest man, and he would pay as much as he was able. If they were willing to come to terms, he would make a compromise with them, for he was not able to pay them everything.

Badman Uses Bankruptcy to Gain Money

The creditors asked what he would give. Badman's friend replied, "One quarter on the dollar." At this, the creditors began to huff, and Badman's delegate would renew his complaint and request, but the creditors would not hear of such a thing. So for that time, the meeting broke up without success. But after his creditors cooled down and began to have second thoughts, they feared that any delay would result in their losing all payment of the debts.

Thus, they consented to a second meeting, came together again, and after much protesting, they agreed to take one-fourth of the debt as full payment. So the money was produced; a certification of payment was drawn, signed, and sealed; account books were checked and all things confirmed; and then Mr. Badman could show himself outside of his house again. After everything was resolved, he would be ahead by many thousands of dollars.

Attentive. Did he take this route more than once?

Wiseman. Yes, I think he went bankrupt two or three times.

Attentive. And did he do it before he had a need to do it?

Wiseman. Need! What do you mean by need? There is no need at any time for a man to play the villain. He did it because of his wicked mind, in order to defraud and deceive his creditors. He had the resources of his father, and also of his wife, to have lived on, with the help of lawful labor, like an honest man. Also, after he had falsely declared his bankruptcy, although he had been a lavish and wasteful spender, he could have paid his creditors what he owed them down to the penny. But if he had done that, he would not have been acting like himself, like Mr. Badman. If he had behaved like an honest man, he would have acted out of character. He did it, therefore, out of a dishonest mind and to a wicked end, namely, that he might have resources, however unlawfully obtained, to follow his pursuit of disreputable women, and to live in the full swing of his lusts, even as he did before.

Attentive. Why, his actions were nothing more than cheating!

Wiseman. His ways were fraudulent indeed. His manner of going bankrupt is nothing more than a clever way of thieving, picking pockets, breaking into shops, and taking from others what belongs to them. But though it seems easy, it is hard to learn; no man who has a godly conscience can ever be successful in this hellish art.

Attentive. Oh, sir, what a wicked man he was!

Wiseman. A wicked man indeed. Through his artful deception, he could tell how to make men send their goods to his shop, and then be glad to take a fourth of what he had promised to pay before he received their goods. I say, he could make them glad to take a quarter for a dollar's worth, and a thousand dollars for what he had promised before to give them four thousand dollars.

Attentive. This proves that Mr. Badman had little conscience.

Wiseman. This indicates that Mr. Badman had no conscience at all; for conscience, the least spark of a good conscience, cannot tolerate this evil.

Attentive. Before we go any further in Mr. Badman's affairs, let me ask you, if you would, to answer these two questions: First, what do you find in the Word of God that speaks against such a practice as this? Second, in your opinion, what should a man do who is in his creditor's debt and can neither pay what he owes nor stay in business any longer?

Wiseman. I will answer you as best as I can. To answer your first question, the Word of God forbids this wickedness; to make it more reprehensible in our eyes, it links it with theft and robbery. God says, "*Thou shalt not defraud thy neighbour, neither rob him*" (Leviticus 19:13). You should not defraud, that is, deceive or cheat. To declare bankruptcy is to defraud, deceive, and betray, which is, as you see, forbidden by the God of heaven. "*Thou shalt not defraud thy neighbour, neither rob him.*" Consequently, it is a kind of theft and robbery thus to defraud and beguile. It is an evil robbing of his business and picking of his pocket; it is despicable to reason and conscience, and contrary to the law of nature. It is a deliberate act of wickedness, and therefore a double sin.

A person cannot commit this great wickedness on a sudden impulse or in a moment of weakness through a violent assault of Satan. He who commits this sin must have time to think about it, creating a disguise that will not easily be uncovered. He who commits this wickedness must first hatch it on his bed, scrutinize the details, and plot a strong plan. Therefore, to the completing of such a wickedness, there must be adjoined many sins, and they, too, must go hand in hand until the sinful act is completed.

But what does the Scripture say? *"[Let] no man go beyond and defraud his brother in any matter: because that the Lord is the avenger of all such"* (1 Thessalonians 4:6). But this kind of bankruptcy is an action that surrounds your brother in order to catch him in a net, and as I said, to rob him and to pick his pocket, and to do so with his consent. His agreement to the repayment plan does not lessen, but instead increases the offense, making it all the more deplorable. For men who are thus cunningly abused cannot help themselves; they are trapped in a deceitful net. But God will pay attention to this crime. He will be the avenger; He will punish all evildoers either now or in the world to come.

The apostle Paul testified to this truth when he said, *"But he that doeth wrong shall receive for the wrong which he hath done: and there is no respect of persons"* (Colossians 3:25). In other words, there is no man, no matter what position he holds, who, if he is guilty of this sin of deceiving and doing wrong to his brother, God will not call to accountability for his actions, for *"there is no respect of persons."* God will *"take vengeance"* (Nahum 1:2) on him, too.

I might add, this sin of defrauding a neighbor is like that first deceitful act that the devil played on our first parents. It is replicated just as the altar that Uriah built for King Ahaz was patterned according to the design of one that Ahaz had seen in Damascus (2 Kings 16:10-11). *"The serpent beguiled me"* (Genesis 3:13), Eve said; Mr. Badman deceived his creditors. The serpent tricked Eve with lying promises of gain (verse 5); in the same way, Mr. Badman tricked his creditors. The serpent said one thing and meant another when he double-crossed Eve (2 Corinthians 11:3); so did Mr. Badman when he double-crossed his creditors.

Therefore, the man who deceives and betrays his neighbor imitates the devil. He takes his example from him and not from God, the Word, or good men, and this is what Mr. Badman did.

And now let me answer your second question: What should a man do who owes his creditors money when he can neither pay them nor work any longer?

First of all, if this is the case, and he knows it, he should not run up one penny's worth of further debt. To incur more debt cannot be done in good conscience. He who knows he cannot pay and yet continues to go into debt knowingly wrongs and defrauds his neighbor and falls under this saying of the Word of God: *"The wicked borroweth, and payeth not again"* (Psalm 37:21). What is worse, he borrows, while at the very same time he knows that he cannot pay again. He craftily takes what belongs to his neighbor. That is, therefore, the first thing that I would propose. Do not go into any further debt.

Second, he should consider how and by what means he was brought into such a condition that he could not pay his debts. Namely, was it through his own negligence in his business? Did he live too far above his means? Was he extravagant in his purchases of food or clothing? Did he lavishly lend what did not belong to him? Or was his current situation brought about by the immediate judgment of God?

If, by searching, he finds that this problem has come upon him through negligence in his business, extravagance in his spending, or something similar, let him labor for a sense of his sin and wickedness, for he has sinned against the Lord. First, the Scriptures speak against being slothful in business and not providing by the sweat of one's brow or other honest ways for those of one's own house (Romans 12:11; 1 Timothy 5:8). Second, he has incurred guilt by being extravagant both in his food and in his choice of clothing for himself and his family. Further, he should feel regret if he has lent to others what belonged to someone else. These things cannot be done in good conscience. They violate both reason and nature; therefore, they must be sins against God.

Therefore, if this debtor has caused his own trouble but desires to live quietly in good conscience, and at peace about his future condition, let him humble himself before God and repent of his wickedness. For *"he also that is slothful in his work is brother to him that is a great waster"* (Proverbs 18:9). To be both slothful and wasteful is to be, as it were, a double sinner.

This man should also consider what steps he has taken that have brought him to this point. Was it the way his parents brought him up or taught him? Was it through an act of providence that he was first thrust into debt? Did he entangle himself in these imprudent ways by not being content with what he had or with what he had received by God's grace and the kindness of his parents? These questions ought duly to be considered.

If, upon examination, a man finds that he is out of the place and calling into which he was put by his parents or the providence of God, and has chosen the wrong paths through pride and greed, then his financial problems are the result of his sin. They are the fruit of his pride and a token of the judgment of God upon him for abandoning his first state. For his bad decisions and the resultant indebtedness, he should be humble and penitent before the Lord.

But if, by an honest examination, he finds that his poverty did not come about because of his bad choices; if, by careful study, he finds that he can say with good conscience, "I did not leave the place and state into which God by his providence has put me, but I have obeyed God in the calling wherein I was called, and have worked hard, have fared fairly well, have been adequately clothed, and have not directly nor indirectly misappropriated my creditors' goods," then these hard times have come upon him by the immediate hand of God, whether by visible or invisible ways. For sometimes they come by visible ways, namely, by fire, by thieves, by loss of cattle, or the wickedness of sinful dealers. And sometimes they come by invisible means, and then no man knows how it happened. We only see that things are going, but cannot see how they are going.

Well now, suppose that a man, through the intervention of God, is reduced to having only a morsel of bread. What must he do then? I believe the best response is still for him to examine if his difficulty is the fruit of some sin. Although it may not be the fruit of sin related to his business affairs, it may be connected to some other sin. *"The LORD will not suffer the soul of the righteous to famish: but he casteth away the substance of the wicked"* (Proverbs 10:3). Therefore, let him still humble himself before his God, because God's hand is upon him. He should say, "What sin is this that brings the hand of God upon me?" For the Bible says to *"humble yourselves therefore under the mighty hand of God, that he may exalt you in due time"* (1 Peter 5:6). And let him be diligent to find it out, for some sin is the cause of this judgment; for God *"doth not afflict willingly nor grieve the children of men"* (Lamentations 3:33). Either his heart is set too much on the world, or religion is neglected too much in his family. There is a snake in the grass, a worm in the gourd, some sin in his bosom, for the sake of which God deals in this way with him.

After this questioning is done, this man should consider if God is changing his condition and state in the world. Perhaps God has allowed him to live in fashion, in fullness, and in abundance of worldly glory, but the man has not improved to the glory of God as he should have. Maybe God's attitude toward him has changed. When Israel ignored God's favor toward them and turned to other gods, God *"abhorred them."* (See Deuteronomy 32:9-20.) Therefore, God will now turn this man loose in barren pastures, that with leanness, hunger, and insufficiency he may spend the rest of his days. But let him do this without murmuring and complaining; let him do it in a godly manner, submitting himself to the judgment of God. *"Let the brother of low degree*

rejoice that he is exalted: but the rich, in that he is made low"
(James 1:9-10).

This is our duty, but it may also be our privilege, to suffer under
the hand of God. And for your encouragement to this hard work,
for this is indeed hard work, consider these four things:

First, it is right to lie down under God's hand, and it is the way
to be exalted in God's time. When God allowed Job to embrace
the dunghill, Job embraced it, and said, *"The LORD gave, and the
LORD hath taken away; blessed be the name of the LORD"* (Job 1:21).
Second, consider the truth that there are blessings that attend a
low condition, more than all the world is aware of. A poor condition has preventing mercy accompanying it. The poor, because
they are poor, are not capable of sinning against God in the same
way the rich can. The psalmist said that the rich can trust and
boast in their wealth (Psalm 49:6). Obviously, the poor cannot do
that. Third, the poor can more clearly see themselves preserved
by the providence of God than the rich. Fourth, it may be that
God has made you poor because he desires to make you spiritually rich. *"Harken, my beloved brethren, Hath not God chosen
the poor of this world rich in faith, and heirs of the kingdom
which he hath promised to them that love him?"* (James 2:5).

I am persuaded that if men upon whom the hand of God rests
would quietly lie down and humble themselves under it, they
would find more peace, yes, more blessings of God attending
them in their humble state than most men are ever aware of. But
this is a hard saying; therefore, I do not expect that many will
either read it with pleasure or desire to take my counsel.

Having thus spoken to the broken man, with reference to his
own self, I will now speak to him as he stands related to his
creditors. In the next place, therefore, let him fall upon the most
honest way of dealing with his creditors.

The first thing he should do is to make them aware of his condition immediately. He should heartily and sincerely ask them
for forgiveness for the wrong that he has done them. He should
also offer them everything he has in the world in order to meet

his debts. He should hide nothing, keeping only the clothes on his back for himself. He should not keep a ring, a spoon, or anything from them. Then, if after seeking forgiveness and offering everything he has does not satisfy them, he should offer his body to be at their disposal, either to go to prison or to be at their service, until he has made amends by working for them as is reasonably appropriate. From his wages, he should only reserve something for the provision of his poor and distressed family, which in reason, conscience, and nature, he is bound to take care of. In these ways, he will make amends as he is able for the wrong that he has done them in wasting and spending their estates.

By thus doing, he submits himself to God's rod and commits himself to the authority of His providence. He casts the lot of his present and future conditions into the lap of his creditors, and leaves the whole verdict to the Lord, even as He will order and incline their hearts to do with him (Proverbs 16:33). And let that be either to forgive him, to take what he has to satisfy the debt, or to let him suffer the lawful consequences of his actions. If he can leave the whole outcome to God, whatever the issue is, that man will have peace of mind afterward. And the comforts of that state, which will include equity, justice, and duty, will be increased to him, because there is more comfort in godliness than there is comfort in the fruits of injustice, fraudulence, and deceit. Besides, this is the way to engage God to favor him by the sentence of his creditors. God can intercede with them to treat him kindly, and He will do it when a man's ways are pleasing in His sight (Jeremiah 15:10-11). *"When a man's ways please the LORD, he maketh even his enemies to be at peace with him"* (Proverbs 16:7). And surely, for a man to seek to make restitution to the utmost of his power for wrongs he has done is the best thing that he can do in this situation.

But he who does otherwise remains in his sin. He refuses to submit to the authority of God and chooses to live in a high estate, although he did not attain it in God's way, when God's will is that he should descend to a lower position. Yes, he defiantly says in his heart and through his actions that he will make his own choices and will follow his own ways regardless of the consequences.

Attentive. I agree with what you have said. But suppose now that Mr. Badman were here. Could he not object to what you have said, and say to you,

> Go teach your fellowmen this lesson, for they are as guilty of mismanaging their money as I was. Yes, I am inclined to think that some of them, too, have declared bankruptcy when they did not need to. But even if they have not done that, still they are guilty of carelessness in their jobs, of living higher than their means—higher than either their profits or their incomes will allow. Besides that, everyone knows that they cheat while they artfully call it making a compromise. They hide their assets, deceive others by casually pulling the wool over their eyes, corrupt their consciences, sin against their principles, and gratify their lusts.

I say, if Mr. Badman were here to object to you in this way, what would be your reply?

Wiseman. What would it be? Why, I would say, "I hope that no good man, no man of good conscience, no man who fears God, values his religion, the peace of God's people, or the salvation of his own soul, would act in this way." False professors of religion there may be, but who on earth can help it? Jade comes in all colors. If men will profess, and make their profession something to hide behind in order to finagle their neighbors out of their possessions, as Mr. Badman did when he tricked the woman who, to her regret, became his wife, who can help it? The churches of old were overcrowded with hypocrites; therefore, it is no surprise that hypocrites still abound during these perilous, difficult times. Notice what the apostle Paul said about this issue:

> *Nay, ye do wrong, and defraud, and that your brethren. Know ye not that the unrighteous shall not inherit the kingdom of God? Be not deceived: neither fornicators, nor idolaters, nor adulterers, nor effeminate, nor abusers of*

themselves with mankind, Nor thieves, nor covetous, nor drunkards, nor revilers, nor extortioners, shall inherit the kingdom of God. (1 Corinthians 6:8-10)

And then again in 2 Timothy :

This know also, that in the last days perilous times shall come. For men shall be lovers of their own selves, covetous, boasters, proud, blasphemers, disobedient to parents, unthankful, unholy, without natural affection, trucebreakers, false accusers, incontinent, fierce, despisers of those that are good, Traitors, heady, highminded, lovers of pleasures more than lovers of God; having a form of godliness, but denying the power thereof: from such turn away. (2 Timothy 3:1-5)

None of these will be saved in this state, nor will their false profession of faith deliver them from the censure of the godly, when their true character is revealed.

We cannot help what they say. How can we help it if men call themselves holy ones, godly ones, zealous ones, self-denying ones, or any other such glorious title when they are involved in evil, sin, and the worst actions imaginable? True, they are a scandal to religion, a grief to those with honest hearts, an offense to the world, and a stumbling block to the weak; and these offenses have come, do come, and will come, no matter what the world does. *"But woe to that man by whom the offence cometh!"* (Matthew 18:7).

Let such hypocrites, therefore, be disowned by all true Christians, and let them be counted among those base men of the world, who by their actions, they most resemble. They are Mr. Badman's kindred. For hypocrites are a shame to religion. I say, these deceitful robbers and pickpockets are a shame to religion, and religious men should be ashamed of them. God judges them among the fools of the world; therefore, let not Christians count them among those who are wise for heaven. *"As a partridge sitteth on eggs, and hatcheth them not; so he that getteth riches, and not by right, shall leave them in the midst of his days, and at his end he shall be a fool"* (Jeremiah 17:11). And Mr. Badman is one of these; therefore, he must expect to fall under this judgment.

One who professes to have religion but who practices such villainies as these—such a one is not worthy to bear the name of Christian any longer! We may say to him as the prophet spoke to this kind, namely, the rebellious who were in the house of Israel, *"Go ye, serve ye every one his idols"* (Ezekiel 20:39). If you will not listen to the law and testament of God and lead your lives in accordance with His laws, you defile His holy name (verse 39).

Go, hypocrites, go. Quit making a profession of faith unless you will lead your lives according to that profession. It is better never to profess than to try to use your profession as a cover for your sin and deceit. The foundational principles of religion do not permit any such thing. The apostle Paul said to the Corinthians, *"Receive us; we have wronged no man, we have corrupted no man, we have defrauded no man"* (2 Corinthians 7:2). These verses suggest that those who are guilty of wronging, corrupting, or defrauding anyone should not be admitted to the fellowship of saints or be counted as their brothers. Nor can these men, with all their rhetoric and eloquent speaking, prove themselves fit for the kingdom of heaven or men of good conscience on earth. Oh, that godly plea of Samuel:

> *Behold, here I am: witness against me before the LORD, and before his anointed: whose ox have I taken? or whose ass have I taken? or whom have I defrauded? whom have I oppressed? or of whose hand have I received any bribe to blind mine eyes therewith? and I will restore it you.*
>
> (1 Samuel 12:3)

These are the words of a man of good conscience indeed. And in his appeal, he was justified in the consciences of the whole congregation so that they could not but with one voice, break out jointly and say, *"Thou hast not defrauded us, nor oppressed us"* (verse 4).

A hypocrite and a fraud, away with him! A Christian should not owe any man anything but love (Romans 13:8). A Christian should provide things, not from what belongs to another man, but from what he has earned through his honest endeavors before God and all men, so that he may honor the doctrine of God our Savior in all things.

Attentive. But suppose that God should strike a man's wealth, and he dies prematurely–before he has time to settle his accounts. Must he be considered to be like Mr. Badman and fall under the same reproach as he?

Wiseman. No, not if he has dutifully done what he could to avoid it. It is possible for a ship to sink at sea, notwithstanding the most faithful endeavor of the most skillful pilot under heaven. It was this way, I imagine, with the prophet who left his wife in debt, endangering his children to become the slaves of his creditors (2 Kings 4:1). He was not an extravagant man, or one who was given to fraud, for the text says he *"feared the Lord"* (verse 1), yet he was more in debt than his wife could pay.

If God blows away what a man has collected, who can help it? (See Haggai 1:9.) And He will do that sometimes, because He will change the state of men's lives and because He will test their virtues. He will also overthrow the wicked with His judgments; all these things are seen in the book of Job. But then, the consideration of this truth should cause men to be careful to be honest, lest this judgment falls upon them for their sin. It should also make them beware of launching further into worldly pursuits other than in a godly, honest way. It should teach them to pray for God's blessings upon their honest and lawful endeavors. And it should set them on a diligent examination of their steps so that if on their path they hear the ice crack, they will have time to go back again.

As long as these things are considered and duly put into practice, if God should reverse a man's fortunes, then he can be content and, like Job, praise God in the middle of misfortune (Job 1:21). Let him give to his creditors what belongs to them and not fight against the providence of God. Instead, let him humble himself under God's mighty hand, even if it comes to strip him naked and bare. He who does otherwise fights against God. He declares himself to be a stranger to Paul's testimony: *"I know both how to be abased, and I know how to abound: every where and in all things I am instructed both to be full and to be hungry, both to abound and to suffer need"* (Philippians 4:12).

Attentive. But Mr. Badman would not, I believe, have made this distinction between things feigned and situations of true need.

Wiseman. If he will not, God will and conscience will—not only our own, but the consciences of all those who have seen the way, and who have known the truth of the condition of such a one.

Attentive. Well, let us at this time leave this matter and return to the life of Mr. Badman.

Wiseman. With all sincerity, I will proceed to relate what was left of his life in order to speak about his death.

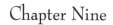

Chapter Nine

Badman's Fraudulent Dealings

Attentive. Please tell it with as much brevity as you can.

Wiseman. Why, are you weary of my relating of things?

Attentive. No, but I like to hear a great deal in a few words.

Wiseman. I do not profess to be an expert in that regard, but yet, as briefly as I can, I will recount what was left of his life. Again, I will begin with his fraudulent dealings. Just as I have shown how dishonest he was with his creditors, now I will tell you how unfairly he treated his customers.

He used deceitful weights and measures. He kept weights to buy by and weights to sell by, measures to buy by and measures to sell by. Those he bought by were too big, and those he sold by were too little.

In addition, he could use a thing called slight of hand, if he had to use other men's weights and measures, and by that means, whether he bought or sold, yes, even though his customer or another merchant looked on, he could turn the situation to his own advantage.

Moreover, he had the ability to miscalculate accounts, whether by weight, measure, or money, and would often do it to his advantage and his customers' losses. And if he was questioned about his accuracy, he had his servants ready to vouch and swear to his books or his word. This was Mr. Badman's practice. What do you think about Mr. Badman's character now?

Attentive. What do I think! Why, I can think nothing except that he was a selfish and wicked man; for these actions, just like his others, were evil. If a tree, as indeed it can, may be judged by its fruits, then Mr. Badman must logically be judged a bad tree. But for my further satisfaction, show me now, by the Word of God, the evil of his practices of using false weights and measures.

Wiseman. The evil of it! Why, the evil is clear to every eye. Heathens, who live like beasts and brutes in many things, abominate and abhor such wickedness as this. Let a man but look on these things as he goes by, and he will see enough in them from the light of nature to make him loathe so evil a practice, although Mr. Badman loved it.

Attentive. But show me something out of the Word against it, will you?

Wiseman. I will willingly do so. First, look into the Old Testament. It says,

> *Ye shall do no unrighteousness in judgment, in mete-yard* [length]*, in weight, or in measure. Just balances, just weights, a just ephah, and a just hin, shall ye have: I am the Lord your God, which brought you out of the land of Egypt.* (Leviticus 19:35–36)

This is the law of God, and what all men, according to the law of the land, should obey. Another verse says, *"Ye shall have just balances"* (Ezekiel 45:10).

Now, having shown you the law, I will also show you how God judges any deviation from this law. *"Divers weights are an abomination unto the Lord; and a false balance is not good"* (Proverbs 20:23). *"A false balance is abomination to the Lord"* (Proverbs 11:1). Some have just weights but false scales, and by virtue of these false scales, regardless of their just weights, they deceive people. Therefore, God commands that the scale be made just. *"A just weight is his delight"* (verse 1). If people's scales are false, they are deceivers, notwithstanding their just weights.

So the Scriptures command first of all that men use a just scale, and they state that a false one is an abomination to the Lord. Then we are told, *"Thou shalt not have in thy bag divers weights, a great and a small"* (Deuteronomy 25:13)—that is, one to buy by, and another to sell by, as Mr. Badman had. *"Thou shalt not have in thine house divers measures, a great and a small"* (verse 14). These Mr. Badman had also.

The Old Testament provides more direction on this subject:

> *But thou shalt have a perfect and just weight, a perfect and just measure shalt thou have: that thy days may be length-ened in the land which the LORD thy God giveth thee. For all that do such things* [that is, use false weights and mea-sures], *and all that do unrighteously, are an abomination unto the LORD thy God.* (Deuteronomy 25:15-16)

See now both how plentiful and how relevant the Scripture is in this matter. But perhaps one might object that all this is old law, and therefore has nothing to do with us under the New Testa-ment—not that I think you, neighbor, would object to this teach-ing. Well, let me answer this foolish notion.

First, he who makes this objection, if he does it to overthrow the authority of those texts, reveals that he is a first cousin to Mr. Badman. For a just man is willing to speak reverently of those commands. The man who objects to this text has, no doubt, but little conscience, if any at all that is good. But let us look into the New Testament, and there we will see how Christ confirmed the same. He commanded that men give to others a good measure, encouraging all to do so with these words:

> *Give, and it shall be given unto you; good measure, pressed down, and shaken together, and running over, shall men give into your bosom. For with the same measure that ye mete withal it shall be measured to you again.* (Luke 6:38)

This verse applies not only to what men will receive back from other men but also how God will repay. God will show His indig-nation against the false man by taking away even what he has, and He will also deliver the false man to the oppressor. Then the extortioner will receive from the oppressor in the same measure he had used against his neighbor.

Another Scripture says, *"When thou shalt make an end to deal treacherously, they shall deal treacherously with thee"* (Isaiah 33:1). That the New Testament also has a warning into the way men operate their businesses is evident from these general exhortations: *"Defraud not"* (Mark 10:19). *"Lie not to another"* (Colossians 3:9). *"No man* [should] *go beyond and defraud his brother in any matter: because that the Lord is the avenger of all such"* (1 Thessalonians 4:6). *"Whatsoever ye do, do it heartily, as to the Lord, and not unto men"* (Colossians 3:23). All these injunctions and commandments concern our lives and conduct among men, with reference to our dealing and trading; consequently, they forbid false, deceitful, yes, all actions that are corrupt.

Having thus in a word or two shown you that these things are bad, I will next, in order to convict those who practice deception, show you where God says these evildoings are to be found.

They will not be found in the houses of good and godly men, for they, like God, abhor them; instead, they will be found in the houses of evildoers, such as Mr. Badman. *"Are there yet the treasures of wickedness in the house of the wicked, and the scant measure that is abominable?"* (Micah 6:10). Are they there yet, notwithstanding God's forbidding, notwithstanding God's tokens of anger against those who do such things! Oh, how a wicked man loathes to let go of a sweet, profitable sin once he has possession of it! Evildoers hold fast to deceit; they refuse to let it go.

Next, these deceitful weights and measures will not be found in the houses of the merciful, but in the houses of the cruel, in the houses of those who love to oppress. *"The balances of deceit are in his hand: he loveth to oppress"* (Hosea 12:7). The wicked man is given to oppression and cruelty; therefore, he uses such wicked things in his occupation. He is a true cheat, and, as was hinted before concerning Mr. Badman's bankruptcy, so I say now, concerning his using these deceitful weights and measures, it is as evil as to steal someone's purse or pick someone's pocket. Clearly, it takes from a man what is his own.

Also, deceitful weights and measures are not to be found in the houses of those who provide food and clothing for the poor. Instead, these evil deeds will be carried out by those who would *"swallow up"* the poor. Listen to what the prophet Amos said:

> *Hear this, O ye that swallow up the needy, even to make the poor of the land to fail, saying, When will the new moon be gone, that we may sell corn? and the sabbath, that we may set forth wheat, making the ephah small, and the shekel great, and falsifying the balances by deceit? That we may buy the poor for silver, and the needy for a pair of shoes; yea, and sell the refuse of the wheat? The LORD hath sworn by the excellency of Jacob, Surely I will never forget any of their works.* (Amos 8:4-7)

So detestable and vile a thing is this in the sight of God.

God hates the thought of calling those who use false weights and measures by any other term than *impure.* He says, *"Shall I count them pure with the wicked balances, and with the bag of deceitful weights?"* (Micah 6:11). No, by no means. They are impure ones. Their hands are defiled; deceitful gain is in their houses; they have gotten what they have by coveting; therefore, they must and will be counted among the impure, among the wicked of the world.

Thus you see how full and plain the Word of God is against this sin, and those who practice it. Mr. Badman, because he used these ways to rook and cheat his neighbors, is rightly rejected from having his name in and among the catalogue of the godly.

Attentive. But I am persuaded that some people do not think that using these deceitful methods is so great an evil.

Wiseman. Whether it is considered an evil or a virtue by men, it does not matter. You can see by the Scriptures how God judges such actions. It was not regarded as evil by Mr. Badman, nor is it by any who are still following in his steps But, I say, it does not matter how men value things. Let us adhere to the judgment of God. This is all the more important, because when we ourselves are done weighing and measuring to others, then God will weigh and measure us and our actions. And when He does, as He will do shortly, then woe to those of whom it will be said, *"Thou art weighed in the balances, and art found wanting"* (Daniel 5:27). God will then repay their evil upon their own heads, when He shuts them out of His presence, favor, and kingdom forever and ever.

Attentive. But it is amazing, since Mr. Badman's common practice was to deceive others, that someone did not find him out and accuse him of this wickedness.

Wiseman. He got away with his roguery among the general public. For what with his false scales but accurate weights, and his slight of hand to boot, he beguiled—sometimes a little, sometimes more—almost everyone with whom he did business. Besides, those who use this wicked trade are either good at blinding men by their pretense of religion or intimidating the buyer with words. I must confess, Mr. Badman was not so skilled at the first, that is, to pretend to be religious. He began to grow tired of this form of deception, even though some of his associates were accomplished in the act. But when it came to intimidating, swearing, or lying to his customers regarding his weights and measures, Mr. Badman had no trouble doing these things.

Attentive. Then it seems that he kept good weights and a bad scale. At least that was better than having both be bad.

Wiseman. Not at all. It showed the depth of his deceitfulness, for if, at any time, his customers found fault and accused him of short-changing them, he would reply, "Why, did you not see them being weighed? Will you not believe your own eyes? If you question my weights, please take them where you will to be checked. I maintain that they are good and just." He would say the same about his scales, so he deceived them by using accurate weights.

Attentive. This is cunning indeed, but something else must have been done or said to conceal the truth from his customers.

Wiseman. Yes, he had many ways to be deceptive, but he was not totally convincing at making a show of religion, even though he had deceived his wife in that way. He was too well known for that, especially by those who lived near him, though he would awkwardly attempt it as best he could. But there are some who are chief villains in this way. They will appear to live an entirely religious life in public while being guilty of the most horrible sins in private. And yet religion in itself is never hurt by true professors of it. But, as Luther said, all evil begins in the name of God. For hypocrites have no other way to bring their evils to maturity than by invoking God's name. Thus they become white-washed walls (Acts 23:3). By the purity of religion—the white of religion—the dirt of their actions is hid. Thus they also *"are like unto whited sepulchres, which indeed appear beautiful outward, but are within full of dead men's bones, and of all uncleanness"* (Matthew 23:27).

Yes, if a doubt arises in the heart of the buyer about the weight and measure being used, often he permits his senses to be deluded as he recalls to mind his merchant's profession of religion. The customer thinks he must be wrong rather than the businessman, for he never dreams that the so-called godly merchant would deceive him. But if the buyer finds out about the false transaction and makes it apparent, then he is placated with apologies. Often the blame is placed on the servants. And so Mr. Cheat maintains his stance as an honest man in the eyes of his customer, even though he will not hesitate to pick the customer's pocket the next chance he gets.

Some excuse their cheating by saying that it is a common prac-tice, as if that should acquit them before the tribunal of God. Others say that they were cheated, so they have to pass on the loss to their customers. Even though they are trying to manipu-late the truth, they must know that they should be doing *"that which is altogether just"* (Deuteronomy 16:20). Suppose that I am cheated; must I therefore cheat another in the same way? If this is a bad practice on the whole, it is also bad in part. Therefore, however you are treated when you are buying, you must deal justly in selling, or you sin against your soul and become like Mr. Badman. And know that justifying yourself because others are doing wrong is not an excuse. It is not custom, but good conscience, that will help at God's tribunal.

Attentive. But I am persuaded that what is acquired by men in this way does them but little good.

Wiseman. I agree, but those who are evil do not hold the same opinion. For if they can make a profit, by whatever means they use, they are content—even if it means they take the devil and all. Little good! Why, do you think they would judge their actions like that? No, they would no more think that way than they would consider what they will do on the day of judgment. All that they think they are getting through their wrong methods is truly worth nothing at all.

But to give you a more direct answer: This kind of getting is so far from doing them little good; in fact, it does them no good at all because thereby they lose their own souls. The Scripture says, *"For what shall it profit a man, if he shall gain the whole world, and lose his own soul?"* (Mark 8:36). He loses, then; he who gains after this fashion loses greatly. This is the man who is "penny-wise and pound-foolish"; this is he who loses his good sheep rather than spend a few dollars for medicine for it; this is the man who loses his soul for a little of the world. And then what does he get but loss and damage? Thus, in his acquiring, he loses his soul in the world to come.

But what does man really get in this world more than hard labor, sorrow, affliction, and disappointment? Men aim at blessedness in getting, I mean, at temporal blessedness, but the man who gains through deceptive means will not be blessed ultimately. For though an inheritance after this manner may be hastily obtained at the beginning, yet in the end, he will not be blessed (Proverbs 20:21). He gathers it indeed, and thinks he will keep it, too, but remember what Solomon said: *"The LORD will not suffer the soul of the righteous to famish: but he casteth away the substance of the wicked"* (Proverbs 10:3).

The time that he does enjoy it will do him no good at all, but be sure, he will not have it for long. For God will either take it away in his lifetime, or else in the generation following. According to the book of Job, *"He* [a wicked man] *may prepare it, but the just shall put it on, and the innocent shall divide the silver"* (Job 27:17).

Consider what is written in Proverbs: *"A good man leaveth an inheritance to his children's children: and the wealth of the sinner is laid up for the just"* (Proverbs 13:22). What then does the man have who acquires his wealth through dishonest means? Why, he receives sin and wrath, hell and damnation. Now tell me how much he possesses?

This, I say, is what he gets. As the psalmist said, we, too, may be so bold to say,

> *I was envious at the foolish, when I saw the prosperity of the wicked....When I thought to know this, it was too painful for me; until I went into the sanctuary of God; then understood I their end. Surely thou didst set them in slippery places: thou castedst them down into destruction. How are they brought into desolation, as in a moment! they are utterly consumed with terrors. As a dream when one awaketh; so, O LORD, when thou awakest, thou shalt despise their image.* (Psalm 73:3, 16–20)

The wicked may huff and puff and make much to-do about nothing for a while, but God has determined that both the man and his riches will melt like grease, and any observant person may see that it is so. Watch as the unrighteous man accumulates much in ways that wrong other people. Before long, what he has stored up will be gone or will have decayed. Then he, or the generation that follows his decline, will return to poverty. And this is what happened to Mr. Badman, notwithstanding his cunning and crafty tricks to get money. When he died, no one could tell if he even had a penny left to his name.

Attentive. He used all of the cunning tricks possible for a man to get money; one would think that he would have been rich when he died.

Wiseman. You stop counting too soon if you think these were the only deceptive means he used to get money, for he had more besides. If his customers' names were written down in his books, he would be hard on them. If he thought he could take advantage of them, then he would be sure to impose upon them his worst, even very bad merchandise, yet charge them the price of the best products. He was like those who sold the bad wheat or the worst of the wheat, *"making the ephah small, and the shekel great, and falsifying the balances by deceit"* (Amos 8:5). This was Mr. Badman's way.

He would sell goods that cost him next to nothing at the price of his most expensive merchandise. He also tried to trick his customers by mixing inferior items with his best goods in order to lessen suspicion. In addition, if his customers at any time paid him cash, they had better beware, for he would usually attempt to collect payment again, especially if he thought that there was any hope of making a profit. If they could not produce sufficient proof of the payment, the odds were a hundred to one that they would pay him again. Sometimes the honest customer would appeal to Badman's servants for proof of the payment of money, but they were trained by Badman to say what he told them. Thus, the sincere person could get no help from them.

Attentive. It is an abominable thing for a man to have this kind of servants. For by such means a poor customer could be ruined and not know how to help himself. Alas, if the merchant was so unconscionable, as I perceive Mr. Badman was, to call for his money twice, and if his assistants would swear that the debt was due, where could the poor customer find any help? He would go under without anyone to help him.

Wiseman. This is a very bad practice that has been going on for hundreds of years. But what does the Word of God say? *"Also will I punish all those that leap on the threshold, which fill their masters' houses with violence and deceit"* (Zephaniah 1:9).

Mr. Badman also had this cunning manner: If he could get an advantage over someone, that is, if his customer could not afford to go elsewhere, or if the product he wanted could not at present be conveniently purchased elsewhere, then he had better look out. Mr. Badman would surely try to control the customer's purse strings and without any pity or conscience make him pay through the nose.

Attentive. That is extortion, is it not? Please tell me your judgment of extortion.

Wiseman. Extortion is exploiting men by taking more than by the law of God or men is right. It is committed sometimes by those who hold political office, but it is most commonly committed by men of trade who, when they have the advantage, will prey on their neighbors. In this way, Mr. Badman was an extortioner. Although he did not charge fees and impose prison time, as bailiffs and court clerks have been known to do, yet he took every opportunity that came his way to cruelly extort money out of his neighbor's pocket. For every man who preys on his neighbor and takes advantage of him by forcing more from him than is reasonable and done in good conscience may very well be called an extortioner. If he charges more than something is worth according to the current prices, he will be judged unworthy to inherit the kingdom of God. The Scriptures say,

> *Know ye not that the unrighteous shall not inherit the kingdom of God? Be not deceived: neither fornicators, nor idolaters, nor adulterers, nor effeminate, nor abusers of themselves with mankind, nor thieves, nor covetous, nor drunkards, nor revilers, nor extortioners, shall inherit the kingdom of God.* (1 Corinthians 6:9-10)

Attentive. Well, this Badman was indeed a sad wretch.

Chapter Ten

A Christian View of Extortion

Wiseman. Yes, you have often said this before. But now that we are talking about extortion, permit me to go on. We have a great many people in this country who live all their days in the practice, and so under the guilt, of extortion. These people would object to being called extortioners.

For example, there is a poor person who lives, we will suppose, many miles from the market. This man wants a bushel of grain, a pound of butter, or cheese for himself, his wife, and his poor children. Since he lives so far from the market, if he goes there, he will lose a day's work, which will be a considerable loss to this poor man. So he goes to a wealthy farmer who lives nearby and asks him to help him by selling him what he needs. Yes, the farmer says, you may have it; but along with the merchandise, the farmer will grumble and perhaps make him pay as much or more for it than he could get for it after having to carry it five miles to a market. In addition, he will sell him the worst of his goods. (But in this practice, women are especially guilty in selling their butter and cheese.) Now this is a type of extortion. It is preying on the needs of the poor. It is oppressing them—in essence, buying and selling them.

But above all, the peddlers who buy up the poor man's food at wholesale and sell it to him for unreasonable gains at retail, or, as we call it, by piecemeal, apply a stinging rate, which is nothing more than extortion. I am talking about those who buy up butter, cheese, eggs, and bacon at wholesale prices, and then sell them in small quantities to the poor during the week after the market is past.

Although I will not condemn them all, many of them bite and pinch the poor by this kind of evil dealing. They destroy the poor because they are poor, and that is a grievous sin. God's Word says,

> *He that oppresseth the poor to increase his riches, and he that giveth to the rich, shall surely come to want....Rob not the poor, because he is poor: neither oppress the afflicted in the gate: for the LORD will plead their cause, and spoil the soul of those that spoiled them.* (Proverbs 22:16, 22-23)

Oh, that he who afflicts and grinds the faces of the poor would take notice of these Scriptures! Here the destruction of the estate, and of the soul, too, of those who oppress the poor is threatened. We will better see where, and in what condition, their souls are, when the Day of Doom comes, but the estates of such usually quickly decay. Sometimes no man and sometimes all men know how.

Besides, these are usurers; yes, they charge interest on food for their brothers, a practice that the Lord has forbidden (Deuteronomy 23:19). And since they cannot do it as well on the market day, they do it when the market is over. That is when the poor go hungry and must have food to eat. Then they are forced to pay high prices for their basic needs. Perhaps some will find fault in my meddling in other people's affairs and for my prying into the secrets of their sinful ways. But to such I would say, since such actions are evil, it is time they were hissed out of the world. For all who do such things offend God, wrong their neighbors, and, like Mr. Badman, provoke God to judgment.

Attentive. God knows there is an abundance of deceit in the world!

Wiseman. Deceit! Yes, but I have not told you the thousandth part of it, nor is it my business now to rake to the bottom of that dunghill. What would you say if I were to analyze some of those vile wretches called pawnbrokers, who lend money and goods to poor people, who are by necessity forced to such an inconvenience. Pawnbrokers will charge, by one trick or another, exorbitant interests on what they lend, notwithstanding the principal is secured by a sufficient item, which they will keep also, if they find any deceitful means to cheat the wretched borrower out of what he pawned.

Attentive. Why, such criminals are the pests and vermin of the country; they are not fit for the society of men. But by some of those things you have said, you seem to imply that it is not lawful for a man to make the best he can.

Wiseman. If by making a good living, you mean to sell for as much as by hook or crook he can get for his commodities, then I say it is not lawful. And if I would say the contrary, I would justify Mr. Badman and all the rest of that gang. That I will never do, for the Word of God condemns them. That it is wrong for a man at all times to sell his goods for as much as he can, I prove by these reasons:

First, if it is lawful for me always to sell my products as expensively, or for as much as I can, then it is lawful for me to lay aside my good conscience in my dealings with others. But it is not right for me, in my dealings with others, to lay aside good conscience. Therefore, it is not lawful for me always to sell my goods for as much as I can. That it is not lawful to lay aside good conscience in our dealings has already been proved earlier in our conversation. But for a man to sell his merchandise for the highest price possible requires that he lay aside his conscience. This is clearly seen in the following points:

First, the man who would make as much profit as possible must sometimes prey on the ignorance of his customer. But he cannot do that with a good conscience, for that is to *"take advantage of and defraud his brother"* (1 Thessalonians 4:6), and that is forbidden. Therefore, he who sells his commodity for an exorbitant price or for as much as he can must lay aside good conscience.

Second, he who would sell his merchandise for a higher cost than he should preys on his neighbor's need, and he cannot do that in good conscience. Once again, that is taking advantage of his neighbor, which is contrary to 1 Thessalonians 4:6. Therefore, to do so would require that he casts off and lays aside a good conscience.

Next, the one who would practice this deceptive act preys on his neighbor's affection. That is also going against what we are taught in 1 Thessalonians 4:6. Therefore, he who will sell his goods at too expensive a price, or for as much as he can, casts off and lays aside a good conscience.

The same may also be said for buying. No one should always buy as cheaply as he can; he must also use good conscience in buying what he can use and keep. If he always buys things as cheaply as he can, he will prey on the ignorance, need, and affection of his salesman, which he cannot do in good conscience.

When Abraham wanted to buy a burial plot from the sons of Heth, he said to them,

> *Entreat for me to Ephron the son of Zohar, that he may give me the cave of Machpelah, which he hath, which is in the end of his field; for as much money as it is worth he shall give it me for a possession of a buryingplace amongst you.* (Genesis 23:8-9)

Abraham would not have tolerated buying something for less than what it was worth. He scorned and abhorred this practice; it would not agree with his religion, reputation, or conscience. Likewise, when David wanted to buy a field from Ornan the Jebusite, he said to him, *"Grant me the place of this threshingfloor, that I may build an altar therein unto the LORD: thou shalt grant it me for the full price"* (1 Chronicles 21:22). His conscience, like Abraham's, would not allow him to pay anything but the full price for the purchase. He knew that there was wickedness in selling at an exorbitant price or in buying too cheaply; therefore, he would not take advantage of another person in this way.

Good conscience ought to be used both in selling and in buying. God will abundantly avenge the wrong of defrauding, as I have forewarned and testified. Listen to what Leviticus 25:14 says: *"If thou sell ought unto thy neighbour, or buyest ought of thy neighbour's hand, ye shall not oppress one another."*

Second, if it is lawful for me always to sell my commodities at the highest price that I can, then it is lawful for me to deal with my neighbor without charity. But it is not lawful for me to lay aside charity, or to deal with my neighbor without it; therefore, it is not lawful for me always to sell my goods to my neighbor for as much as I can. A man in dealing should consider his neighbor's good, profit, and advantage as his own, for this is to exercise charity in his dealing.

That I should exercise charity toward my neighbor in my buying and selling with him is evident from the general command: *"Let all your things be done with charity"* (1 Corinthians 16:14). The fact that a man cannot exercise charity who sells to make as much profit as he can or who buys as cheaply as he can is evident by these reasons:

- First, the one who sells his goods for as much money as he can seeks good for himself, and himself only. But love *"seeketh not her own"* (1 Corinthians 13:5). So then, he who thinks only of himself when he sells things as expensively as he can does not exercise charity in his dealing.

- Next, the one who sells his product for as much as he can get hardens his heart against all reasonable entreaties of the buyer. He who does so cannot exercise charity in his dealing; therefore, it is unlawful for a man to sell overpriced merchandise.

- Third, if it is lawful for me to sell my goods for as much I can, then there can be no sin in my trading in unreasonable ways in the management of my business. Whether I lie, swear, curse, or cheat, in order to sell my merchandise at the highest price, it does not matter. But that there is sin in these practices is evident. Ephesians 4:25 says, *"Wherefore putting away lying, speak every man truth with his neighbour: for we are members one of another."*

- Fourth, he who sells at the highest price possible violates the law of nature that says, *"All things whatsoever ye would that men should do to you, do ye even so to them"* (Matthew 7:12). Now if the seller were the buyer, he would not want to be charged an exorbitant price for what he was buying; therefore, he should not charge outrageous prices when he is the seller instead of the buyer.

- Fifth, the one who sells at too high a price takes advantage of others, using his specialized knowledge to abuse God's law and to wrong his neighbor. God has given you more skill, more knowledge and understanding about your product than he has given to him who would buy from you. But can you think that God has given you this information so that you might prey on your neighbor? Is your knowledge given to you so that you might beguile your neighbor? No, He has given it to you so that you might help him. You can serve as eyes to the blind and save your neighbor from damage that his ignorance, need, or inordinate desire to possess would cause. In this way, God can use you to help your neighbor escape from temptation that is too great for him to endure on his own. (See 1 Corinthians 10:13.)

- Next, in all that a man does, he should have an eye to the glory of God, but he cannot have that if he sells his merchandise at a higher price than is fair.

- In addition, all that a man does, he should do *"in the name of the Lord Jesus"* (Colossians 3:17), that is, as being commanded and authorized to do it by Him. But he who sells at unreasonable prices cannot even pretend to do this without horrid blaspheming of that name, because the Scripture commands otherwise.

- Last, in all that a man does, he should have an eye to the day of judgment. He should consider how his actions will be measured in that day. (See Acts 24:15-16.) Therefore, no man can or should always sell at unfair prices unless he will risk the consequences of those actions. Yes, in so doing, he must say that he will run the hazard of the trial of that day, for the Bible says, *"If thou sell ought unto thy neighbour, or buyest ought of thy neighbour's hand, ye shall not oppress one another"* (Leviticus 25:14).

A Christian View of Extortion

Attentive. But why do you add the cautionary words that one should not always sell too high or buy too low? Do you not thereby suggest that a man may sometimes do so?

Wiseman. I do indeed suggest that sometimes the seller may sell at the highest price he can, and the buyer may buy at the cheapest price he can. Either of these actions is allowable only in these cases: when he who sells is a swindler and lays aside all good conscience in selling, or when the buyer is a crook and lays aside all good conscience in buying. If the buyer or the seller has the principles of a rogue, then let him look to himself; however, you are not to lay aside your conscience because the one with whom you are dealing does so. No matter how vile or base the customer is, keep your merchandise at a reasonable price; or, if you buy, offer reasonable gain for the thing you would have. If godly principles are not acceptable to the buyer or seller, then seek more honest people with whom to do business. If you object and say that you do not have the skill to know the actual value of things, then ask someone who has more skill than yourself in that affair, and let him set the terms for what you buy or sell. But if there were no underhanded people in the world, these objections would not need to be made.

Thus, my very good neighbor, I have given you a few of my reasons why a man who has something to sell should not always sell it too expensively or buy as cheaply as he can; instead, he should use good conscience toward God and charity toward his neighbor in both.

Attentive. But were some men to hear you, I believe they would laugh in your face.

Wiseman. I do not question that at all, for so Mr. Badman used to do when any man told him of his faults. He used to think that he was wiser than anybody else. He considered, as I have hinted before, that anyone who hesitated because of his scruples to defraud someone else was unmanly. But let Mr. Badman and his fellows laugh. I will put up with it and still give them good counsel. (See Luke 16:13-15.) But I will remember also, for my further relief and comfort, that those who were covetous of old served the Son of God Himself in this way. It is their time to laugh now, that they may mourn in time to come (Luke 6:25). And I will say again, when they have laughed out their laugh, then he who does not use good conscience toward God and charity toward his neighbor in buying and selling dwells next door to an infidel, and is related to Mr. Badman.

Attentive. Well, but what will you say to this question? You know that there is no settled price set by God for any items that are bought or sold under the sun, but all things that we buy and sell ebb and flow in price like the tide. How then will a man with a tender conscience avoid doing wrong to the seller, buyer, or himself in making business transactions?

Chapter Eleven

Instructions for Christians in Business

Wiseman. This question is thought to be frivolous by all who are like Mr. Badman. It is also difficult in itself, yet I will endeavor to answer it in two parts. First, how should a businessman, in trading, keep a clear conscience, whether he is a buyer or seller? Second, how should he prepare himself to do this work and live in the practice of it? To address the first question, I believe that he must observe what has been said before; namely, he must follow his conscience before God, practice charity to his neighbor, and show much moderation in dealing. Let him therefore keep within the bounds of the positive side of those eight reasons that were presented to prove that men should in their dealings act justly and mercifully between man and man. Then there will be no great fear of wronging the seller, buyer, or himself. But I offer the following advice to prepare or instruct a man in doing the right thing in his business affairs.

First, people should consider that to strive to accumulate an abundance of wealth is not as rewarding as most men think. All that a man has over and above what meets his present needs serves only to feed the lusts of the eye. For *"when goods increase, they are increased that eat them: and what good is there to the owners thereof, saving the beholding of them with their eyes?"* (Ecclesiastes 5:11). Many times, when men are consumed by acquiring riches, they *"fall into temptation and a snare, and into many foolish and hurtful lusts, which drown men in destruction and perdition"* (1 Timothy 6:9). Few people end up with something good

153

in their efforts to accumulate wealth. But this truth Mr. Badman could not comprehend.

Consider that the pursuit of wealth through dishonest means—as he does who gets it without good conscience and charity to his neighbor—is a great offense against God. Consequently, God says, *"I have smitten mine hand at thy dishonest gain which thou hast made"* (Ezekiel 22:13). It is a manner of speech that shows anger in the very mention of the crime.

Therefore, realize that a little, honestly gotten, though it may yield you but a dinner of herbs at the time, will yield more peace than will a fatted calf that is acquired by ill-gotten means. (See Proverbs 15:17.) *"Better is a little with righteousness than great revenues without right"* (Proverbs 16:8).

Be confident that God's eyes are upon all your ways, and that *"He pondereth all* [your] *goings"* (Proverbs 5:21). Also, He notes them, writes them down, and seals them in a bag against the time to come (Job 14:17).

Be sure to remember that you do not know the day of your death. Remember also that when death comes, God will give your material possessions, for which you have labored and for which perhaps you have hazarded your soul, to one whom you do not know will be wise or foolish (Ecclesiastes 2:18-19). And then, *"what profit hath he that hath laboured for the wind?"* (Ecclesiastes 5:16).

Besides, you will have nothing that you may so much as carry away in your hand. Guilt will go with you if you have acquired your riches dishonestly, and those to whom you will leave an inheritance will receive it to their hurt. Duly consider these things and prepare your heart to your calling of buying and selling.

I come, in the next place, to show you how you should live in the practical part of this art. Are you to buy or sell?

If you sell, do not praise; if you buy, do not belittle. Assign the things that you sell their just value and worth. You cannot knowingly do anything else, unless you have a covetous and wicked mind. Otherwise, commodities are overvalued by the seller, and also undervalued by the buyer. *"It is naught, it is naught, saith the buyer: but when he is gone his way, then he boasteth"* (Proverbs 20:14). What has this man done but lied in the devaluing of his bargain? And why did he discount its worth to wrong and beguile the seller? Because he has a covetous mind.

Are you a seller, and do things become increasingly expensive? Do not contribute to keeping the prices high. To do this requires a wicked heart, like those who seek to make *"the ephah small, and the shekel great, and falsifying the balances by deceit"* (Amos 8:5). Are you a buyer, and do things become increasingly costly? Do not use cunning or deceitful language to pull the prices down, for that cannot be done except through wickedness, also. What then should we do, you say? Why, I answer, leave things to the providence of God and submit to His hand. When products become more and more expensive, the hand that upholds the price—that is, the hand of the seller, who loves high prices that bring him more profit—for the time being, is stronger than the one that would pull the prices down. Therefore, I say, take heed and do not have a hand in it. Otherwise, you may hurt yourself and your neighbor. Instead, take the following advice:

First, do not announce a shortage of goods beyond the truth and state of things; especially be careful of predicting shortages in the future. It was for not believing in the provision of God that the officer was trodden to death at the gate of Samaria. (See 2 Kings 7:1-2, 17-20.) This sin has a double evil in it. It belies the present blessing of God among us, and it undervalues the riches of His goodness, which can make all good things abound toward us (2 Corinthians 9:8).

Next, this wicked thing may be done by hoarding when the hunger and needs of the poor cry out against it. God may show His dislike against storing things up only for yourself by, as it were, permitting the people to curse one who hoards. *"The people shall curse him: but blessing shall be upon the head of him that selleth it"* (Proverbs 11:26).

Finally, if prices do rise and you are distressed, still be moderate in all your selling; be sure to let the poor have their money's worth. Sell to those in need. Show mercy to the poor man in your selling to him, and because he is poor, give him the lowest price you can. This is to buy and sell with good conscience; in this way, you do not wrong the buyer or your conscience, for God will surely reward you in the same way that you have treated others (Obadiah 15; Luke 6:38). I have spoken concerning selling your merchandise, but in all things, your duty is to *"let your moderation be known unto all men. The Lord is at hand"* (Philippians 4:5).

Chapter Twelve

The Sin of Pride

Attentive. Well, sir, now that I have heard enough about Mr. Badman's immoral character, please proceed to describe his death.

Wiseman. But, sir, the sun is not that low; we have at least three hours before nightfall.

Attentive. I am not in any great hurry. I just thought that you were done telling about his life.

Wiseman. Done! No, I have much more to say.

Attentive. Then he was more wicked than I thought.

Wiseman. That may be, but let us proceed. To all of his wickedness, Mr. Badman added pride. He was a very proud man. He was exceedingly proud and haughty in spirit. He acted as if what he said should never be contradicted or opposed. He considered himself as wise as the wisest man in the country, as good as the best, and as handsome as they come. He took as much delight in praising himself as he did in receiving compliments from others. He could not tolerate that anyone should think himself better than he, or that any person's wit or personality should be judged better than his. He barely accepted those he judged to be his equal. But those who were of an inferior rank, he would look over in great contempt. If at any time he had a remote occasion of having to deal with them, he would show great snobbery and a very domineering spirit. The words of Solomon describe his character well: *"Proud and haughty scorner is his name, who dealeth in proud wrath"* (Proverbs 21:24). He never felt that his meals were prepared well enough, his clothes made fine enough, or his praise refined enough.

Attentive. Pride is a sin that sticks as close to nature, I think, as most sins. I do not know of any two grosser sins that adhere closer to men's nature than immorality and pride. They have, as I call it, an interest in nature; it likes them because they most satisfy its lust and fancies. Therefore, it is no surprise that Mr. Badman was tainted with pride, since he had so wickedly given himself up to work all iniquity with greediness (Ephesians 4:19).

Wiseman. You speak the truth. Pride is a sin that sticks close to nature, and is one of the first follies wherein it shows itself to be polluted. For even in little children, pride will first of all show itself; it is an early appearance of the sin of the soul. It is that corruption that strives for predominance in the heart; therefore, it usually comes out first. But though children are so prone to it, yet I think that those who are older should be ashamed of it. I could have started Mr. Badman's story by describing his pride, but I do not think that childish pride is as evil as pride demonstrated by the more mature. Therefore, I passed over it; but now, since he had no more respect for himself and shame for his vile and sinful state but to be proud as an adult, I have taken the occasion in this place to mention his pride.

Attentive. Friend, if you can remember them, tell me some of the places in Scripture that speak against pride. I desire to know these verses because pride is now a reigning sin. Sometimes, I happen to fall into the company of those who are in my judgment very proud, and I have a mind to tell them about their sin. When I tell them, unless I bring God's Word to bear, I do not doubt but that they will laugh me to scorn.

Wiseman. Laugh you to scorn! The proud man will laugh you to scorn no matter what text you show him, unless God smites his conscience by the Word. In addition, when you have said what you can, they will tell you that they are not proud, but rather that you are the one who is proud; otherwise, you would not judge, nor so boldly meddle in other men's matters as you do.

Nevertheless, since you asked, I will mention several texts that speak against pride. *"Pride, and arrogancy, and the evil way, and the froward mouth, do I hate"* (Proverbs 8:13). *"A man's pride shall bring him low"* (Proverbs 29:23). *"And he shall bring down their pride"* (Isaiah 25:11). *"And all the proud, yea, and all that do wickedly, shall be stubble: and the day that cometh shall burn them up"* (Malachi 4:1). This last is a dreadful text; it is enough to make a proud man shake. God says that He will make the proud ones as stubble, that is, as fuel for the fire. On the judgment day, which will be like a burning oven, they will be consumed. But Mr. Badman could never stand to hear pride spoken against, or that anyone should say of him, "He is a proud man." He used to mistreat those who told him of his faults.

Attentive. What was the reason for that?

Wiseman. He did not tell me the reason, but I imagine it is the same reason common to all vile persons. They love their vices, but they do not care to bear their names. The drunkard loves the sin, but does not love to be called a drunkard. The thief loves to steal, but he cannot stand to be called a thief; the whore loves to commit immorality, but does not love to be called a whore. And so Mr. Badman loved to be proud, but could not tolerate being called a proud man. The fragrance of sin is desirable, but it pollutes and corrupts man. To name a man's sin is to put a blot on his honor.

Attentive. It is true what you have said, but how many kinds of pride are there?

Wiseman. There are two types of pride: pride of spirit and pride of body. The first of these is mentioned in these Scriptures: *"Every one that is proud in heart is an abomination to the LORD"* (Proverbs 16:5). *"An high look, and a proud heart, and the plowing of the wicked, is sin"* (Proverbs 21:4). *"The patient in spirit is better than the proud in spirit"* (Ecclesiastes 7:8).

Bodily pride is also mentioned in the Scriptures:

> *In that day the LORD will take away the bravery of their tinkling ornaments about their feet, and their cauls, and their round tires like the moon, the chains, and the bracelets, and the mufflers, the bonnets, and the ornaments of the*

legs, and the headbands, and the tablets, and the earrings, the rings, and nose jewels, the changeable suits of apparel, and the mantles, and the wimples, and the crisping pins, the glasses, and the fine linen, and the hoods, and the veils. (Isaiah 3:18-23)

By these expressions, it is evident that there is pride of body, as well as pride of spirit, and that both are sinful and thus abominable to the Lord. But these texts Mr. Badman could never bear to read. They were to him as Micaiah was to Ahab—they never spoke good of him, but evil (1 Kings 22:8).

Attentive. I doubt that Mr. Badman was the only one who would malign those texts that speak against his vices. I believe that most ungodly men, where the Scriptures are concerned, have a secret antipathy against the words of God that most clearly and fully rebuke them for their sins.

Wiseman. That is true, without a doubt, and by their enmity, they show that sin and Satan are more welcome to them than are wholesome instructions of life and godliness.

Attentive. To return to our discussion of Mr. Badman and his pride, will you show me some symptoms of one who is proud?

Wiseman. Yes, I will. First, I will show you some signs of pride of heart. A proud heart is seen by outward things. Pride of body, in general, is a sign of pride of heart, for all proud gestures of the body flow from a proud heart. As Solomon said, *"There is a generation; O how lofty are their eyes! and their eyelids are lifted up"* (Proverbs 30:13). He also said that *"he that exalteth his gate seeketh destruction"* (Proverbs 17:19). Now, lofty eyes and exalting one's gate are signs of a proud heart, for both these actions come from the heart. Jesus said, *"There is nothing from without a man, that entering into him can defile him: but the things which come out of him, those are they that defile the man"* (Mark 7:15).

Specifically, heart pride is revealed by a stretched-out neck and by a pretentious manner. For the proud assume a lofty behavior. This is what makes them look scornfully, speak harshly, and act contemptuously toward their neighbors. A proud heart is a persecuting heart. *"The wicked in his pride doth persecute the poor"* (Psalm 10:2). A prayerless man is a proud man (Psalm 10:4). A contentious man is a proud man (Proverbs 13:10). A disdainful man is a proud man (Psalm 119:51). The man who oppresses his neighbor is a proud man (Psalm 119:122). He who does not listen to God's Word with reverence and fear is a proud man (Jeremiah 13:15-17). And be sure, he who calls the proud blessed is a proud man (Malachi 3:15). All those with pride in their hearts reveal themselves to be proud men. (See Jeremiah 43:2.)

As to bodily pride, it is characterized by all the particulars mentioned before, for though they are said to be symptoms of a proud heart, they reveal themselves within the body. You know that diseases that are within are often seen by outward and visible signs, yet by these very signs even the outside is defiled also. So all those visible signs of heart pride are signs of bodily pride, too. Some outward signs of pride include wearing gold, pearls, and expensive clothes; elaborate arranging of the hair; following fashion trends; seeking to imitate the proud, either by speech, looks, dress, actions, or other foolish trifles. (See 1 Peter 3:3-5; 1 Timothy 2:9-10.) The world is full of people who are concerned only with their outward appearance. All these examples, and many more, are signs of a proud heart and of bodily pride.

But Mr. Badman would not permit, by any means, that his excessive concern for the way he looked should be called pride; instead, he thought of it as neatness, handsomeness, comeliness, cleanliness, and maintaining a sense of fashion. He would not concede that he was proud, even though he wanted his neighbors to regard him as exceptional and outstanding.

Attentive. But I have been told that when some have been criticized for their pride, they have turned the reprimand toward those by whom they have been rebuked, saying, *"Physician, heal thyself!"* (Luke 4:23). Look at your own household and your friends, even the wisest of you, and see if you are blameless. For who is prouder than you who profess to be religious—scarcely the devil himself!"

Wiseman. My heart aches at this answer, because there is too much truth in it. This very answer Mr. Badman would give his wife when she, as she did sometimes, would reprove him for his pride. He would say, "We will have great corrections in living now, for the devil has turned into a reformer of vice. No sin reigns more in the world than pride among Christians."

And who can contradict him? Let us give the devil his due; the reality is too apparent for any man to deny. And I doubt not but that the same answer is ready in the mouths of Mr. Badman's friends; for they may and do see pride display itself in the dress and behavior of Christians, one may say, almost as much as among any people in the land. More is the pity. Yes, and I fear that extravagances among Christians have hardened the hearts of many, as I perceive they did to an extent in the heart of Mr. Badman himself.

For my own part, I have seen many, and I am talking about church members, too, so excessively adorned with their newfangled trinkets, even when they have been at their solemn appointments with God. I have wondered how such made-up persons could sit in the place of worship without fainting. But certainly, the holiness of God, and their own pollution by sin, must be far from the minds of such people, no matter what profession they make.

I have read of the shamelessness of a harlot (Jeremiah 3:3) and of Christian modesty (1 Timothy 2:9). I have read of costly array, and of what is becoming to women who profess godliness and good works (1 Peter 3:1-5). But if I might speak, I know what I know, and could say without being wrong, about the evil present among some Christians (Jeremiah 23:15), but I will hold my peace.

Attentive. You seem greatly concerned over this issue, but what if I say more? It is whispered that some good ministers have sanctioned their people regarding their frivolous and extravagant apparel; yes, they have excused their gold, pearls, and expensive clothes.

The Sin of Pride

Wiseman. I do not know what they have excused, but it is easily seen that they tolerate, or at least ignore or pretend to be ignorant about such things, both where their wives and children are concerned. And so, *"from the prophets of Jerusalem is profaneness gone forth into all the land"* (Jeremiah 23:15). And when the hands of the rulers are chief in a trespass, who can keep their people from being drowned in that trespass (Ezra 9:2)?

Attentive. This is deplorable.

Wiseman. So it is, and I will add, it is a shame, it is a reproach, it is a stumbling block to the blind; for though men are as blind as Mr. Badman himself, yet they can see the foolish thoughtlessness that is at the root of all these apish and wanton extravagances. But many have their excuses ready. They blame their parents, their husbands, their training, and the like. Yes, even the examples of good people prompt them to it, but all these excuses will be blown away as easily as a spider's web when the thunder of the Word of the great God rattles from heaven against them. It will do so at the time of their death or judgment, but I wish that it might do so before. Alas, these excuses are but bare pretenses; these proud ones love to have it so.

I once talked with a maid by way of reproof for her foolish and gaudy garment. But she told me that the tailor made it that way. In truth, it was the poor, proud girl who gave the order to the tailor to make it like that. Many blame parents, husbands, tailors, and others in an effort to direct the fault elsewhere. But the original cause of all these evils is their evil hearts and their giving way to their wicked desires.

Attentive. Now that you are speaking of the cause of pride, please show me why pride is now so prevalent.

Wiseman. I will tell you what I think are the reasons for it. First, such persons are led by their own hearts rather than by the Word of God (Mark 7:21-23). I told you before that the original fountain of pride is the heart, for out of the heart comes pride (verses 21-22). Therefore, pride is so prevalent because people are led by their hearts, which naturally tend to lift them up in pride. This pride of heart tempts them, and by its deceits overcomes them (Obadiah 3). It puts a bewitching virtue into their peacock's feathers, and then they are swallowed up with the vanity of them.

Another reason why some who profess to be religious are so proud is that they are more apt to follow the example of those who are of the world than those who are saints. Pride is of the world. *"For all that is in the world, the lust of the flesh, and the lust of the eyes, and the pride of life, is not of the Father, but is of the world"* (1 John 2:16). From the world, therefore, those who profess religion learn to be proud. But they should not look to worldly examples. Some will object that the saints of today should not be used as examples either, for they are as proud as others. Let those who are guilty be ashamed. But when I say Christians should follow the example of saints, I mean what Peter said,

> *Likewise, ye wives, be in subjection to your own husbands; that, if any obey not the word, they also may without the word be won by the conversation of the wives; while they behold your chaste conversation coupled with fear. Whose adorning let it not be that outward adorning of plaiting the hair, and of wearing of gold, or of putting on of apparel; but let it be the hidden man of the heart, in that which is not corruptible, even the ornament of a meek and quiet spirit, which is in the sight of God of great price. For after this manner in the old time the holy women also, who trusted in God, adorned themselves, being in subjection unto their own husbands.* (1 Peter 3:1-5)

Another reason for the prevalence of pride is that some have forgotten the pollution of their natures. Remembering our carnal natures should keep us humble, and being kept humble, we will be kept at a distance from pride. The proud and the humble are set in opposition; *"God resisteth the proud, and giveth grace to the humble"* (1 Peter 5:5). And can it be imagined that a sensible Christian should be a proud one? A sense of humility tends to make one modest—not fill one up with pride. But when a person begins to forget what he is, then he tends to become proud. I think it is one of the most senseless and ridiculous things in the world for a man to be proud of what is given to him for the purpose of covering the shame of his nakedness.

Persons who are proud have lost sight of God and His holiness. If God were before them, as He is behind them, and if they saw Him in His holiness, as He sees them in their sins and shame, they would take little pleasure in their slavish imitation of the world. The holiness of God makes the angels cover their faces and crumbles Christians, when they view it, into dust and ashes (Isaiah 61:1-3, 5). And as His majesty is, such is His Word (Isaiah 66:2). Therefore, those who sanction pride disgrace His name.

Finally, what can be the end of those who are proud of the way they adorn themselves? Why do they favor ridiculous fads or styles that show their naked shoulders or their breasts hanging out like a cow's udder? Why do they paint their faces, stretch out their necks, and impose all the formalities that pride leads them to? Is it because they desire to honor God? Is it because they would adorn the Gospel? Is it because they would beautify religion and make sinners fall in love with their own salvation? No, no, it is rather to please their lusts, to satisfy their wild and extravagant whims. I hope that no one does it to stir up lust in others, to the end that they may commit immoral acts. I believe, whatever their purposes, that this is one of the great plans of the devil.

Also, I believe that Satan has enticed more into immoral practices by the glittery show of fine clothes than he could possibly have drawn without it. I wonder what it was that in ancient times was called *"the attire of an harlot"* (Proverbs 7:10); certainly it could not have been more bewitching and tempting than the garments of many so-called Christians today.

Attentive. I heartily agree with what you have said, and I wish that all the proud women who profess to be Christians were within the reach and sound of your voice.

Wiseman. What I have said, I believe is true; but as for the proud women who profess religion, they have Moses and the prophets, and if they will not listen to them, how then can we hope that they will receive any good from the words of one like me? (See Luke 16:29-31.) I may sound as dull as a ram's horn, but I have spoken my mind. Now, if you will, we will move on to some other of Mr. Badman's doings.

Attentive. Before you tell me anything else about Mr. Badman, would you mind showing me the specific consequences that result from this sin of pride?

Wiseman. I will sincerely try to honor your request. First, pride makes man so much like the devil in hell that he cannot reflect the image and likeness of God. The angels became devils through their being puffed up with pride. (See 1 Timothy 3:6.) It is pride also that lifts or puffs up the heart of the sinner, thereby making him bear the very image of the devil.

Pride makes a man so odious in the sight of God that he will not, must not, come near His majesty. *"Though the LORD be high, yet hath he respect unto the lowly: but the proud he knoweth afar off"* (Psalm 138:6). Pride sets God and the soul at a distance; pride will not let a man come near to God, nor will God let a proud man come near to Him. Now this is a dreadful thing!

I repeat, pride keeps God and the soul at a distance. *"God resisteth the proud"* (James 4:6). *"Resisteth,"* that is, He opposes him, He distrusts him, He condemns him and all his actions. The proud man may approach God's laws, but he cannot come into His presence, have communion with Him, or receive blessing from Him. For the high God resists the proud man.

God's Word says that *"the LORD will destroy the house of the proud"* (Proverbs 15:25). He will destroy his house; it may be understood that God will destroy him and his household. So he destroyed proud Pharaoh (Exodus 15:19); so he destroyed proud Korah (Numbers 16:32), and many others.

Pride, where it comes, and is entertained, is a certain forerunner of some judgment that is not far behind. When pride goes before, shame and destruction will follow. *"When pride cometh, then cometh shame"* (Proverbs 11:2). *"Pride goeth before destruction, and an haughty spirit before a fall"* (Proverbs 16:18).

Persisting in pride makes the condition of a poor man as without a remedy, as are the devils themselves. (See 1 Timothy 3:6.) And this, I fear, was Mr. Badman's condition, and this was the reason that he died as he did, as I will show you before long.

But why do I need to talk of the particular actions, or rather the prodigious sins of Mr. Badman, when his whole life and all his actions went, as it were, to the making up of one massive body of sin? Instead of believing that there is a God, his mouth, his life, and his actions declared that he did not believe.

His sinfulness led him to say within his heart that he had no fear of God (Psalm 36:1). Instead of honoring God and giving Him glory for any of His mercies or His providence toward him—for God is good to all, and He lets His sun shine and His rain fall upon the unthankful and unholy (Matthew 5:45)—he would ascribe the glory to other causes.

If good things happened, he would attribute them to his own intelligence, labor, care, industry, or cunning. If bad things happened, he would consider them the result of bad luck, chance, mismanagement of matters, or the ill will of his neighbors. He would also attribute any misfortune to his wife's being religious, and spending, as he called it, too much time in reading, praying, or the like. It was not his way to acknowledge God, that is, to graciously recognize God's hand in all things. But, as the prophet said, *"Let favour be showed to the wicked, yet will he not learn righteousness"* (Isaiah 26:10). And again, *"For the people turneth not unto him that smiteth them, neither do they seek the LORD of hosts"* (Isaiah 9:13). This was Mr. Badman's character.

Neither mercies nor judgments would make him seek the Lord (Psalm 119:156). Again, he would not recognize the works of God or regard the operations of His hands either in mercies or in judgments (Isaiah 26:10; Psalm 145:9). But further, when by providence he was placed under the best means for his soul, he never put any of these helpful influences to good use. For instance, he had a good master; and before that, a good father; and after that, a good wife. Sometimes, when on a journey, he would, for novelty's sake, go to hear a good preacher and then he would hear a good sermon, but none of these godly influences affected him for the good. Even though grace was shown to him, *"he* [would] *not learn righteousness; in the land of uprightness* [would] *he deal unjustly, and* [would] *not behold the majesty of the LORD"* (Isaiah 26:10).

Instead of reverencing the Word, when he heard it preached, read, or discussed, he would sleep, talk about others' business, or else object to the authority, harmony, and wisdom of the Scriptures. He would compare the Scriptures to a ball of wax and say that a man could twist them into whatever he wanted them to say. He would argue,

> How do you know that they are the Word of God? How do you know that these sayings are true? One Scripture says one thing, and another says quite the contrary. Besides, they mention a thousand impossibilities. They are the cause of all dissensions and discords that are in the land. Therefore, you may still think what you will, but in my mind, they are best at ease who have the least to do with them.

Instead of loving and honoring those who bear Christ's name (Galatians 6:10) and reflect the image of Christ in their lives, he would make them the subjects of his jokes and the objects of his slander. He would either mock their sober deportment, their gracious language or quiet behavior, or he would desperately swear that they were full of deceit and hypocrisy. He would endeavor to render godly men as odious and contemptible as he could; any lies that were told to disgrace them, he would vouch for their truth. He was much like the one of whom the psalmist spoke who would sit and slander his mother's son (Psalm 50:19-20). Yes, he would even speak reproachfully of his wife, though his conscience told him, and many would testify, that she was a very virtuous woman. He would also slander his wife's friends, affirming that their doctrine tended to lasciviousness, and that in their meetings they acted in ways that were unbecoming to men and women, and that they committed immoral acts. He was much like those who accused the apostle Paul of saying, *"Let us do evil, that good may come"* (Romans 3:8).

And if he heard any scandalous gossip related in any way to those who professed to be religious, no matter how false it was, he would delight, laugh, and be glad. He was much like those of whom it is written, *"Report, say they, and we will report it"* (Jeremiah 20:10). He would blame all Christians and say, "Hang those rogues. There is not a good apple among them. 'Like to like,' said the devil to the coal miner; they all come from the same group." Then he would curse them all.

Attentive. If those who profess to be religious are wise, Mr. Badman's observations and words will make them more wary and careful in all things.

Wiseman. You say the truth. For when we see that men are watching for us to stumble, and rejoice to see us trip up and fall, it should make us much more careful in how we act and what we say.

I think it was as enjoyable for Mr. Badman to hear, raise, and tell lies and false stories about those who fear the Lord as it was for him to go to bed when he was weary. But we will let these things pass for now. For as bad as he was in these things, so he added many more similar evils to his life.

He was an angry, wrathful, envious man, a man who did not know what meekness or gentleness meant, nor did he desire to learn. His natural temperament was to be surly, huffy, harsh, and worse. Because he gave way to his temper, it caused him to be furious and unrestrained in all things, especially against goodness itself, and against other things, too, when he was displeased.

Attentive. Solomon said, *"The fool rageth, and is confident. He that is soon angry dealeth foolishly"* (Proverbs 14:16-17).

Wiseman. Moreover, he said, *"Anger resteth in the bosom of fools"*

(Ecclesiastes 7:9). Truly, if it is a sign of a fool to have anger residing in his heart, then Mr. Badman was a fool of no small size, notwithstanding the conceit that he had of his own abilities.

Attentive. Fools are mostly wise in their own eyes.

Wiseman. True, but as I was saying, if it is a sign that a man is a fool when anger resides in his heart, then what is it a sign of, do you think, when malice and envy also abide there? For, to my knowledge, Mr. Badman was as malicious and as envious a man as you have ever known.

Attentive. Certainly, malice and envy flow from pride and arrogance, and from ignorance, and ignorance comes from the devil. And I thought, since you mentioned the pride of Mr. Badman, we would also be hearing about these other evil characteristics before we were done with his story.

Wiseman. Envy flows from ignorance indeed. And Mr. Badman was so envious that when provoked, he would swell up like a toad swells with poison. He whom he maligned might at any time have read envy in his face wherever he met him, or in whatever he had to do with him. His envy was so rank and strong that if it at any time he lost control of it, he could hardly regain control. He would watch over a man to do him evil as a cat watches over a mouse to destroy it. Yes, he would wait seven years, but if the opportunity to hurt his enemy came, he would take it and make him feel the weight of his envy.

Envy is a devilish thing. The Scripture suggests that none can stand before it:

> *A stone is heavy, and the sand weighty; but a fool's wrath is heavier than them both. Wrath is cruel, and anger is outrageous; but who is able to stand before envy?*
>
> (Proverbs 27:3–4)

Envy, because of its offensiveness, is counted among the worst evils that exist:

> *Now the works of the flesh are manifest, which are these; adultery, fornication, uncleanness, lasciviousness, idolatry,*

witchcraft, hatred, variance, emulations, wrath, strife, seditions, heresies, envyings, murders, drunkenness, revellings, and such like. (Galatians 5:19-21)

Yes, it is so malignant a corruption that it rots the very bones of him in whom it dwells. *"A sound heart the life of the flesh: but envy the rottenness of the bones"* (Proverbs 14:30).

Attentive. Envy is the very father and mother of a great many hideous and monstrous evils. Envy both begets them and nourishes them, until they come to their cursed maturity in the heart of him who entertains them.

Wiseman. You have described envy accurately in calling it the father and mother of a great many other monstrous evils, for it is so venomous and vile a thing that it puts the whole course of nature out of order. Envy causes confusion and is a container of every evil thing. *"For where envying and strife is, there is confusion and every evil work"* (James 3:16). That is why I say you have rightly called it the very father and mother of a great many other sins.

Now, for our further edification, I will tally up some of the offspring of envy. First, envy rots the very bones of the person who entertains it. And, as you have also hinted, it is heavier than a stone or than sand; yes, it falls like a millstone upon the head. Therefore, it kills the one who throws it, and the one at whom it is thrown. *"Envy slayeth the silly one"* (Job 5:2). That is, it destroys the person in whom it resides, and also the one who is its object. It was envy that killed Jesus Christ Himself, because it was envy that led His adversaries to persecute Him (Matthew 27:18; Mark 15:10). It was envy that was behind the plan of Joseph's brothers to sell him into slavery in Egypt (Acts 7:9). It is envy that lends a hand in causing dissension among God's saints (Isaiah 11:13). It is envy in the hearts of sinners that stirs them up to expel God's ministers from their midst (Acts 13:45-50; 14:1-6). What more can I say? It is envy that is the very nursery of gossip, arguments, backstabbing, slander, criticism, and murder.

It is not possible to list all the specific fruits of this sinful root.

Therefore, it is no surprise that Mr. Badman was such an ill-natured man, for the great roots of all manner of wickedness were in him unchecked, unharmed, and untouched.

Attentive. But it is a rare case, even for Mr. Badman, that he was never at any time filled with remorse for his ill-spent life.

Chapter Thirteen

God's Judgment on Drunkenness

Wiseman. I cannot say that he was ever remorseful, if by remorse you mean repentance for his evil actions. Yet twice I remember that he was troubled by his condition—once when he broke his leg as he came home drunk from the tavern, and another time when he became sick and thought he was going to die. Besides these two times, I do not remember any other time when he experienced any regret over his manner of living.

Attentive. Did he break his leg then?

Wiseman. Yes, once as he came home drunk.

Attentive. How did he break it?

Wiseman. He was at an alehouse, that wicked place about three miles from his home. Having drunk hard the greater part of the day, when night came, he could stay no longer. He called for his horse, mounted him, and rode him like a madman, as drunken persons usually ride. Away he went, as fast as the horse could go. Thus he rode, until he came to a muddy spot, where his horse stumbled, fell, and threw his master. When Badman fell, he broke his leg, and there he lay. You cannot imagine how much he swore at first. But after a while, coming to his senses and feeling the pain and the uselessness of his leg, he realized how bad a situation he was in. He feared that this fall might result in his death. He began to cry out in this manner, "Lord, help me. Lord, have mercy on me. Good God, deliver me." So there he lay, until he was rescued by someone who came by, lifted him up, and carried him home, where he lay for some time before he was able to go out again.

Attentive. You say he called upon God?

Wiseman. Yes, he would cry out in his pain, and would say, "O God," and "O Lord, help me." But whether he was praying for his sins to be pardoned and his soul to be saved, or to rid himself of his pain, I do not know for sure. I fear it was for the latter because when his pain was gone, and he had hopes of mending, even before he could go out, he quit praying and began his old game again—namely, to be as bad as he was before. He started to send for his old companions. His brutish friends would come to his house to see him, and with them he would be, as well as he could because of his lame leg, as corrupt as they could be from the wickedness of their hearts.

Attentive. It was a wonder he did not break his neck.

Wiseman. He would have broken his neck instead of his leg if it had not been for God's mercy toward him; he deserved punishment ten thousand times over. I have heard of many who, when drunk as he, have taken their horses and have traveled from the tavern to the grave. They have broken their necks between the alehouse and their homes. Some people have drunk themselves to death and have died in their drink.

Attentive. It is a sad thing to die drunk.

Wiseman. So it is, but I wonder that no more do so. For considering the heinousness of that sin, and with how many other sins it is accompanied, such as oaths, blasphemies, lies, reveling, whoring, and brawling, it is a wonder to me that any who live in that sin escape such a blow from heaven that should tumble them into their graves. In addition, when they are as drunk as beasts, they will ride like lunatics and madmen without any fear of danger. It is as if they are daring God to meddle with them because they are drunk. I wonder why He does not withdraw His protecting providence from them and leave them to those dangers and destruction that by their sins they have deserved, and that by their madness they would rush into. But then I remember that He has appointed a day wherein He will hold them accountable (Acts 17:30-31). Often, He does make examples of some to show that He takes notice of their sins, abhors their evil ways, and will settle up with them at the set time.

Attentive. It is worth noticing how God shows His abhorrence for the sins of men and strikes some of them down with a blow. For example, when Mr. Badman broke his leg, it was undoubtedly a stroke from heaven.

Wiseman. It is worth noticing indeed. It was a visible sign that fell on him while he was in the height of his sin. It reminds me of a passage from Job:

> *Therefore he knoweth their works, and he overturneth them in the night, so that they are destroyed. He striketh them as wicked men in the open sight of others; because they turned back from him, and would not consider any of his ways.* (Job 34:25-27)

God punishes evildoers in plain sight. That is just what happened to Mr. Badman. His injury was noticed by everyone, and his broken leg was the talk of the town. "Mr. Badman has broken his leg," one person said. "How did he break it?" asked another. "As he came home drunk from the tavern," said a third. "It is the judgment of God upon him," said a fourth. Thus, his sin, his shame, and his punishment were all made conspicuous to those who were around him. I will tell you a few stories that come to mind.

I have read in Mr. Clarke's *Looking Glass for Sinners* that, once upon a time, a certain drunken fellow boasted as he drank that there was neither heaven nor hell. He also said that he believed that man had no soul, and that, for his own part, he would sell his soul to anyone who would buy it. Then one of his companions bought it from him for a cup of wine. Presently, the devil, in man's shape, bought it from that man for the same price, and in the presence of them all, took hold of the soul-seller and carried him away through the air, so that he was never heard from again.

Clarke also told about a man from Salisbury who was in the prime of health. He was drinking and carousing in a tavern. He made a toast, wishing health for the devil. He said that if the devil would not come and toast to his health in return, he would not believe that there was either God or devil. Whereupon his companions, stricken with fear, hurried out of the room. Soon after, hearing a hideous noise and smelling a stinking odor, the wine merchant ran up into the barroom. He found that his customer was missing, the window was broken, and the iron bars of the window were bent downward and all bloody. But the man was never heard of again.

Clarke also told about a bailiff from Hedley who, on the Lord's Day, being drunk, got on his horse and rode through the streets, saying that his horse would carry him to the devil. Presently, his horse threw him and broke the man's neck. These things are worse than Mr. Badman's breaking his leg. They should be a caution to all of his friends who are living, lest they also fall by their sin into these sad judgments of God.

But, as I said, Mr. Badman quickly forgot all. His conscience was choked before his leg was healed. Therefore, before he recovered from the fruit of one sin, he tempted God to send another judgment to seize him. And so God did quickly after. For not many months after Badman's leg was well, he had a very dangerous bout of sickness. Then he began to think that his death was imminent indeed.

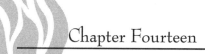

Chapter Fourteen

False Repentance

Attentive. Well, what did he think and do then?

Wiseman. He thought he would go to hell. I know that because he could not keep from saying so. To my best recollection, he lay one whole night crying out in fear. At times, he would tremble so that he would make the bed shake under him. But oh, how the thoughts of death, of hellfire, and of eternal judgment wracked his conscience. Fear could be seen in his face, and in his tossings to and fro. It could also be heard in his words and understood in his heavy groans. He would often cry, "I am undone! I am undone! My vile life has undone me!"

Attentive. Then his former atheistic thoughts and principles were too weak now to support him from the fears of eternal damnation.

Wiseman. Yes, they were too weak indeed! They may serve to stifle a man's conscience when he is in the midst of prosperity or to harden his heart against all good counsel when God has left him and given him *"over to a reprobate mind"* (Romans 1:28). But, alas, atheistic thoughts, notions, and opinions must shrink and melt away when God sends, yes, comes with sickness to visit the soul of such a sinner for his sin.

A man who lived about twelve miles from us had so immersed himself in his atheistic notions that, at last, he attempted to write a book against Jesus Christ and against the divine authority of the Scriptures. But I think it was not printed. Well, after many days, God struck him with a sickness, from which he later died.

So, while he was sick and musing upon his former doings, the book that he had written came to his mind, and with it such a sense of his evil in writing it that it tore his conscience as a lion would tear a young goat. He lay, therefore, upon his deathbed in a sad way. His conscience was greatly troubled. Some of my friends went to see him, and as they were in his room one day, he quickly called for pen, ink, and paper. When it was given to him, he took it and wrote words to this effect: "I, such a one, in such a town, must go to hellfire, for writing a book against Jesus Christ and against the Holy Scriptures." He would have leaped out of the window of his house to have killed himself, but was prevented from that by his friends. Thus, he died in his bed, such a death as it was. It will be well if others take warning from him.

Attentive. This is a remarkable story.

Wiseman. It is as true as it is remarkable. I heard it from reliable witnesses, who were present and caught him in their arms and saved him when he tried to leap out of his bedroom window in order to destroy himself.

Attentive. Well, you have told me what Mr. Badman's thoughts were when he was sick; please tell me now what he did during that time.

Wiseman. Did? He did many things that, I am sure, he never thought he would ever do, and that, to be sure, his wife and children never expected him to do. In this fit of sickness, his thoughts were quite altered about his wife. I say his thoughts, as far as could be judged by his words and behavior toward her. Now he called her his good wife, his godly wife, his honest wife, his precious dear, and such. Now he told her that she had the best of it. She had a good life to stand by her, while his debaucheries and ungodly life always stared him in the face. He said that the counsel that she often gave him was good, though he was bad for not heeding it.

Now he would listen to her talk to him, and he would lie sighing by her while she did. He would ask her to pray for him, so that he might be delivered from hell. He would also consent to some of her good ministers coming to comfort him, and he would seem to show them kindness when they came. He would treat them courteously and pay diligent attention to what they said. He preferred that they did not talk much about his ill-spent life, because his conscience was burdened by that already. He did not care to see his old companions, and the thoughts of them were a torment to him. Now he would speak kindly to that child of his who followed in his mother's footsteps, though before he could not stand to have the child in his presence.

He also welcomed the prayers of good people, hoping that God in His mercy would spare him a little longer. He promised that if God would let him recover this once, he would become a new man. He would be penitent toward God, and a loving husband to his wife. He would grant her liberty to go to hear her ministers, and he would even attend the services with her. He pledged that they would go hand in hand to heaven together.

Attentive. Here was a fine show of things! I guarantee his wife was glad for these changes.

Wiseman. His wife! Yes, and many good people besides. The news spread all over the town about what a great change had come over Mr. Badman. They heard how sorry he was for his sins, how he had begun to love his wife, and how he desired good men to pray to God to spare him. They heard about the promises he had made to God that if God would raise him from his sickbed to health again, what a new, penitent man he would be toward God, and what a loving husband to his good wife.

Well, ministers prayed, and good people rejoiced, thinking that they had truly rescued a man from the devil. There were some of the weaker sort who lacked the faith to believe that God had begun a work of grace in Badman's heart, but his wife, poor woman, you cannot imagine how inclined she was to believe that her husband had changed. She rejoiced and hoped that her prayers had been answered. But alas, in a little time, things all proved otherwise.

After he had stayed in bed for a while, his pain began to lessen, and he began to feel like himself again. Before long, he was so much better that he could walk around the house, and his appetite returned to normal. Now, his wife and her good friends stood by, hoping to see Mr. Badman fulfill his promises of becoming new toward God and loving to his wife; sadly, the opposite happened. As soon as he started to see signs of improvement in his health and found that his strength had begun to renew, his troubled conscience gradually disappeared. His great fears became like a stranger to him, and he acted as if he had never been worried about dying.

Chapter Fifteen

Badman's Return to Sin

Wiseman. Truthfully, I am inclined to think that one reason he no longer regarded or remembered his sickbed fears, and was no better for having experienced them, was because of a conversation he had with the doctor who supplied him with medicine during the time he was recuperating. As soon as Mr. Badman began to mend, the doctor came and sat down by him in his house. There they conversed about the nature of his disease. Among other things, they talked about Badman's troubled mind, and how he would cry out, tremble, and express his fears of going to hell when his sickness lay pretty hard upon him. Regarding these fears, the doctor told him that his anxieties and outbursts arose as a result of his illness. The doctor said that it was natural for someone suffering from that disease to experience light-headedness. He explained that it was caused by the sick person's inability to sleep, and that the lack of sleep affected one's mental and emotional state. The doctor pointed out that as soon as he was able to sleep and to rest, he quickly mended, and his mind calmed down. That was the doctor's explanation for why Badman was no longer troubled.

"And so it was indeed," thought Mr. Badman. "My fears were only the effects of my illness, and my emotional distress was only natural. Then surely, since my physician was my savior, my lust will again be my god." So he never paid any more attention to religion, but committed himself again to worldly lusts and wicked companions. That was the end of Mr. Badman's conversion.

Attentive. I thought, as you told me about him, that this conclusion would result from his sickbed confession, for I discerned, by the way you told the story, that the true symptoms of conversion were lacking in him. Those that appeared to be genuine were only substitutes for the real thing; they were the kind of promises that reprobates make.

Wiseman. You speak the truth, for even when he was most sensible, he lacked an understanding of the pollution of his nature. He experienced the kind of guilt for his sinful actions that reprobates before him have felt. Take, for example, Cain (Genesis 4:13-14); Pharaoh (Exodus 9:27-30); Saul (1 Samuel 15:24-26); and Judas (Matthew 27:3-5).

Besides, what he really desired was to be delivered from going to hell, and who would willingly go there? The other thing he wanted was for his life to be extended in this world. We do not find by anything that he said or did that He desired Jesus Christ to be his Savior. He did not express any sense of a need to be clothed in the righteousness of the Lord (Isaiah 61:10) or for His Spirit to sanctify him (1 Thessalonians 5:23). His confidence was in his own strength, and he saw nothing of the treachery of his own heart. If he had, he would never have been so free to make promises to God that he would change his ways. Instead, he would have been afraid that if he had made amends, he would have returned to his old ways like a dog returns to his vomit (Proverbs 26:11). He would have begged the saints to pray for him and pleaded for assistance from heaven on that account, that he might have been kept from doing so. It is true; he did beg for the prayers of good people, as did Pharaoh of Moses and Aaron (Exodus 9:28), and Simon of Simon Peter (Acts 8:24). His heart also seemed to be softened toward his wife and child, but alas, it was because of the conviction that God had given him concerning their happy estate compared with his miserable one rather than for any true love toward the work of God that was in them. True, he showed them some acts of kindness, but so did the rich man who, when in hell, asked Abraham to send someone to warn his five brothers who were yet in the world about *"this place of torment"* (Luke 16:28). Even a sinner can love others enough to wish that they would go to heaven instead of to hell.

Attentive. Sickbed repentance is seldom good for anything.

Wiseman. It is very rarely good for anything indeed. Death is an unwelcome guest to the sinner, and usually, when sickness and death visit, this is what happens: Sickness takes the sinner by the shoulder, and death stands at the bedroom door, waiting to receive him. Then the sinner begins to look around him and to think to himself, "These enemies will take me away to stand before God. I know that my life has not been lived as it should have been. What will happen to me when I appear before God?"

Often, a sense of what the sinner's punishment will be and a realization of the place of punishment startles the defiled conscience that has been roused by death's lumbering presence at the door. Thus, usually, a sickbed repentance is primarily a last-ditch effort to be saved from hell and from death. It is a plea to God that He will restore health until the sinner has the chance to change his evil ways, concluding that it is in his power to reform himself. This fact is evident by his large and lavish promises to do so. I have known many who, when they have been sick, have had huge measures of this kind of repentance, and while it has lasted, the noise and sound of it have spread around the town. But alas, how long has it lasted? Often, it scarcely remains until the sick person becomes well. It passes away like a mist and is transient. But this kind of repentance is compared to the howling of a dog. God says of this kind of repentance, *"They have not cried unto me with their heart, when they howled upon their beds"* (Hosea 7:14).

Attentive. Yet one may see by this the desperateness of men's hearts, for what is it but a rash evil to make promises to God to change, if God will just spare them, and then, as soon as they are recovered, or quickly thereafter, to fall into sin as they did before and never regard their promises again.

Wiseman. It is a sign of desperate madness indeed. Surely, they must realize that God took notice of their promises, that He heard the words that they spoke, and that He has laid them up against the time to come. (See Isaiah 30:8-9.) Then He will bring out their promises and testify to their faces that they flattered Him with their mouths and lied to Him with their tongues when they were sick (Psalm 78:34-37). When they believed they were dying, they made promises to change their ways if God would only heal them, but then, when they recovered, they did not keep their vows to God.

As I have told you, Mr. Badman did these things. He made great promises that he would be a new man, that he would leave his sins behind and become a convert, and that he would love his godly wife. Yes, many fine words Mr. Badman spoke in his sickness, but he took no good actions when he was well again.

Chapter Sixteen

A Christian's Death

Attentive. How did his good wife take it when she saw that he had not really changed, but that he had returned like a dog to its vomit (Proverbs 26:11) and was back to his old ways again?

Wiseman. Why, it broke her heart. It was a worse disappointment to her than knowing how he had deceived her into marrying him. At least, she took his insincere repentance more to heart and could not handle it as well. Of course, she had prayed often for him before, even all the time that he had mistreated her. Now, when he was so alarmed by his sickness and so desirous that he might live and change his ways, the poor woman thought that the time had come for God to answer her prayers. Even though she did not permit herself to share her gladness by whispering it among her friends, when she saw herself disappointed by her husband's turning rebel again, she could not stand up under it. She fell into a languishing illness, and in a few weeks, she gave up the ghost.

Attentive. How did she die?

Wiseman. She died bravely. She was comforted by the sense of well-being that came from her faith in Christ, and through Him, of the assurance of the world to come. She spoke bravely throughout her sickness, and she gave many signs of her salvation to those who came to visit her. The thoughts of the grave, and especially of her rising again, were sweet thoughts to her. She welcomed death, because she knew it would be her friend. She behaved herself like those who were making themselves ready to go to meet the bridegroom. (See Matthew 25:1-13.)

She said,

Now I am going to rest from my sorrows, my sighs, my tears, my mourning, and my complaints. I have longed to be among the saints, but I had no means to be allowed to join them. Now I am going, and no one can stop me, to the great meeting, *"to the general assembly and church of the firstborn, which are written in heaven"* (Hebrews 12:23). There I will have my heart's desire; there I will worship without temptation or other impediment; there I will see the face of my Jesus, whom I have loved, whom I have served, and who now I know will save my soul. I have prayed often for my husband's conversion, but there has been no answer of God in that matter. Are my prayers lost? Are they forgotten? Are they cast away? No, they are hanged upon the horns of the golden altar (see Psalm 118:27), and I will have the benefit of them myself, the moment that I will enter into the gates, those gates through which *"the righteous nation which keepeth the truth may enter in"* (Isaiah 26:2). I can say of my husband, as holy David said of his enemies, *"But as for me, when they were sick, my clothing was sackcloth: I humbled my soul with fasting; and my prayer returned into mine own bosom"* (Psalm 35:13). My prayers are not lost; my tears are still in God's bottle (Psalm 56:8). I desired a crown and glory for my husband, and for those of my children who follow in his steps, but as far as I can see, I must rest in the hope of having all these joys myself.

Attentive. Did she say these things openly?

Wiseman. No, she spoke these words only to one or two of her most intimate acquaintances, who were permitted to come and see her while she lay languishing upon her deathbed.

Attentive. Well, please continue with your story. I am glad to hear the blessed end that came to Badman's wife. This news is good medicine to my heart while we sit talking under this tree.

Wiseman. When she drew near her end, she called for her husband.

A Christian's Death

When he came to her, she told him that now he and she must part. She said,

> God knows, and you know, that I have been a loving, faithful wife to you. My prayers have been many for you, and as for all the abuses that I have received at your hand, those I freely and heartily forgive. I will still pray for your conversion as long as I have breath in this world. But husband, I am going where no bad man will ever come, and if you do not convert, you will never see me again. Please do not let my frank words offend you. I am your dying wife, and out of my faithfulness to you, I leave this exhortation with you. Stop sinning; flea to God for mercy while mercy's gate stands open. Remember that the day is coming when you, though now you are healthy and well, will lie at the gates of death as I do. What will you do then if you are found with a naked soul when you meet the cherubim with their flaming swords? Yes, what will you do then if death and hell come to visit you while you are in your sins and under the curse of the law?

Attentive. This was honest and plain speech, but what did Mr. Badman say to her?

Wiseman. He did what he could to divert her talk by throwing in other things. Also, he showed some pity to her and would ask her if she needed anything. With various words, he would distract her from talking about his need of salvation. When she saw that he was not listening to her, she sighed deeply, and lay still. So he went away, and then she called for her children and began to talk to them.

First, she spoke to those who were vulgar, and told them of the danger of dying before they had grace in their hearts. She told them also that death might be nearer to them than they knew, and she asked them to look when they went through the churchyard again to see if there were not little graves there. "Oh, children," she said, "will it not be dreadful to you if we only meet on the day of judgment, and then we are parted again, never to see each other anymore?" With that, she wept, and the children also wept, so she continued her conversation with them. She said,

> Children, I am going from you. I am going to Jesus Christ, and with Him there is neither sorrow, nor sighing, nor pain, nor tears, nor death (Revelation 21:4). I long for you to go there, too, but I can neither carry you nor take you there. But if you will turn from your sins to God, and will beg mercy at His hands by Jesus Christ, you will follow me, and will, when you die, come to the place where I am going, that blessed place of rest. Then we will be together forever, beholding the face of our Redeemer, to our mutual and eternal joy.

So she reminded them to remember the words of their dying mother when she was cold in her grave, and they were hot in their sins, if perhaps her words might put a check to their vices, and that they might remember and turn to God. Then they all went away from her except for her darling, namely, the child that she had the most love for because he followed her ways. So she addressed herself to him and said,

> Come to me, my sweet child. You are the child of my joy. I have lived to see you become a servant of God. You will have eternal life. I, my sweetheart, will go before you, but you will follow after, if you will *"hold the beginning of [your] confidence stedfast unto the end"* (Hebrews 3:14). When I am gone, remember my words. Love your Bible, follow the teachings of God's faithful ministers, deny ungodliness, and if troublesome times come, set a higher price upon Christ, His Word, His ways, and the testimony of a good conscience than upon all the world besides. Treat your father kindly and dutifully, but do not choose any of his ways. If you may go to service, choose that rather than to stay at home, but then be sure to choose a service where you may be helped forward in the way to heaven. In order to arrange for such a service, speak to my minister. He will help you, if possible, to find such an apprenticeship.

A Christian's Death

I also desire, my dear child, for you to love your brothers and sisters, but do not learn any of their naughty tricks. *"Have no fellowship with the unfruitful works of darkness, but rather reprove them"* (Ephesians 5:11). You have grace; they have not responded to any. Therefore, see that you beautify the way of salvation before their eyes by living a godly life and speaking conversation that reflects your submission to the revealed will of God. In these ways, your brothers and sisters may see and be more pleased with the good ways of the Lord. If you live to marry, take heed of being deceived as I was, that is, of being beguiled with fair words and the flatteries of a lying tongue. But first be sure of godliness, yes, as sure as it is possible for one to be in this world. Do not trust your own eyes, or your own judgment, as to that person's godliness that you are invited to marry. Ask counsel of good men, and do nothing without my minister's advice, if he is still living. I have also asked him to look after you.

Thus she talked to her children and gave them counsel. After she had talked to this beloved child a little longer, she kissed him and bid him to go downstairs.

In short, her time drew on, and the day that she must die arrived. So she died, with a soul full of grace and a heart full of comfort. By her death, she ended a life full of trouble. Her husband arranged a funeral for her—perhaps because he was glad to be rid of her, but we will leave that to be revealed at the Judgment.

Attentive. This woman died well. And now that we are talking about the death of a Christian, I will tell you a story of one who died some time ago in our town. The man was a godly old Puritan. After a long and godly life, he fell sick of the sickness from which he would die. As he lay dying, becoming increasingly more feeble, the woman who looked after him thought that she heard music. It was the sweetest music that she had ever heard in her life. It continued to play until he gave up the ghost. Now, when his soul departed from him, the music seemed to withdraw and to go farther and farther away from the house, and so it went until the sound was completely gone.

Wiseman. What do you think that music was?

Attentive. For all I know, it was the melodious notes of angels that were sent by God to carry him to heaven.

Wiseman. I cannot say but that sometimes God works in ways that are out of the ordinary with us poor mortals. I do not know if that is what happened with Badman's wife, but she had better music in her heart than sounded in this woman's ears.

Attentive. I believe so, but please tell me, did any of her other children respond to her words to the betterment of their souls?

Wiseman. One of them did, and he became a very hopeful young man. I can say nothing for the rest.

Attentive. And what did Badman do after his wife died?

Wiseman. Why, just as he did before. He scarcely mourned two weeks for her, and his mourning then was, no doubt, more for show than from his heart.

Attentive. Did he not sometimes talk about his wife after she died?

Wiseman. Yes, when the mood suited him, and he would commend her extravagantly, saying she was a good, godly, virtuous woman. But this practice is not a thing to cause wonder. It is common with wicked men to hate God's servants while they are alive and to commend them after they are dead. That is how the Pharisees treated the prophets. Those of the prophets who were dead, they commended; those who were alive, they condemned. (See Matthew 23:29-39.)

Chapter Seventeen

Badman Receives His Own Medicine

Attentive. Did Mr. Badman marry again quickly?

Wiseman. No, not for a good while. When he was asked why he did not remarry, he would offer this unseemly response: "Who would keep a cow of their own who can have a quart of milk for a penny?" Meaning, who would pay to support a wife when he could have a prostitute whenever he chose? So villainous, so abominable were his actions after the death of his wife. Yet at last, there was one who was too hard for him to manipulate. After getting him sufficiently drunk, she cunningly extracted a promise of marriage from him, and so she held him to it and forced him to marry her.

And she was as good as he at all his vile and ranting tricks. She had her companions just as he had his, and she would meet them at the tavern and alehouse more often than he was ever aware. To be blunt, she was a true whore. She had many men who came to her at an appointed time and place. Yes, he detected what was going on, but he did not know what to do about it. For if he began to talk, she could throw in his face the names of the whores that she knew he had visited, and she could match him also in cursing and swearing, for she would return oath for oath, and curse for curse.

Attentive. What kind of oaths would she say?

Wiseman. Why, damn her, and sink her, and the like.

Attentive. These are provoking things.

Wiseman. So they are, but God does not altogether let such things go unpunished in this life. Something of this I have shown you already, but I will mention one or two more instances.

In the year 1551, in a city of Savoy, there lived a man who was a monstrous curser and swearer, and though he was often admonished and condemned for it, he would by no means mend his ways. At length, a great plague occurred in the city, and he withdrew himself, along with his wife and a relative, into a garden. There he was again admonished to repent of his wickedness, but he hardened his heart even more, swearing, blaspheming God, and giving himself to the devil. Immediately, the devil snatched him up, while his wife and relative looked on. The devil positively carried him away. When the local officials were notified, they went to the place and questioned the women, who confirmed the truth of the story.

Clarke, in his book *Looking Glass for Sinners*, wrote about a wicked woman from Olster who used to give herself body and soul to the devil as she cursed. Reproved for it, she continued the practice. Then one day, while she was at a wedding feast, the devil came in person and carried her up into the air. He carried her around the town in that way as she emitted horrible outcries so that the inhabitants were ready to die from fear. By and by, he tore her into four pieces, leaving her four quarters on four different highways. Then he brought her intestines to the marriage feast and threw them on the table in front of the mayor of the town, saying, "Behold these dishes of meat belong to you, and the same destruction awaits you if you do not rectify your wicked life."

Attentive. Although God refrains from dealing the same way with all men who desecrate and denounce His name, and immediate judgments do not overtake them, yet He makes their lives bitter to them by other judgments, does He not?

Wiseman. Yes, yes, and for proof, I need go no further than to this Badman and his second wife, for their railing, cursing, and swearing did not end in words alone. They would fight and fly at each other like cats and dogs. But it must be looked upon as the hand and judgment of God upon him for his depravity. He had an honest woman before, who would not join in his evil-doing; therefore, God took her away and gave him one as bad as himself. Thus, that measure that he meted to his first wife, his second wife meted to him again (Matthew 7:2). And this is a punishment with which God will sometimes punish wicked men. As the Lord said to Amaziah, *"Thy wife shall be an harlot in the city"* (Amos 7:17).

Mr. Badman lived quite a while with this last wife, but, as I told you before, in a most sad and hellish manner. Now he would bewail his first wife's death—not out of love for her godliness, for he could never put up with that, but for the ways in which she always used to keep the home. This wife would go out and neglect her responsibilities. His first wife was also honest and faithful, but his last wife misused her body in prostitution. The first woman loved to keep things together, but this last one could whirl things about as well as he. The first would be silent when he chided her and would take it patiently when he abused her, but his second wife would give him word for word, blow for blow, and curse for curse. Mr. Badman had met his match! God had a mind to make him see the baseness of his own life in the wickedness of his wife. But that would not do with Mr. Badman; he would be Mr. Badman still. This judgment did not work any reformation upon him, no, not toward God or man.

Attentive. I guarantee you that Mr. Badman thought, when his first wife was dead, that next time he would make a far better match.

Wiseman. What he thought I cannot tell, but he could not hope for it in this match. He knew that he was caught. He knew that he was entrapped by this woman and would have escaped if he could. He knew her to be a prostitute before; therefore, he could not expect to have a happy life with her. For she who would not be true to her own soul could not be expected to be true to him.

Solomon said, *"A whore is a deep ditch"* (Proverbs 23:27), and Mr. Badman found this to be true. For when she had caught him in her pit, she would not leave him until she had extracted a promise of marriage. When she had taken him so far, she forced him to marry her. After that, they lived the life that I have described.

Many of his neighbors, even many of those who were carnal, said, "It is a righteous judgment of God upon him for his abusive behavior and language to his other wife." For they were all convinced that she was a virtuous woman, and that he, the vile wretch, had killed her with his lack of kindness.

Chapter Eighteen

A Death in Sinful Security

Attentive. And how long did they live together that way?

Wiseman. Some fourteen or sixteen years. Even though she, too, had brought money with her into the marriage, they sinned it all away and parted as poor as church mice. And how could it reasonably be otherwise? He would have his way, and she would have hers; he among his companions, and she among hers; he with his harlots, and she with her rogues. Thus, they reduced their wealth to poverty.

Attentive. Of what disease did Mr. Badman die, for now I perceive we are come to the point of his death?

Wiseman. I cannot accurately say that he died from one disease, for there were many that consented and put their heads together to bring him to his end. He suffered from edema, tuberculosis, obesity, gout; and some say that he had a trace of syphilis. Yet the captain of all these men of death, which came against him to take him away, was tuberculosis, for that is what brought him down to the grave.

Attentive. Although I will not say that good men cannot die of tuberculosis, edema, or obesity—yes, these may result in a good man's death—yet I will say again, many times these diseases come through man's excessive use of things. Much drinking leads to many diseases. Undoubtedly, Mr. Badman's death resulted from his abuse of himself in the use of lawful and unlawful things. I base my judgment upon the detailed report of his life that you have given to me.

Wiseman. I do not think that you need to revoke your sentence, for it is thought by many that Badman brought himself to destruction through his wicked ways with prostitutes. He was not an old man when he died, nor was he naturally very feeble; instead, he was strong and of a healthy complexion. Yet, as I said, he languished to his grave, decaying and rotting away. And what made him stink when he was dead, I mean, what made him stink in his name and reputation? It was that he died with a foul odor of disease upon him. He was a man whose life was full of sin and whose death was without repentance.

Attentive. These were blemishes sufficient to make him stink indeed.

Wiseman. They were and they did. No man will be able to speak well of him now that he is gone. His name will rot above the ground as his carcass rots beneath. And this is according to the saying of the wise man, *"The memory of the just is blessed; but the name of the wicked shall rot"* (Proverbs 10:7).

Both aspects of this text are fulfilled in the lives of Mr. Badman and his first wife. For her name still flourishes, even though she has been dead almost seventeen years, but his name will began to stink and rot before he has been buried seventeen days.

Attentive. To the man who dies with a life full of sin and with a heart void of repentance, although he would die of the most golden disease, if there were anything that might be called such, I guarantee that his name will stink both in heaven and on earth.

Wiseman. You speak the truth; therefore, the names of Cain, Pharaoh, Saul, Judas, and the Pharisees, though dead thousands of years ago, stink as fresh in the nostrils of the world today as if they were but newly dead.

Attentive. I fully agree with you in this assessment. But since you have charged him with dying impenitent, please let me see how you will prove it—not that I altogether doubt it, because you have affirmed it, but I love to have proof for what men say in such weighty matters.

A Death in Sinful Security

Wiseman. When I said he died without repentance, I meant insofar as those who knew him could judge when they compared his life, the Word, and his death together.

Attentive. Well said. They went the right way to find out whether or not he had repented. That is, whether he had clearly shown that he had or had not repented. Now then, please show me how they proved that he had not repented.

Wiseman. So I will. The first sign was that, in all the time of his sickness, he showed no recognition or sense of his sins; instead, he was as secure and as quiet as if he had never sinned in all his life.

Attentive. I agree that this is a sign that he had no guilt for his sins, for how can a man repent of what he has neither recognition nor knowledge of? But it is strange that he had no sense of his sins now, when he had such an awareness of his evil ways when he was sick before.

Wiseman. He was as secure now as if he had been as sinless as an angel—though all men knew what a sinner he was, for his sins were revealed in his face. His debauched life was read and known by all men; his repentance was read and known by no man, for, as I said, he had none. And for all I know, the reason that he had no sense of his sins now was that he no longer profited by the conviction that he had felt before. He no longer liked to retain the knowledge of God that caused his sins to come to his remembrance (Romans 1:28). Therefore, *"God gave* [him] *over to a reprobate mind"* (verse 28), to hardness and stupidity of spirit; thus was this Scripture fulfilled in him:

> *Make the heart of this people fat, and make their ears heavy, and shut their eyes; lest they see with their eyes, and hear with their ears, and understand with their heart, and convert, and be healed.* (Isaiah 6:10)

And this Scripture as well: *"Let their eyes be darkened that they may not see"* (Romans 11:10). For a man to live in sin and to leave this world without repentance is the saddest judgment that can overtake a man.

Attentive. Although both you and I have agreed that without a recognition and knowledge of sin there can be no repentance, yet that is but our opinion; therefore, let us now see if by the Scripture we can support our position.

Wiseman. That is easily done. The three thousand who were converted on the day of Pentecost did not repent until they had a sense of their sins (Acts 2:37-41). Paul did not repent until he a sense of his sins. (See Act 9:1-6.) The Philippian jailer did not repent until he understood that he needed to be saved (Acts 16:30). Of what should a man repent? The answer is, of sin. What is it to repent of sin? The answer is, to be sorry for it, to turn from it. But how can a man who does not know he has sinned be sorry for his sin? David not only committed sins, but also remained impenitent for them until Nathan the prophet was sent from God to show him how he had sinned. Then, but not until then, did David repent of them. (See 2 Samuel 12:1-13.) Job, in order to repent, cried to God, *"Show me wherefore thou contendest with me"* (Job 10:2). And again, *"That which I see not teach thou me: if I have done iniquity, I will do no more"* (Job 34:32). He was not asking God to show him the sins that he knew he had done but to show him any that he did not have a sense or knowledge of in order that he might repent of them. Also, Israel's repentance came after they were made aware of their sins, and after they were instructed about the evil of them (Jeremiah 31:18-20).

Attentive. These are good testimonies of this truth. They prove indeed the need for repentance. If it is true that Mr. Badman did not repent, then he lived and died in sin. Without repentance, a man is sure to die in his sins, for they will lie down in the dust with him, rise at the Judgment with him, and hang about his neck like cords and chains when he stands at the bar of God's tribunal (Proverbs 5:22). They will go with him, too, when he is sent away from the judgment seat with the words, *"Depart from me, ye cursed, into everlasting fire, prepared for the devil and his angels"* (Matthew 25:41). They will fret and gnaw his conscience, because they will be to him as a never-dying worm (Isaiah 66:24; Mark 9:44).

A Death in Sinful Security

Wiseman. You say well, and I will add a word or two more to what I have said. Repentance does not occur without a recognition and a sense of sin, but not everyone who knows that he has sinned repents, that is, repents and receives salvation. As the Scripture says, "*Godly sorrow worketh repentance to salvation not to be repented of: but the sorrow of the world worketh death*" (2 Corinthians 7:10). For it is fresh in our minds that Mr. Badman realized how sinful he was when he had the terrible illness, but his conviction died without procuring any such godly fruit as true repentance, as was manifest by his hasty return to sin when he became well. He returned to his sin "*as a dog returneth to his vomit*" (Proverbs 26:11).

Many people also think that repentance is the same thing as confession of sin, but they are very much mistaken; for repentance, as was said before, is being sorry for sin, and turning from transgression to God by Jesus Christ. Now, if this is true, that every recognition and sense of sin will not always result in repentance, then repentance certainly cannot occur where there is no recognition and sense of sin. It is clear that not all conviction of sin leads to repentance when we examine the lives of Cain, Pharaoh, Saul, and Judas, all of whom had a sense, a great sense, of sin, but none of whom repented and found new life.

Now, I conclude that Mr. Badman died impenitent, and so his death was most miserable.

Attentive. But please, before we finish our conversation about Mr. Badman, give me another proof of his dying in his sins.

Wiseman. Another proof is this: he did not desire a sense of his sins that he might have repentance for them. Did I say he did not desire it? I will add, he greatly desired to remain in his false security, and that I will prove by what follows. First, he could not endure for any man to talk to him about his sinful life, and yet that was the way to produce a sense of sin that would lead to repentance of it in his soul. But he could not tolerate such talk. Those men who did offer to talk to him about his ill-spent life were as unwelcome to him, during the time of his last sickness, as Elijah was when he went to meet with Ahab as Ahab was going to take possession of Naboth's vineyard. (See 1 Kings 21:17-20.) *"Ahab said to Elijah, 'Hast thou found me, O mine enemy?'"* (verse 20). So Mr. Badman would say in his heart to and of those who came to him, even though they came out of love to convince him of his evil life in order that he might have repented of it and have obtained mercy.

Attentive. Did good men then go to see him in his last sickness?

Wiseman. Yes, those who were his first wife's acquaintances went to see him and to talk with him to see if perhaps now he might, at last, reconsider and cry to God for mercy.

Attentive. They did well to try to urge him to save his soul from hell. But how can you tell that he did not care for the company of these godly visitors?

Wiseman. Because of the different way that he acted with them compared with his behavior when his old carnal companions came to see him. When his old friends came to see him, he would go out of his way, both by words and actions, to signify that he was glad they had come to visit. He would also talk with them freely and look pleasantly at them, though their conversation could not be anything but what David said carnal men would offer to him when they came to visit him in his sickness. *"If he comes to see me, he speaketh vanity: his heart gathereth iniquity to itself"* (Psalm 41:6). But these kinds of talks, I say, Mr. Badman could put up with much more than he did the conversations of better men.

But I will more particularly give you a description of his behavior toward good men, and good conversation, when they would come to see him. First, when they arrived, his spirits would seem to drop at the sight of them. Then he would not care to answer any of their questions when they sought to determine whether or not he had a sense of sin, death, hell, and judgment. He would either say nothing, evade their questions, or else tell them that he was too weak and exhausted, so he could not speak much. Next, he would never initiate conversation with them, and he was glad when they held their tongues. He would ask them no questions about his state and the world to come, or how he could escape the damnation that he knew he deserved. At last, he made a practice of asking his wife, when these good people attempted to come to see him, to tell them that he was asleep or that he wanted to go to sleep or that he was so weak from a lack of sleep that he could not tolerate any noise. After he had treated them in this way time after time, at last they were discouraged from coming to visit him anymore.

Now, in this time of his sickness, he was so hardened that, when his wicked companions came to visit him, he would talk disparagingly about those good men, and about their good doctrine, too. He would belittle those who came to see him out of love—those who labored diligently to convert him. Moreover, when these good men were leaving his house, he would never say, "Please, when will you be able to come again, for I desire more of your company so that I may hear more of your good instruction?" No, he never said a word like that; instead, when they were visiting, he would never offer them any refreshment, and when they were leaving, he would never thank them for their good company and good instruction.

When his evil friends visited him during his final illness, he would talk to them about worldly matters, such as business, houses, lands, famous men, great titles, renowned places, outward prosperity or outward adversity, or some other carnal thing. From all of his conversations, I conclude that he did not desire a sense and understanding of his sin in order that he might repent and be saved.

Attentive. It must be as you say, if these things are true that you have asserted about him. I do believe them, because I know you would not dare to tell a lie about the dead.

Wiseman. I was one of those who visited him and observed his behavior and actions, and I have given you an accurate account of what happened.

Attentive. I am satisfied. But please, if you can, show me now, from God's Word, what sentence God passes upon such men.

Wiseman. Why, the man who is averse to repentance, who does not desire to hear about his sins in order that he might repent and be saved, is said to be like the man who said to God, *"Depart from [me]; for [I] desire not the knowledge of thy ways"* (Job 21:14). He is a man who says in his heart and with his actions, *"I have loved strangers* [foreign gods]*, and after them will I go"* (Jeremiah 2:25). He is a man who shuts his eyes, stops his ears, and turns his spirit against God (Zechariah 7:11-12; Acts 7:57-58; 28:25-27). Yes, he is a man who is at enmity with God, who abhors God with his soul.

Attentive. What other sign can you give me that Mr. Badman died without repentance?

Wiseman. Why, he never heartily cried out to God for mercy during the time of his affliction. True, when seizures or sharp, sudden pains took hold of him, then he would say, as other carnal men do, "Lord, help me; Lord, strengthen me; Lord, deliver me," and the like. But to cry to God for mercy, he did not, but acted, as I hinted before, as if he had never sinned.

Attentive. That is another bad sign indeed, for crying to God for mercy is one of the first signs of repentance. When Paul was repenting of his sins, the Lord said of him, *"Behold, he prayeth"* (Acts 9:11). But he who does not show the first sign of repentance reveals that he is impenitent. I do not say that there will be no crying. There can be tears without true repentance. (See Hebrews 12:16-17.) David said, *"They cried, but there was none to save them; even unto the LORD, but he answered them not"* (Psalm 18:41). God would have answered if their cries had been the fruit of repentance. But, I say, if men can cry to God and still be unrepentant, be sure that those who do not cry at all are not repentant. It is said in Job, *"They cry not when he bindeth them"* (Job 36:13); that is, they do not cry to God because they have no repentance. No repentance, no cries; false repentance, false cries; true repentance, true cries.

A Death in Sinful Security

Wiseman. I know that it is as unlikely for a man to refrain from crying to God when he is repentant as it is for a man to withhold groaning when he feels excruciating pain. He who looks into the book of Psalms, where repentance is most vividly described, will find that crying–strong crying, hearty crying, great crying, and incessant crying–has been the fruit of repentance, but Mr. Badman exhibited no form of repentance; therefore, he died in his sins.

That crying to God is an inseparable effect of repentance is seen in these Scriptures:

> *Have mercy upon me, O God, according to thy lovingkindness: according unto the multitude of thy tender mercies blot out my transgressions.* (Psalm 51:1)

> *O Lord, rebuke me not in thine anger, neither chasten me in thy hot displeasure. Have mercy upon me, O Lord; for I am weak: O Lord, heal me; for my bones are vexed. My soul is also sore vexed: but thou, O Lord, how long? Return, O Lord, deliver my soul: oh save me for thy mercies' sake.* (Psalm 6:1-4)

> *O Lord, rebuke me not in thy wrath: neither chasten me in thy hot displeasure. For thine arrows stick fast in me, and thy hand presseth me sore. There is no soundness in my flesh because of thine anger; neither is there any rest in my bones because of my sin. For mine iniquities are gone over mine head: as an heavy burden they are too heavy for me. My wounds stink and are corrupt because of my foolishness. I am troubled; I am bowed down greatly; I go mourning all the day long. For my loins are filled with a loathsome disease: and there is no soundness in my flesh. I am feeble and sore broken: I have roared by reason of the disquietness of my heart.* (Psalm 38:1-8)

I might give you many more of the holy sayings of good men whereby they expressed how they were, what they felt, and whether they cried or not as they were brought to repentance. It is as likely for a man, when the pangs of guilt are upon him, to hold back from praying, as it is for a woman, when the pangs of travail are upon her, to keep from crying out. If all the world told me that such a man has repentance, if he is not a praying man, I could not be persuaded to believe it.

Attentive. I know no reason why you should, for there is nothing that can demonstrate that such a man has repented. But, sir, what other sign do you have by which you can prove that Mr. Badman died in his sins, thus in a state of damnation?

Wiseman. I have this fact to prove it: His old, sinful companions in the time of his health were those whose company and carnal talk he most delighted in during his sickness. I have hinted at this before, but now I suggest it as an argument of his lack of grace, for where there is indeed a work of grace in the heart, that work not only changes the heart, thoughts, and desires, but also the conversation and the company one keeps as well. When Paul had a work of grace in his soul, he tried to join himself to the disciples. He no longer wanted to be associated with his old companions and their loathsome deeds. Now he was Christ's disciple, and he favored the company of His other disciples. *"And he was with them* [the apostles] *coming in and going out at Jerusalem"* (Acts 9:28).

Attentive. I thought of something before when you mentioned his preference for his wicked friends over the godly men who visited with him. I thought, this is a dangerous sign that he did not have grace in his heart. As the saying goes, "Birds of a feather will flock together." If this man were one of God's children, he would congregate with God's children. His delight would be with and in the company of God's people. As the psalmist said, *"I am a companion of all them that fear thee, and of them that keep thy precepts"* (Psalm 119:63).

Wiseman. You speak well, for what fellowship has he who believes with an infidel (2 Corinthians 6:14-15)? And although it is true that all who associate with the godly are not godly themselves, yet those who inwardly choose the company of the ungodly and openly profane, rather than the company of the godly, as Mr.

A Death in Sinful Security

Badman did, surely are not godly men, but ungodly. He was, as I told you, out of his element when good men came to visit him, but he was among his own kind when his worthless companions came around.

Truly, grace alters everything—hearts, lives, choices of companions, and all—for by it the heart and man are made new. And a new heart and a new man must have objects of delight that are new. *"Old things are passed away"* (2 Corinthians 5:17). Why? Because *"all things are become new"* (verse 17). Now, if *"all things are become new,"* namely, heart, mind, thoughts, desires, and delights, it follows by consequence that the choice of one's companions will be affected; hence, it is said that *"all that believed were together"* (Acts 2:44); that they were *"added to the church"* (verse 47); that *"they went to their own company"* (Acts 4:23); and that they *"were of one heart and of one soul"* (verse 32).

Now, someone could object and say that Mr. Badman was sick; therefore, he was unable to go to the godly. But he had a tongue in his head, and he could have spoken to others, if his heart were so inclined, asking them to call or send for the godly to visit him. Then the company of the ungodly, especially his fellow sinners, would, whenever he saw them, have been a burden and a grief to him. If his heart and affection were inclined toward the good, then good companions would have suited him best. But his chosen companions were his old associates, and his delight was in them; therefore, his heart and soul were still ungodly.

Attentive. Please tell me how Badman acted when he drew near to death; for, I perceive that what you say of him now has reference to him and to his actions at the beginning of his sickness. Then he could endure company and much talk; besides, perhaps then he thought that he would recover and not die. Later, when he had cause to think, when he was wasting away, when he was at the grave's mouth, how did he act then? I mean, when he was, as we say, within a step of death, when he saw and could not but know that shortly he must die and appear before the judgment of God, what were his actions then?

Wiseman. Why, there were not any other changes in him other than the changes to his body caused by the effects of his disease. Sickness, you know, will alter the body, and pain will make men groan, but as for his mind, he remained unchanged. His mind was the same; his heart was the same. He was the selfsame Mr. Badman—not only in name but also in his behavior—until the very day of his death; yes, so far as could be observed, he was the same up to the very moment in which he died.

Attentive. What was his death like? Was it difficult, or did he die easily and quietly?

Wiseman. He died as quietly as a lamb. To bystanders, it appeared that there was no struggle. As for his mind, it seemed to be totally quiet. But why do you ask me this question?

Attentive. Not for my own sake, but for the sake of others. For there is an opinion among the uninformed that if a man dies, as they call it, like a lamb, that is, quietly, and without terrifying fear, which some show in their deaths, they conclude, beyond all doubt, that such a person has gone to heaven and has certainly escaped *"the wrath to come"* (1 Thessalonians 1:10).

Chapter Nineteen

A Quiet, Hardened Death

Wiseman. No judgment regarding the eternal state of a man can be made by a quiet death. Suppose that one man dies quietly, another dies suddenly, and a third dies with a fearful spirit. No one can judge their eternal condition by the manner of their deaths. Those who die quietly, suddenly, or fearfully may go to heaven or to hell. No one can determine a man's final destination by the death he dies. The judgment that we make of the eternal outcome of a man must be gathered from another consideration, namely, Did the man die in his sins? Did he die in unbelief? Did he die before he was born again? If so, then he has gone to the devil and hell, even though he may have died ever so quietly. Or we ask, Was the man a good man? Did he possess faith and holiness? Was he a lover and a worshipper of God by Christ according to God's Word? If so, then he has gone to God and heaven no matter how suddenly or with what state of mind he died. But Mr. Badman died without faith. His life was evil, and his ways were evil to his end; therefore, he went to hell and to the devil, no matter how quietly he died.

Indeed, in some cases, there is a judgment to be made about a man's eternal condition by the manner of his death. For instance, suppose that a man murdered himself or lived a wicked life, and after that, died in utter despair. These men, without a doubt, do go to hell. Here I will take the opportunity to speak about two of Mr. Badman's brothers, for you know I told you before that he had two brothers, and of the manner of their deaths. One of them killed himself, and the other, after a wicked life, died in utter despair. Now, I would not be afraid to conclude that both of these brothers went to hell.

Attentive. Please tell me how the first brother killed himself.

Wiseman. Why, he took a knife and cut his own throat; immediately, he gave up the ghost and died. Now, what can we judge of such a man's condition, since the Scripture says, "*No murderer hath eternal life abiding in him*" (1 John 3:15). By that, it must be concluded that one like this has gone to hell. He was a murderer, a self-murderer, and that is the worst kind, one who kills his own body and soul. Nor do we find mention made in the Holy Bible of any but cursed ones who did such kinds of deeds.

And this is a painful judgment of God upon men, when God will, for the sins of such, give them up to be their own executioners, or rather to execute His judgment and anger upon themselves. And let me earnestly give this caution to sinners: Take heed, sirs, and stop sinning, lest God treats you as He treated Mr. Badman's brother, that is, lest He gives you up to be your own murderer.

Attentive. Now that you mention this, I once knew a man, a barber, who took his razor and cut his own throat. Then he stuck his head out of his bedroom window to show the neighbors what he had done. Before long, he died.

Wiseman. I can tell you a more dreadful thing than that, I mean in regard to the manner of committing suicide. About twelve years ago, a man who lived at Brafield, by Northampton, named John Cox, murdered himself. Here is how he did it. He was a poor man who had been sick for some time, and the time of his sickness fell at the beginning of harvest. He was consumed with worry over how he and his family would survive if he was unable to work during this season. He fell into deep despair and cried out to his wife, "We are ruined!"

Right after saying that, he asked his wife to leave the room so that he could try to get some rest, so she left. But instead of sleeping, he took his razor and cut a great hole in his side. Then he cut his own throat. His wife, hearing him sigh and gasp for breath, came into the room. When she saw what he had done, she ran out and called in some neighbors. When they saw what he had done to himself, one of them said to him, "Oh, John, what have you done? Are you not sorry?"

He answered harshly, "It is too late to be sorry."

Then, the same person said to him, "Oh, John, pray to God for forgiveness for your terrible actions."

Upon hearing that exhortation, he seemed to be very offended, and in an angry manner said, "Pray!" With that word, he flung himself against the wall, and, after a few gasps, died desperately.

I cannot confirm all the particulars, but the general point to the story is true. I heard it from a sober, credible person, who himself was the eyewitness who talked with the man.

Many other such dreadful things could be told, but these are enough.

Attentive. This is a dreadful story. I would to God that it might be a warning to others, to instruct them to fear Him and to pray, lest He should give them up to do the same as John Cox did. For surely those who deliberately take their own lives cannot go to heaven; therefore, as you have said, he who has died by his own hands certainly has gone to hell. But speak a word or two about Badman's other brother.

Wiseman. The wicked man who was dying in despair?

Attentive. Yes.

Wiseman. Well then, Mr. Badman's other brother was a very wicked man, both in heart and life. Nothing could reclaim him—neither good men, good books, good examples, nor God's judgments. After he had lived a great while in his sins, God struck him with a sickness, from which he died. Now, during his illness, his conscience began to be awakened, and he began to bellow so loudly about his ill-spent life that the people of the town began to talk about him. As the word spread, many neighbors came to see him and to read to him, as is the common custom. But everything they tried could not abate his terror. He would lie in his bed gnashing his teeth and wringing his hands, convinced of the damnation of his soul. In horror and despair he died. He did not call on God; instead, he distrusted God's mercy and blasphemed His name.

Attentive. This brings to mind a man who a friend of mine told me about. He had lived wickedly, and when he came to die, he fell into despair. Having concluded that God had no mercy for him, he asked the devil for a favor, saying, "Devil, be good to me."

Wiseman. This is almost like Saul, who being forsaken of God, went to the witch of Endor, and so to the devil, for help (1 Samuel 28:7-20). Unfortunately, if I purposed to collect these dreadful stories, it would be easy before long to come up with hundreds of them. I will conclude as I began; those who are their own murderers, or who die in despair, after they have lived a life of wickedness, will surely go to hell.

Here I would add a word of caution. Everyone who dies troubled in spirit, that is, confused and afraid, does not necessarily die in despair. For a good man may have these feelings during his death, and yet go to heaven and glory. For, as I said before, he who is a good man, a man who has faith and holiness, and loves and worships God through Christ, according to His Word, may die distressed in spirit. Satan will not quit trying to assault good men on their deathbeds, but they are secured by the Word and power of God. Yes, even though they may be agonized in spirit, they are also helped to exercise themselves in faith and prayer. That is something that the one who dies in despair can by no means do. But let us return to Mr. Badman and talk further about the manner of his death.

Attentive. I think you and I are of the same mind, for I was just thinking about calling you back to that topic. And now, since it was your own idea, let us converse a little more about his quiet, calm death.

Wiseman. We were speaking before of the manner of Mr. Badman's death—how he died calmly and quietly. At that time, you made the observation that many people conclude that if a man dies quietly, as they call it, like a lamb, he has certainly gone to heaven.

A Quiet, Hardened Death

To the contrary, if a wicked man dies quietly, a man who has all his days lived in notorious sin, his quiet dying is far from being a sign of his being saved; instead, it is an absolute proof of his damnation. This was Mr. Badman's case. He lived wickedly even to the end, and then he went quietly out of the world; therefore, Mr. Badman has gone to hell.

Attentive. Well, since you speak so confidently in this matter, please tell me what proof you have for your opinion.

Wiseman. My first argument is drawn from the need for repentance. No man can be saved unless he repents. Neither can he repent unless he recognizes that he is a sinner. I guarantee that he who knows he is a sinner will be tormented for a time by that knowledge. This truth is testified to by all the Scriptures and by Christian experience. He who knows himself to be a sinner suffers conviction, especially if that knowledge does not come to him until he is cast upon his deathbed. The man is distressed, I say, before he can die quietly. Yes, he is anxious, dejected, and cast down. He also cries out in hunger and thirst for Christ's mercy. If, in the end, he dies peacefully, with that calm assurance that comes through faith and hope in God's mercy—what Mr. Badman and his brothers were complete strangers to—his serenity is discerned by all judicious observers. They witness what came before it, what flows from it, and what fruit follows it.

I confess that I am not an admirer of sickbed repentance; I think it is seldom good for anything. But I repeat, he who has lived in sin and profanity all his days, as Mr. Badman did, and yet dies quietly before repentance steps in, is assuredly going to hell and is damned.

Attentive. This sounds like a strong proof indeed. Repentance must be sought, or else we will go to hellfire. If a wicked person is impenitent until the day of his death, even if he leaves this world silently, it is a sign that he has died without repentance; thus, he is damned.

Wiseman. I am satisfied that repentance is necessary because God calls for it, and He will not pardon sin without it. *"Except ye* *repent, ye shall all likewise perish"* (Luke 13:3). This is what God has said, and anyone who thinks he can go to heaven and glory without repentance will prove how foolhardy he is. Repent, for *"the ax is laid unto the root of the trees: therefore every tree which bringeth not forth good fruit is hewn down, and cast into the fire"* (Matthew 3:10). There can be no good fruit where there is not sound repentance.

This was true in Mr. Badman's case. He led a sinful life to the very end. He died calmly, but without repentance; therefore, he has gone to hell and is damned. A quiet death that follows a sinful life leads to hell.

My second argument is drawn from these blessed words of Christ:

When a strong man armed keepeth his palace, his goods are in peace: but when a stronger than he shall come upon him, and overcome him, he taketh from him all his armour wherein he trusted, and divideth his spoils.

(Luke 11:21–22)

The fully armed, strong man kept Mr. Badman's house, that is, his heart, soul, and body, for he went from a sinful life quietly out of this world. The stronger man did not disturb him by intercepting with sound repentance his sinful life and his quiet death. Therefore, Mr. Badman has gone to hell.

The strong man who is fully armed is the devil, and quietness is his defense. The devil never fears losing the sinner, if he can keep him calm. If the devil can keep the sinner composed in a sinful life and through a quiet death, the sinner becomes the devil's own. There is no fear of the devil's losing such a soul, because Christ, who is the best Judge in this matter, said, *"his goods are in peace"* (verse 21)—in quiet and out of danger.

Attentive. Without a doubt, being at peace with sin is one of the greatest signs of a damnable state.

Wiseman. So it is. Therefore, when God expressed the greatness of His anger against sin and sinners, He said, "They are *'joined*

A Quiet, Hardened Death

to idols: let [them] *alone'* (Hosea 4:17). Do not disturb them; let them go on without control; let the devil enjoy them peaceably; let him carry the unconverted quietly out of the world." This is one of the saddest judgments, and speaks of the burning anger of God against sinful men.

My third argument comes from this saying of Scripture:

> *He hath blinded their eyes, and hardened their heart; that they should not see with their eyes, nor understand with their heart, and be converted, and I should heal them.*
>
> (John 12:40)

I want to mention three things from this Scripture. First, there can be no conversion to God when the eye is darkened and the heart is hardened. First the eye must be opened, and then the heart must turn from sin and yield to God; otherwise, there can be no conversion. This was clearly Mr. Badman's case. He lived a wicked life and died with his eyes shut and his heart hardened. His sinful life united with a calm death. Because he refused to be converted, he will partake of the fruit of his sinful life in hellfire.

Second, this hardened condition of man is a clear sign of God's anger against man for his sin. When God is angry with men, this is one of the judgments that He gives them up to, namely, to blindness of mind and hardness of heart. Also, He allows this condition to accompany them to the gates of death. Then and there, and not any sooner, their eyes are opened.

Thus it is said of the rich man mentioned in Luke, *"And in hell he lift up his eyes, being in torments"* (Luke 16:23). This verse implies that he did not lift them up before. He neither saw what he had done, nor where he was going, until he came to the place of execution, to hell. He died asleep in his soul. He died dulled and dazed; consequently, he died meekly, like a child or a lamb, just as Mr. Badman did. This was a sign of God's anger. He had a mind to damn him for his sins; therefore, He would not let him see or have a heart to repent, lest he should convert. Then his damnation, which God had appointed, would be frustrated.

"That they should not see with their eyes, nor understand with their heart, and be converted, and I should heal them" (John 12:40).

The third thing I notice in this verse is that a sinful life followed by a quiet death is the common highway to hell. There is no surer sign of damnation than for a man to die quietly after having lived a sinful life. I am not saying that all wicked men who are troubled at the time of their deaths with a sense of sin and fear of hell repent, and therefore go to heaven. Instead, I believe that some are made to see, but are left to despair; they are not converted by seeing, and they leave this world loudly bemoaning their lost condition.

But I say that there is no surer sign of a man's damnation than for him to die quietly after having lived a sinful life, for him to sin and die with his eyes shut, for him to sin and die with a heart that cannot repent. *"He hath blinded their eyes, and hardened their heart; that they should not see with their eyes, nor understand with their heart"* (John 12:40).

God not only has a judgment for wicked men but also fair treatment. He will *"render to every man according to his deeds"* (Romans 2:6). God knows how *"to reserve the unjust unto the day of judgment to be punished"* (2 Peter 2:9). And this is one of His ways by which He does it. Thus it was with Mr. Badman.

Fourth, it is said in the book of Psalms, concerning the wicked, *"There are no bands* [pangs] *in their death: but their strength is firm"* (Psalm 73:4). By *"no bands"* or pangs, the psalmist meant no troubles, no gracious chastisement, no correction for sin as God's people experience, often at the time of their deaths. Therefore, the psalmist added, concerning the wicked, *"They are not in trouble as other men; nor are they plagued like other men"* (verse 5). Instead, they go as securely out of the world as if they had never sinned against God, and they jeopardize their own souls to the danger of damnation. They seem to go unbound, set at liberty, out of this world, although they have lived notoriously wicked lives all of their days. The prisoner who is to die at the gallows for his wickedness must first have the chains removed from his legs. It seems as if he is being given his liberty, when instead he is going to be executed for his transgressions. Wicked men also have *"no bands"* or pangs in their deaths. They seem to be more at liberty when they are winding up their sinful lives than at any other time.

Hence, you may hear them boast of their faith and hope in God's mercy when they lie upon their deathbeds. Yes, you may hear them speak confidently of their salvation as if they had served God all their days. The truth is, behind all their boasting is a seared conscience. Their sinful, base life does not come into their minds to correct them and bring them to repentance; instead, presumptuous thoughts and a hope and faith as fragile as a spider's web, woven by the devil himself, possess their souls, to their own eternal undoing (Job 8:13-14).

Chapter Twenty

Final Judgment

Wiseman. Hence, wicked men's hopes are said to die, not before, but with them. They give up the ghost together. And thus it was with Mr. Badman. His sins and his hopes went with him to the gate, but there his hope left him, because he died there. His sins went in with him, to be a worm gnawing at his conscience forever and ever (Isaiah 66:24).

The opinion, therefore, of the general public concerning this kind of dying is frivolous and foolish. Mr. Badman died like a lamb, or, as they call it, like a newborn child, quietly and without fear. I am not referring to the struggle between the natural body and death, but to the struggle between the conscience and the judgment of God. I know that nature will struggle with death. I have seen a dog and a sheep die with difficulty. A wicked man may have a hard, physical death because there is a natural antipathy between nature and death. But even while death and nature are struggling for mastery, the soul, the conscience, may be as numb, as senseless and ignorant of its miserable state, as the bed on which the sick man lies. Thus, the outward death of sinners may appear to be easy, but in truth, by the judgment of God, they are bound over to eternal damnation. By that same judgment, they may be kept from seeing who they are and where they are going, until they plunge down among the flames.

It is a very great judgment of God on wicked men for them to die in this manner, for it cuts them off from all possibility of repentance, and thus of salvation; therefore, it is as great a judgment upon those who survive them, those who were their companions in evil. For by the manner of their deaths, their seemingly peaceful passing, their wicked friends become even more hardened to the consequences of sin and take courage to continue on in their course.

When they compare their sinful, cursed lives with their child-like, lamblike deaths, they think that all is well. They believe that no damnation has happened to them. Although they lived like devils incarnate, yet they died like harmless ones. There was no whirlwind, no tempest, no affliction in their deaths. They died as quietly as the most godly of them all. They had as great a faith and hope of salvation as the godly possess, and they would talk as boldly of salvation as if they had assurance of it.

But as was their hope in life, so were their deaths. Their hope was without trial, because it was not of God's working, and their deaths were without anxiety, because this was the judgment of God concerning them.

Again, their survivors are encouraged to follow in their steps and to continue to live in open violation of God's law. Remember the words of the psalmist regarding the wicked:

> *For there are no bands in their death: but their strength is firm. They are not in trouble as other men; neither are they plagued like other men. Therefore pride compasseth them about as a chain; violence covereth them as a garment.*
>
> (Psalm 73:4-6)

Therefore, they take courage to do evil. They pride themselves in their iniquity. Why? Because their wicked companions died, after they had long lived the most profane and wicked lives, as quietly and as like lambs as if they had been innocent.

Yes, by seeing this kind of death, they are emboldened to conclude that God either does not, or will not, take notice of their sins. *"They are corrupt, and speak wickedly concerning oppression: they speak loftily"* (Psalm 73:8). They make sin better than it is pronounced to be by the Word. They speak wickedly concerning oppression. They commend it and consider it a prudent act. They also speak loftily. *"They set their mouth against the heavens"* (verse 9). They go so far as to say, *"How doth God know? and is there knowledge in the most High?"* (verse 11). And all this, as far as I can tell, arises in their hearts as a result of observing the quiet, lamblike deaths of their companions. *"Behold, these are the ungodly, who prosper in the world"* (verse 12); that is, by their wicked ways, *"they increase in riches"* (verse 12).

Therefore, this is a great judgment of God, both upon the man who dies in his sins, and also upon his companions who watch him die. He sins, he dies in his sins, and yet he dies quietly. What will his companions say to this? What conclusion will they make in how God will deal with them when they see the lamblike death of their companion? Be sure that they cannot, from such a sight, say, "A miserable death lies ahead for us if we do not repent." They cannot comprehend from the childlike death of Mr. Badman that sin is a dreadful, bitter thing. Instead, if they judge according to what they see, or according to their corrupted reason, they will conclude, with the wicked ones of old, *"Every one that doeth evil is good in the sight of the LORD, and he delighteth in them; or, where is the God of judgment?"* (Malachi 2:17).

Yes, this is enough to puzzle the wisest man. The psalmist himself was put to the test by observing the quiet death of ungodly men. He said,

> *"Verily I have cleansed my heart in vain, and washed my hands in innocency"* (Psalm 73:13). From outward appearance, they fare far better than I. *"Their eyes stand out with fatness; they have more than heart could wish"* (verse 7). *"All the day long I have been plagued, and chastened every morning"* (verse 14).

The good fortune of evil men made the psalmist wonder, yes, and Job and Jeremiah, too. But when the psalmist went into the sanctuary and sought God's wisdom, he understood their end in a way that he could not have understood it before. He did not understand *"until* [he] *went into the sanctuary of God"* (verse 17). What place was that? Why, it was where he might inquire of God.

By seeking understanding from God, he resolved this matter. He said, *"Then understood I their end"* (verse 17). He saw that God had *"set them in slippery places"* (verse 18) and *"castedest them down into destruction"* (verse 18). *"Castedest them down,"* that is, suddenly, or, as the next words say, *"As in a moment! they are utterly consumed with terrors"* (verse 19). These terrors did not seize them on their sickbeds, for they had *"no pangs"* (verse 4) in their deaths. The terrors, therefore, seized them there in judgment, where they will remain forever. This truth the psalmist found out, but not without great pain, grief, and heartfelt searching—so deep, so hard, and so difficult. It was no easy thing for him to come to a right understanding in this matter.

Indeed, this is a deep judgment of God toward ungodly sinners. It is enough to stagger a whole world. Only the godly who are in the world have a sanctuary in which to go, where the oracle and Word of God is found, by which His judgments, and the reason for many of them, are made known and understood.

Attentive. Indeed, this is a staggering state. It is full of the wisdom and anger of God. And I believe, as you have said, that it is full of judgment to the world. Who would have imagined, who had not known Mr. Badman and yet had seen him die, that he had not been a man who had lived a holy life and practiced godly conversation, since he died so quietly, so like a lamb or a newborn child? Would they not, I say, have concluded that he was a righteous man? Or if they had known him and his life, yet to see him die so quietly, would they not have concluded that he had made his peace with God? Even further, if some had known that he had died in his sins, and yet that he had died so like a lamb, would they not have concluded that either God does not know our sins, or that He approves of them? Or that He lacks the power, the will, the heart, or the skill to punish them, since Mr. Badman himself went from a sinful life so quietly, so peaceably, and so lamblike as he did?

Wiseman. Without question, this is a heavy judgment of God upon wicked men. One goes to hell in peace while another goes to hell in trouble; one goes to hell being sent there by his own hands, while another goes to hell being sent there by the hand of his companion; one goes there with his eyes shut while another goes there with his eyes open; one goes there bellowing while another goes there boasting of heaven and happiness all the way (see Job 21:23); one arrives there like Mr. Badman himself while others find their way there as his brothers did. But above all, Mr. Badman's death, as to the manner of his dying, is full of snares and traps to wicked men; therefore, those who die as he died are the greatest stumbling block to the world. They go on and on peaceably from youth to old age, and then to the grave, and so to hell, without noise. They go *as an ox goeth to the slaughter, or as a fool to the correction of the stocks"* (Proverbs 7:22), that is, both senselessly and confidently.

Oh, the horror of arriving at the gates of hell! Oh, how terrible to see those gates are open for them! And when they see that hell is their home, and that they must go there, then their peace and quietness flies away forever. Then they roar like lions, scream like banshees, howl like dogs, and tremble at their judgment, as the devils do themselves. Oh, when they see that they must cross the gulf and descend into the throat of hell! When they see that hell has shut her ghastly jaws upon them, then they will open their eyes and find themselves within the bowels of hell! Then they will mourn and weep and gnash their teeth for pain (Matthew 22:13). But their torture rarely begins until they are out of the sight and hearing of those mortals whom they leave behind alive in this world.

Attentive. Well, my good neighbor Wiseman, I perceive that the sun grows low, and that you have come to a conclusion with Mr. Badman's life and death; therefore, I will take my leave of you. Only first, let me tell you that I am glad that I met with you today and that we had the opportunity to discuss Mr. Badman's state. I also want to thank you for your kindness to me in answering all of my questions. I would only ask for your prayers that God will give me much grace, that I may neither live nor die as Mr. Badman did.

Wiseman. My good neighbor Attentive, I wish you health in soul and body. If anything that I have said about Mr. Badman's life and death may be of benefit to you, I will be sincerely glad. But I desire for you to thank God for it, and to pray wholeheartedly for me that I, along with you, may be *"kept by the power of God through faith unto salvation"* (1 Peter 1:5).

Attentive. May it be so. Farewell.

Wiseman. I wish you a hearty farewell.

God has set a Savior against sin,
a heaven against a hell,
light against darkness,
good against evil,
and the breadth and length
and depth and height of grace
that is in Himself for my good,
against all the power and strength
and subtlety of every enemy.

—John Bunyan

The Holy War
John Bunyan

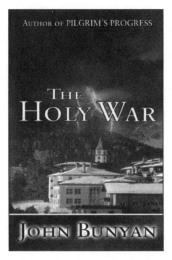

A fierce battle rages to take control away from the rightful Prince of Mansoul. Who will be the conquering prince? Diabolus or Emmanuel? And what can the inhabitants do to resist the attacks of the evil one? Through this powerful allegory, you will learn how to build up your defenses and prepare for war because your soul is under attack from the forces of evil. Bunyan will illuminate your understanding and show you that, with Christ the Conqueror on your side, you have nothing to fear!

ISBN: 978-0-88368-706-2 • Trade • 320 pages

The Pilgrim's Progress
John Bunyan

Acclaimed as "one of the greatest literary masterpieces in the world," John Bunyan's beloved allegory captivates the reader's attention while providing insight into the Christian life. Join Bunyan as he tells the story of "Christian," a man on an adventurous journey across rough terrain, over sunlit hills, and through dark valleys. His trek is an intriguing allegory for today—mixed with the chivalric adventure of yesterday—as the pilgrimage takes you from the City of Destruction to the Celestial City whose builder and maker is God.

ISBN: 978-0-88368-096-4 • Pocket • 400 pages

---

www.whitakerhouse.com